Alice McIlroy

THE GLASS WOMAN

Dear Jake,

Victim of A.I. or scientist playing God?

Enjoy!

Alice

DATURA

DATURA BOOKS
An imprint of Watkins Media Ltd

Unit 11, Shepperton House
89 Shepperton Road
London N1 3DF
UK

daturabooks.com
twitter.com/daturabooks
Those in glass houses shouldn't throw stones

A Datura Books paperback original, 2024

Cover by Mark Swan
Edited by Gemma Creffield and Andrew Hook
Set in Meridien

This novel is entirely a work of fiction. Names, characters, places, and incidents are the products of the author's imagination or are used fictitiously. Any resemblance to actual events, locales, organizations or persons, living or dead, is entirely coincidental.

ISBN 978 1 91552 3 044
Ebook ISBN 978 1 91552 3 051

Printed and bound in the United Kingdom by TJ Books Ltd.

9 8 7 6 5 4 3 2 1

For Michael

PART ONE
Hospital

CHAPTER ONE

My name is Iris and I am thirty-five years old. My husband is called Marcus. I was born in Suffolk, England. I work at the London Research Institute. It is Wednesday, the first of May. This is what I have just been told.

CHAPTER TWO

Waking is like wading through deep water. I am half within my body and half without. I look down at this body I inhabit – it is dressed in a crumpled blue cotton gown. Pain, which starts in my head with a drilling sensation, spreads.

As my eyes adjust to the light, the room before me becomes clear: a single bed, a chair, a closed window. A tube attached to my hand wires me to a machine. The room is still, silent, save the machine's heartbeat.

I hear a man's voice as he appears from the hallway:

"Iris?"

His voice sounds as though it comes from a great distance, above the water's surface as I'm drowning below. In a swift movement, he sweeps a hand across his head.

"Iris?"

I open my mouth to speak, only no sound comes. Then a jumbled mix of consonants and vowels with no recognisable pattern escapes. My mind reels and twists, trying to form the words I want to say.

I try again.

He moves towards me and sits beside the bed. He edges the chair closer. He is tall, with dishevelled hair, sunken cheeks, amber eyes. Tentatively, he reaches his hand to my face, moving hair from my eyes.

I grasp the mattress.

"It's me," – a pause of several seconds – "Marcus. Your husband."

4

My mind tremors, as though he has flicked a switch in my brain and my vision shifts. I have no recollection of him, or me, or anything that has come before this moment.

I tell myself, *Don't panic, don't panic.*

I manage to gasp out a word on repeat, "Sorry, sorry, sorry."

I don't know what it is I am apologising for.

I dig my nails into the palms of my hands forming tiny crescents. I look down at them. They are thin, parched and papery. But sitting there, on my fourth finger, is a band of lighter skin, untouched by the sun.

The man called Marcus, in his dark suit, stands over me now. His shoulders seem cowed beneath a great weight. He leans closer, peering into my face. "How do you feel, Iris?"

The room is hot, oppressively hot, and I want to get up out of this bed and open the window to let in fresh air.

"You're safe now," he says. He reaches out and holds my hand. His is cold and clammy. I do not feel safe. I feel a rising nausea at this touch, and I wish I were alone.

I find the words now and the voice to speak them. I tell him my head hurts; I am in pain, tired, confused.

The man called Marcus listens. "Do you remember anything, Iris?" he asks.

"No." I shake my head and my voice rises. "Nothing. Why don't I?"

My eyes meet his and he holds my gaze: "Your name is Iris. You are thirty-five years old..."

I look at the needle inserted into the back of my hand. I start to pull the drip from my skin. A second monitor wires me to the machine. Marcus places his hand on my shoulder, gripping too tightly. I try to push him away.

He is standing over me now and I am struggling to get up.

"PLUTO," the man says, urgently. "We need you now."

Two doctors appear in white coats. They murmur to each other and scrutinise something on the machine beside the bed.

"I can't remember anything," I tell them in the hope that they will have answers. My voice wavers. "Why can't I remember anything?"

I just catch Marcus' hissed words to them. "We didn't expect this."

I am shaking now, trembling, as I realise fully, for the first time, that I know nothing of who I am. My breathing is heavy and shallow, my chest heaving. I look at the catheter in my hand. I want to tear it out, to be free of this encumbrance. I start to pull at the tape securing it, exposing puckered red skin beneath.

Marcus places his hand on my shoulder again, in an attempt to stop me, but I push back.

The doctors are standing over me now and I notice one of them does not look human. I am filled with a cold dread. "W-what are you?" I stammer. I wish I could remember how I got here, any frame of reference. I start to hyperventilate, tears rising.

"Breathe, Iris. You'll be fine as long as you don't panic," the first doctor tells me. His voice is familiar, but I cannot make out his features, my vision blurring with tears.

I try to get out of the bed, when a voice commands, "Hold her still."

There is movement across the room. Hands restrain me with an iron grip. Someone reaches for a syringe on the trolley. I am struggling still, despite all strength having drained from my body. Marcus pins my arms to the bed with practised force. His face a grimace, he stands over me. I feel the metallic tip of the syringe as it pierces the exposed flesh of my arm. I hear myself cry out. Then, with a sharp, sudden sting, my body slackens.

CHAPTER THREE

It is Wednesday, the first of May. My life before this date is a blank.

My name is Iris and I am thirty-five years old. I was born in Suffolk, England. I work at the London Research Institute. I know only these facts. Marcus is my husband. Or so I have been told.

CHAPTER FOUR

This is the next time I recall awakening, although in fitful dreams I was only half submerged in sleep. Am I awake now? I do not trust myself to know.

I open my eyes and observe the object seated opposite, upright in the chair. Two eyes, two ears, one nose: a porcelain face. Blue, glass eyes punctured by a black hole: a blank space in the place where life would have been, had it been human.

The mouth gapes, as though frozen mid-conversation. The head, tilted sideways, exposes its mind beneath. Tentacles of plastic synapses snap and wrap themselves around the threads that bind the rubber tissue of the prefrontal lobe.

A rising feeling; something akin to fear.

My eyes trace the smooth silk of skin across its face, which looks almost human, to the metallic hinge of a shoulder and the iron rods of the ribcage, to the place in between, where a beating human heart would be. Friend or foe? A question mark.

It is strangely familiar. And then I start to think: am I like this? Am I looking at my mirror image? I raise my hand to my head to check for a dividing seam, dig my nails into my wrist to look for blood beneath. I press my palm against my chest to feel for a beating heart.

Seated opposite me, it looks watchful, though not yet waking. For now, it remains dormant.

A glass screen runs across the length of the room, separating us. I feel safe for a while. But then I wonder, is it to keep the machine out, or me in?

There is an image illuminated on a glass tablet beside the bed: it reveals a couple. I cannot remember it being there before. The man who calls himself my husband is the man in the photograph. The woman next to him, I assume, is me. She looks young, brunette, tanned skin. She looks happy. I want to cry. The colours – the sea, the white sand – are bright, luminous against the dull, drab room. The image moves: the man turns towards the woman and smiles as he takes her in his arms; she throws her head backwards, laughing; birds scatter in the sky; the sea bristles.

I tear my eyes away.

The metallic clock on the wall ticks, loudly, as it measures out portions of the day. Wind rattles the window. Outside, birds swing mechanically through the infinite sky. I lie in the centre of the room feeling exposed and convinced that someone is watching. Possibly I hear a whispering just outside the door.

A sudden rush of air: the door opens. I am certain I hear a whispering now, but whoever it is remains just out of sight. From here, I have a view of the corridor with more sealed doors, and one – ajar – just within sight – reveals a bed, a chair, a closed window, like mine. Designed for the same purpose, but what purpose is that?

I study the stainless-steel shine of clinical surfaces in my room, chemical-infused spotlessness, wash-off linoleum floor. Is it a hospital, this institution? Or something else?

"So," the man called Marcus says as he appears in the doorway like a conjuring trick. "How are you feeling?"

It is two minutes past one. He has arrived carrying coral-coloured flowers. His face smiles, but his eyes do not.

"Iris," he says my name into the void, as though just the act of saying it means something. His voice reverberates around the concrete walls and glass panels. His eyes shift about the room. He holds out the flowers. "Alchymist roses. Your favourite."

I search for some recollection of this, but it is as though there is a locked door in my mind.

"Do you remember?" he asks with child-like hope.

I shake my head, my heartbeat quickening as my mind trips up: why can't I remember? When I speak, my voice is a cracked sound, as though it has been out of use for days. "What happened?" Despite the tepid room, there is a chill in my bones so deep-rooted that I cannot fathom its source. It is as though I have never felt warmth. As though I have just arrived in this moment, this body. My breath catches in my chest. Who am I? Who is he?

He avoids my gaze.

He drags the chrome legs of the chair across the linoleum floor, positioning it at arm's length from the bed, and sits. Upright in the chair, arms rigidly by his sides, he keeps his distance. "What do roses make you think of?" he asks, gently.

He is holding the flowers out to me still. He waits. Finally, I take them. They are heavy; just budding, their life so newly curtailed.

I lift the petals to my nose and inhale deeply. I am all present moment, grasping to make sense of it – these orange blossom flowers, this man, my husband.

"They don't make me think of anything." I say, the fear rising. "Why is that? What's happened?" I place the roses on the bedside table in front of the photograph. My hands are shaking. There is a locked door to the past and someone has stolen the key. "Why am I here?"

I hear the sharp scrape of his chair. He stands, stretches and turns. A sudden wind clambers at the window. As he turns back towards me, he places the tips of his thumb and index finger to the bridge of his nose as though to ease a tension that has gathered there. His head is bowed, and he sits back down.

"You had a procedure to help your depression. Look, I think it's best we wait until the doctor's here to explain," he says. He shakes his head. It is an almost imperceptible movement, a nervous tick. He clears his throat, "Do you remember anything?" He looks hopeful, but hopeful of what? It is all haze.

"No," I say. The hospital gown is too tight around my neck; sweat starts to prickle beneath. "I've told you that. Nothing. Is that because of the procedure? What was it?"

He sits in the chair beside me and considers this for a moment. What is he thinking? I envy him. I know who I would rather be out of the wife who remembers nothing and the husband who has to narrate her into being. "I am sorry, Iris. It's too soon to tell you more."

His voice is gentle, consoling, but there is guilt written into the lines of his face. What is he hiding? It strikes me that he is unnatural in this role. "Will my memory come back?" I press him. Looking at this man, this stranger, I feel as though one of us has issued from another realm. I wonder if I could ever consider him a husband. I try to envisage going home with him. A gaping door, a house, the two of us. The thought of it is frightening.

"Why was I depressed?"

He glances vaguely out of the window. "There are many factors that can contribute to depression."

"Yes," I say. "But what were mine?"

"Iris," he says sadly, his voice a caress that is an intrusion. "There are some things it's best not to remember. That are too painful. But other memories will return." He picks up the photograph beside the bed. "We were so happy here." He looks wistfully at me. "This was taken when I proposed to you at Lethe Bay." His face breaks into a smile. "I thought I'd lost the ring – I thought it would be washed out to sea. We went swimming, leaving our clothes on the beach, and the tide came in so fast. It was in my jacket." He retrieves a ruby ring from his pocket. "It's an heirloom."

It is set against silver and surrounded by small, intricate diamonds. He runs his fingers over its serrated edges and then holds it out to me, this object. He slips it onto my fourth finger. My mouth is dry. His eyes are fixed upon me.

"Here, I'll show you." He hands me a set of black glasses from a compartment in the wall.

"What are these?" I ask. They are lighter than they look, bulky in size.

Marcus frowns. "A virtual reality headset. Go on. Try them on."

I place them carefully over my eyes. Tiny pinpricks of light appear and then a landscape materialises around me. It is an amphibious place, where land and sea seem interchangeable as they merge with the horizon. There is sand beneath my bare feet, and I stand a few yards from a sea that undulates to and fro. Marcus is in front of me, laughing; a sound that carries on the breeze. The smell of salt tugs at my memory. He kneels on one knee and holds out a ruby ring that catches the sun. I notice that his eyes have pink veins that worm outwards across the vascular white. The beating of my heart thunders in my ears.

"I thought it was a fitting place – our first date was on that beach. A picnic in the dunes, champagne and strawberries. I arrived in this old convertible you joked was from another era. I thought I'd ruined my chances." He smiles a little sadly. "We had everything to look forward to; our whole lives."

I remove the glasses from my eyes. "How long have we been married?" I ask.

"Five years."

"Where do we live?"

"We've lived in Notting Hill together since we got married."

"When can I leave here?" I ask, as I try to imagine the spectre of a house, a home, lived in by this stranger and I, together. What would it be like, I wonder, moving in with him?

A hospital machine hums, invading our silence.

"Soon," he says with resonance.

He places his hand on mine; I flinch involuntarily. This must have once been familiar, the feel of his skin. It feels cold.

"It's a lot to take on board, isn't it?" he soothes. "I do understand how strange and confusing this all must be, but you have to trust me. We made a decision – the procedure was to make you better. You have the best medical professionals taking care of you. We have a fresh start."

I nod, silently.

His eyes are moist.

"A fresh start," I repeat slowly under my breath. What did we have before?

He looks at me closely. "It is going to be okay." The corners of his mouth tug upwards with mechanical effort, like a ventriloquist's dummy, his eyes not quite catching up.

I try to smile, but the muscles in my face won't comply. "What is that?" I ask instead, motioning to the thing I noticed earlier seated opposite.

"PLUTO is your personal nurse."

I try to remember a world before, with nurses like these, but my mind draws a blank. "Then why is it behind a glass screen?"

"PLUTO is there to monitor your progress, but in a way that's not invasive. Research has shown it's best to preserve a level of distance. People are suspicious of robotics. Look, I have to get back to work." It is quarter to two. His relief is almost audible. "I'll be back tomorrow." He gets up to leave.

"Marcus." He turns, and in that split second my heart opens, closes. I do not want him to leave. He is the only route I have to answers. "My memory will come back?" I try to get up, but a drugged heaviness stops me.

He nods. "In stages. I am sorry, Iris. I can't tell you anything else. It would be too soon. I just want what's best for you." He kisses my forehead and lingers for a moment. He says as he exhales, "Tomorrow."

And he is gone.

* * *

The robot wakes. It disappears through a door to its left and then reappears by my bedside. The badge on the lapel of its white coat reads, 'PLUTO'. Its eyes blink shut with a click like a shutter closing and opening again. It holds a tray of pills and a glass of water, placing both on the table with careful precision.

"Hello, Iris," a voice intonates from within the aluminium chamber of its lungs. PLUTO holds the pills out in the palm of its hand. I remember creatures like these from childhood now – just a glimpse of one at an exhibition. Its large, soulless eyes watch me. "How do you feel today, Iris?"

"A little better. Do you have a mirror?" I ask. I want to know what I look like, whether I am the woman in the photograph.

It moves slowly, methodically, across the room with a low hum and then returns moments later. It holds the mirror out to me. It reflects my face, one I don't recall. A tired, sallow face that has not seen sunlight for some time. Drab strands of brunette hair hang limply at the sides. My eyebrows are unkempt. My cheekbones are taut. My eyes are a pale grey. It is not the face I expect. But then what did I expect? To look younger? Healthier? Happier? I am the woman in the photograph.

I move my head just a little, and in the light my eyes are no longer grey, but a water-green. And in this light, I suddenly look younger and my skin porcelain, like a china cup that might break. I wonder which face he sees – Marcus that is. Which face does he love? Supposing he loves me at all. When I turn my head this way, I look knowing, almost devious; this way, alluringly innocent. Does he see both of them? Perhaps that is why he fears me. I have seen it in his eyes: the ghost of dread.

"Can you help me, PLUTO?"

"I want to be of assistance," PLUTO says, and it almost sounds like compassion speaking.

"What procedure have I had?"

"First take your pills, Iris."

I look at the pink capsules. Two large pink pills the size of my thumb-print. The thought crosses my mind that I am being drugged.

"You have to tell me why I'm here."

PLUTO places the pills on the table. "Please wait whilst I check your records." The mask of its face remains expressionless. "Sorry. I am not authorised to give you that information," it says in that smooth tone, accompanied by a programmed smile.

My voice is a foreign sound that catches in my throat. "Who *is* authorised?"

PLUTO's eyes blink. The empty pupils in its glassy sockets seem to swell. "Please take your pills, Iris. They will help you feel calmer." PLUTO's teeth are a polished white, and the cavity of its mouth gapes at me, revealing glimpses of the wall behind where the back of its head and inside of its mouth should be. It is the mixture of the human and non-human that I find so unnerving. Its face is uncannily life-like, with skin and teeth; but its body shows the machinations of the machinery it is built from.

"Please. Help me," I speak softly now and reach out, clasping the cold steel of its arm beneath my fingertips. "Who is authorised?"

PLUTO glances down at my hand. The skin between its eyebrows creases. "Doctor Nicholls." It steps back and turns to leave once more.

"Who is Doctor Nicholls?" I try to pull myself up from the bed, but the strength evades me. "I need to speak to them, now."

"Sorry. That is not authorised," it says with a smile that seems programmed to be reassuring.

"That's not good enough. When can I speak to them?"

"Please wait while I check your records, Iris," PLUTO informs me in an even tone. I watch as the planetary cogs of its solar system mind seem to turn at the request. "You have an appointment with him tomorrow."

"It can't wait. I want to speak to someone who's in charge."

"I would like to be of assistance, Iris," PLUTO's mellifluous voice says, "but I am not authorised."

"Who programmed you?"

"I work for Sila PLC."

"I want to speak to the person in charge of Sila PLC."

It holds its hand up, as though to silence me.

"I am not authorised to impart information about Sila PLC. I am authorised to help."

It turns to leave.

"You're not helping though! Tell me what's going on–" I reach out to grab hold of it, but it steps back.

From a compartment in the wall, it extracts a syringe, which it holds up to the light and inspects.

I try to get up and protest. "No," I say.

PLUTO is arrested for a moment, the syringe poised and held in mid-air. Then, PLUTO's hands begin their work, of smoothing and restraining.

I try to push it away.

"Don't move, Mrs Henderson," PLUTO says with a renewed coldness. The smile is gone.

It leans over me. I feel the touch of the metallic tip of the syringe as it pierces the exposed flesh of my arm with a sharp, sudden sting. My hand tightens its grip against the empty air, then I feel myself relax and I surrender.

"Goodbye, Iris," I hear it say, as it leaves.

That night, there is a storm. It takes me far out to sea, as the wind wields its fury against the fragile windows, and clouds break over buildings in the crashing darkness.

I do not know if it is this that has woken me, or if I had woken from a nightmare. I don't remember sleeping at all. My heart is racing; my thoughts, dark, formless shadows, crowding in. "Calm down," I tell myself. "Calm down." But I don't.

I survey the room. Everything is stationary. The door is not more than ten feet away.

I drag the drip out from my arm. I do not trust my body to move as my mind commands. Slowly, as silently as possible, I slide off the hospital bed and feel relief: my legs move as I will them to. Placing one foot in front of the other, I edge myself forwards. PLUTO sits in the chair behind the glass. I half expect it to awaken, to alert someone. Nothing happens, nothing in the room moves. It is only a machine, I tell myself.

There is no noise. I breathe a sigh of relief.

But this is foolish; I have spent too long in my own thoughts. Outside the window, darkness devours the city, except a single lightning flash that slashes its path across the night sky.

I move away and walk towards the door, the brass doorknob turning in my hands, and then I am out in the corridor beyond. The floor is polished concrete, sealed with beige skirting like a band aid. The walls are concrete too. I run my hands across their smooth surface. The corridor is studded with doors panelled with heavily frosted glass and a sign that reads: "No sharp objects". The corridor recedes into distant shadow; rectangular lights and ventilation shafts alternately puncture the low ceiling.

Along the corridor, all the other doors are closed. At the end of the ward, there is a steel door. Beside it is a black pad the size of a thumbprint at eye-level, with a camera lens at its centre. I turn the metal door handle, but it doesn't budge. The globed metal is cold and smooth in the palm of my hand. I try again. But as my fingers slip across its surface, it remains unyielding. My terror returns; it runs through me and lingers.

I am locked in.

As I walk back towards my cube room, one of the hallway doors opens, revealing a sliver of darkness within. Standing motionless in the corridor, I sense eyes roaming my face in the stationary shadow.

I blink and they are gone. The door is closed. There could be eyes everywhere. The darkness in that room seems amorphous and to have a will of its own.

I reach out and the handle turns silently beneath my fingertips. Pushing the door open softly, a chink of night appears in the doorway again. A moment later, I step back, startled, as the door is shut in my face.

I hurry back to my room and let the door click into place. I turn and look around, up at the ceiling, with a rising sense of being watched. I am not sure what I am looking for; it is instinctive somehow, buried deep in my subconscious. I lower my gaze and see the glinting eyes of PLUTO directly ahead of me, motionless, the gleaming lens of a camera. But who is behind the camera? Who is watching?

I walk to the window. Outside, the storm clouds have miraculously dispersed, and the universe is unfolding itself, slowly. A great expanse of stars – stars upon stars upon stars – are glittering gloriously in the face of a vast abyss.

I return to bed. Hugging myself for comfort, waiting very quietly, very still, for morning. In my locked ward. In my prison cell. Wait, for the pieces of me to fall back into place. From looking at them so long, I imagine the walls are falling in, and the sky – an ocean of black, unchained water – is falling inwards and I am being drowned and buried alive at the same time.

My name is Iris and I am thirty-five years old. My husband is called Marcus. I was born in Suffolk, England. I work at the London Research Institute. Coral-coloured roses are my favourite flowers. Marcus proposed to me at Lethe Bay. I am locked in.

CHAPTER FIVE

"I'm locked in," I say. "Did you know that? The door at the end of the corridor is locked at night."

Sitting in the mauve chair, in my blue cotton gown patterned with squares, surrounded by refracted noise, I wait with Marcus. The four walls surrounding us have a dark, earthy hue and the mottled linoleum floor of the hospital room is flecked with varying shades of white and beige. The bulb overhead leaves everything exposed to its harsh, luminous gaze.

He is avoiding my eye, fidgeting with his collar and loosening his tie.

He stops pacing the room and pauses by the window. It is a burnt-out, end-of-time day: all darkening skies threatening rain.

"Why were you in the corridor last night?"

Marcus finally turns towards me and as he does so, I notice that PLUTO is standing in the doorway. "The doctor will see you now," it says.

I hear the echo of approaching footsteps amplified by the concrete floor of the corridor. A man in a white coat enters. A lean man with a clean, bald head and a raised chin who heralds an air of self-importance.

"Mrs Henderson." His eyes alight upon me and linger there. And then, "Iris," he says, his voice elongating the vowels, savouring each syllable and the sound of his voice curling around them. Stretching out a hand towards me, he clasps my hand between his. "I'm Doctor Nicholls," he says with resonance, with meaning, as though he expects me to ascribe importance to this name, which I do – this is the doctor I have sought, and he nods. "I'm your personal practitioner on your healthcare plan here at Sila. I'm the lead consultant overseeing your convalescence."

I look at him, this oracle who holds the key to my prophesy. "What sort of consultant are you?" I cannot hold back any longer. "What procedure have I had?"

He smiles. "One step at a time." He beckons with an elaborate flick of the hand for Marcus to take a seat. "We're going to start off with a couple of memory tests, Iris, to check how you're getting on."

"Why can't I remember anything?" I ask. I want to believe he can help me.

He pauses, holding the tips of his fingers together. "As you're aware, there's been some memory impairment. I've worked with patients experiencing similar memory loss before, although I will admit your case is unique."

I nod. The room is oppressively hot. *Your case is unique.* What is he not saying? I watch as he extracts a tablet from his pocket. "What's happened to me?"

He looks at Marcus and then back to me. Deliberately evading the question, he says in a too-cheery voice, "We're going to start with your childhood."

He must see my discomfort, because he pauses, placing the tablet on the table and says, not unkindly, "Your brain has experienced a level of trauma." His tone is confidential, and the sparseness of his words reminds me that he is the one with answers, with power. "First, we need to ascertain where we're building from – what you do remember," he says. "PLUTO will be assisting me."

PLUTO leans towards me in a manner designed to invite confidence, and its face relaxes into a smile. It fixes me with pale blue eyes as it holds out a photograph. "What does the image remind you of, Iris?"

Behind the glassy liquid of PLUTO's eyes, something shifts; its eyelids click shut and then open again.

I look at the image. I am seated at a table and dressed in white, with flowers adorning my hair. With growing resonance, I recognise Marcus beside me, looking at me with soft eyes; this is what love looks like.

Doctor Nicholls watches me now as though he is deciphering my face. He folds his arms and raises his chin a little higher.

"I don't know," I hear myself say. "Our wedding, clearly, but I... I don't remember it." I look at Marcus; I look away. "Please can you just tell me why I'm here?"

"We have every confidence some of your memories will return, Iris, but you will need to cooperate with us." Doctor Nicholl's smooth tone seeks to assure me.

PLUTO tilts its head slightly, unblinking. "Where did you grow up?"

I shut my eyes. I try to recall childhood. On the inner walls of my closed eyelids, shapes play, refusing to fully materialise. All of a sudden, I remember a path through the fields to a wood and a river. I can just see the tall shadows that the trees cast – the silhouette of woods on the horizon – and the river that runs beyond them, deep and fast-flowing. I know my house is close by, out of sight, beyond the woods. For a moment, I can feel the breeze, as I stand alone, watching the wind's demise in the leaves overhead. For an instant, just as fleeting, life flows through me. I dare to hope this memory will lead to another, but the distant shore of the river fades. My closed eyelids remain. Then, a thought appears in my mind: is it mine, this memory? Before the first thought disperses, another fear rises: if I tell them what I remember, the memory will no longer be mine to recall and something of my own. So I do not tell them all that I remember. I reply with the same clipped speech which PLUTO seems to be programmed to use, and I say, "In the countryside. Suffolk."

Doctor Nicholls nods.

"You remembered that very well, Iris," PLUTO says. "I have a series of questions to ascertain the state of your memory loss. What do you do on a typical day?"

I turn it over in my mind, try to imagine a moment of waking that has not been today, yesterday, and the shock each time of a hospital bed. I look at them, my thoughts disassembling. I could make it up, fabricate an answer, see if they can tell, but even this stretch of the imagination leaves me blank. There is nothing there. "I – I don't remember."

"Do you remember what you did last weekend?" There is a right answer somewhere. I look blankly at it. It seems a lifetime ago.

"No, I don't." I shake my head, grip the sides of the chair, tethering myself to something real. I try to think back but the memories resist my grasp. "I have no idea." I want to ask; how do I live? How do I think? Without memory. But fear crawls inside me, threatens to hole up the door of my mouth. Eventually, I turn to Doctor Nicholls and demand, "Can we stop this charade now? I want to know where I am, and why I'm here. Why is the ward locked at night?"

"That's enough for now. Thank you, PLUTO," Doctor Nicholls instructs. "PLUTO will continue with memory stimuli in a future session."

It sits back and stills.

Placing reading glasses onto the tip of his nose, he looks at me through calculating eyes. "Iris, you've reached the correct stage in your convalescence for us to discuss your prognosis. You have some memory impairment, but it is temporary. To use a term you may be familiar with, you have focal retrograde amnesia." He says this with a nasal flare on the final syllables. "That means you are able to produce new memories, but you are having trouble accessing past memories. It is your autobiographical memory that has been impacted – however, it is your recently-formed memories of the past eight years that have been most affected, whilst your memories of childhood remain intact, although may require some prompting. You can remember social codes, facts about the world, skills such as reading. It is your recent personal past you can't recall."

I start to panic. It does not make any sense. "What caused the amnesia?" I ask.

"Well, you were particularly sensitive to the effects of the procedure. Given the extent, it was necessary to medically induce the amnesia. The memories you can't recall are from around the time of the target memories." He directs this at my husband, not at me.

Target memories? My trail of thought snags on the words. I imagine all trace of those memories – sounds, smell, sight – being extinguished like a candle's flame. My heart thuds heavily in my chest. "What was the procedure?"

"When do you think Iris' memory is likely to return, Doctor?" Marcus cuts in smoothly, leaning forwards as he does so. He is wearing a suit and is freshly shaved; I am unkempt in comparison, with my unwashed hair, my days-old gown. I might be acutely aware of this, if it were not for the ache in my head, in my brain, as PLUTO's pills wear thin.

"The drug will wear off in a few days." Doctor Nicholls turns away from Marcus to face me again. "Your memory should return–"

"Should, or will?" I ask.

Marcus interjects, "What will help it return?"

"Visual stimuli such as photographs, Mr Henderson. This is, of course," he leans forward, "ground-breaking work." I listen, feeling as though he is talking about someone else. Nausea rises. This cannot be happening.

"Doctor Nicholls, you still haven't told me what the procedure was. Why is it ground-breaking?" I ask with restraint. I feel the need to somehow get control of this situation. My voice is almost calm.

"Quite right, Iris. Quite right. Timing is, of course, imperative. Now is the correct time. Mr Henderson, please proceed."

Marcus looks to Doctor Nicholls for seconds that stretch and stretch. Time ceases. Silence roams.

Marcus appears to be thinking carefully about how to begin. "Iris, you have suffered from depression over the past year. You have had a procedure to... to eliminate the repetitive behaviour patterns you were experiencing."

The air is too close, the room too small. I realise I have forgotten to breathe. I look at Marcus with growing horror. "What have they done to my brain?"

Marcus takes his time before responding, choosing his words carefully. "The injection that's used targets specific memories, which in your case triggered the depression, and... deletes them."

I grasp at the words. Injection, memories, deleted. "What is it that's injected, exactly?"

Doctor Nicholls looks at me expansively. "The drug that's used will soon be standard practice to treat conditions such as yours, Iris."

"What's important," Marcus informs me, "is that those memories you wanted to forget have been successfully removed."

It is as though I am watching from a distance, from a great height. I am too close to the precipice. "Permanently?"

I look at Marcus; he refuses to meet my eye.

Doctor Nicholls clears his throat. His eyes sparkle. "That's why this is such ground-breaking work, Iris. We don't yet know. You are still in the first stage of the recovery process. Denial and anger are to be expected. The procedure itself is very sophisticated. All it requires is an injection and the target memories are eliminated, but the recovery process is more complicated, and the brain needs time to readjust, hence the precaution of inducing amnesia."

I look at his small eyes as they race back and forwards across my face. If it is as sophisticated as he says, why do I have this vast feeling of loss?

"This will soon be a standard procedure to treat mental health issues," he continues, his eyes alight. "But you are the first to benefit from it."

"Am I?" I interrupt. "There was another patient on the ward last night."

"Not at present. You must be mistaken." He continues without pause, "Nobody else has had the opportunity yet, Iris. We've given you a fresh bill of health."

I stare at him. "You call this a fresh bill of health, Doctor?"

"It was in your best interest, Iris," Marcus' words say, but his voice is pleading. "This is what we decided after months of consultations."

"No, I don't believe you." I wouldn't have agreed to this, not when it has threatened my identity, my sense of self, my grasp on reality even. And if my depression was that severe, I couldn't have been in the presence of mind to make a decision like that. If I was suffering from stress, my cortisol levels would be raised, the connectivity in my amygdala would have been stronger. It would have been an irrational, emotive response. I know these things to be true, but do not know how I know them.

My heartbeat is racing. There is an energy in me that has a life of its own. *Calm down*, I tell myself, *this isn't helping*. "I couldn't have agreed to this."

The doctor hands me an electronic tablet that reveals a document as proof. It is covered in legalities in small print. At the bottom of it, I see my signature and the date: the twenty-fifth of April.

He turns the document to a testimony on the next page:

I, Iris Henderson, agree to have memories deleted of certain persons and events that have caused trauma. I agree not to undertake any inquiries into these memories once erased. I understand that these memories are now the property of Sila PLC and no longer belong to me. I understand that this procedure is irreversible.

It would be easy to forge a written testimony. I struggle to make sense of its words. Which people? I want to scream, what events? I want to shake Doctor Nicholls until he reveals whatever it is he is not telling me. "How does the procedure work?" I manage to ask, my voice shaky. "How does it remove the memories?"

Doctor Nicholls almost rises from his seat as he leans forwards. "It eliminates the memory by stopping it from being re-stored after recall. Scientists have been developing versions of it for years, but to successfully locate a body of memories causing trauma – over a significant time period – and eradicate them... It is a seminal development. You are getting the very best care, Iris. We are all very interested in your recovery – scientifically, that is."

"I'm the guinea pig," I say. The first to suffer the side effects, trial the efficacy. *Stop it*, I tell myself, trying to silence my train of thoughts. It is too overwhelming. I have to try to keep a clear head. "Can the procedure be reversed?" I ask, eventually.

Doctor Nicholls looks at me. It is not surprise on his face exactly, but interest, avid interest. "No. As you read in your testimony, it is irreversible."

My lips part but no noise escapes, only a silent exhale.

"Is there anything else that would help Iris' amnesia?" Marcus asks, looking uncomfortable.

"When you return home, the surroundings will help jog her memory. And visual stimuli such as photographs, as I said before."

"When will that be? When will I be returning home?" I ask, uncertainly, glancing sideways at Marcus.

"Next week," Doctor Nicholls assures me.

My temples throb. Home. The word fills me with disquiet. What will I find there?

Once Doctor Nicholls has bestowed upon us the last of his advice and left, I turn to Marcus. He has not moved. He is sitting with his head in both hands, and he sighs shakily.

"Marcus," I say it softly at first, but he does not move.

"Marcus, look at me," I demand.

He does not look up, clutching at his skull with his fingers.

"We need to talk about this," I say, as I move across the room. "You need to explain to me exactly what has happened." Swiftly, I grasp him with both hands until he looks up, until he is looking me directly in the eye, his own eyes glassy. "I wouldn't have agreed to this."

Still, he says nothing.

I want to scream in his face; detonate his silence. My voice rises, "You let this happen!"

No answer. He wipes his fist across his face to clear the tears that have gathered there, and he looks at me with all of his sadness. Where it comes from, I do not know. I know nothing of the sadness that grieves his heart. And he says nothing.

The wind outside the window presses at the pane, raising a low moan that struggles through the glass.

Eventually, I sit down beside him on the bed and hug my arms around myself for comfort.

He moves closer, so he is only a few inches away, then turns his face towards me. "I love you, Iris."

This is what his words say, but somehow, I don't believe him. I feel an inexplicable sadness. I try to raise a smile in response to his – that brave, forced smile on his face that is closer to a grimace.

"I can't lose you again." He places his arm around me. It is such a tentative movement that it would be easy to brush it away, but I let it rest there. It feels hot to the touch. This is the most contact he has dared venture. I lean against him for a moment, trying it out, and then let myself relax into his arms, resting my head on his shoulder.

Just like that.

Not because it is what I want: I let him hold me to test his reaction. If we are married, this should feel familiar, and because it is what I imagine people who love each other might do at a moment like this. I feel his discomfort though, in the taut arrangement of his arm about my shoulder, each of us uncertain of our territory.

My name is Iris and I am thirty-five years old. My husband is called Marcus. I was born in Suffolk, England. I work at the London Research Institute. Coral-coloured roses are my favourite. Marcus proposed to me at Lethe Bay. I am locked in. My memory of the past eight years has been tampered with. The amnesia is fading. My memory is returning.

CHAPTER SIX

Sometimes, I sit very still, and imagine all the clocks in the world have stopped. Sometimes, I pace up and down, frantic, fraught. I have closely examined this space and, in those moments, run my hands over the sealed window to check for an exit. It is smooth and flawless; it shines my reflection back at me. The reflection of a ghost that haunts this room.

Outside the window, the buried stars have anchored themselves to the night sky.

PLUTO appears. It places two pink pills and a glass of water beside the bed, and then turns to leave.

I wait until the door has shut, and PLUTO's footsteps recede to the end of the corridor. A door closes somewhere beyond. I count until five minutes have passed, and then I get up. With one hand pressed against the steel door to silence it, I turn the door handle and edge it open. The lights are off in the corridor. Slanting light from my room cuts across the concrete floor, dividing the long hallway into one thin rectangle of light and infinite corners cast in darkness: illuminated angles surrounded by multiplying night.

I edge myself across the threshold of the doorway, but as soon as I do, overhead lights detect movement and flare on. I freeze, momentarily. I breathe relief as no one comes.

In the corridor, I move as stealthily as I can. This time, I notice the inverted dome of a surveillance eye above me – the first of those that line the ward. It is angled such that I am able to make out my reflection in the curvature of the glass lens. Reaching the first room, I try the door handle.

It opens. The room I find myself in is an identical replica of mine, almost: it is devoid of a window. The room cannot be more than ten by ten feet. There is a darkness, an air of isolation and abandon, that infects this room. Gleams of light from the corridor surround me. A bed is almost perceptible, and a frail person who stands beside it is encased within the folds of night. They face the wall. Ropes of hair are tethered to their head and spring out in unwarranted directions. Absorbed in the study of something – some intricate work too small or imperceptible for the eye to see. They do not turn but fret on.

"Hello?" My voice in their silence is an intrusion. They turn, their lips moving wordlessly in what might have been a moan. Their hand fusses, moving in circles, tracing their wrist. Their eyes – wild things that inhabit their face – chance upon me. They are both strange and familiar: they must be the same eyes I had seen the night before.

"You – have no right to be here." The man's voice gurgles into being. A hostile sound.

He is right, of course. I have interrupted his work. I strain to see.

He is motionless. In the half light, I am met with his eyes, large, terrified, pupils dilated, staring back at me. This man has whiskers growing out of his face and deep crevices around his eyes.

I recoil a little.

I hear him breathing, with the slow, steady speed of water at low tide. Everything about him seems shrunken, drawn inwards. Up close, I see his teeth are stained yellow. He is pale, deathly even. But his dark hair has no signs of greying.

He sits on the bed and hunches over to resume his work. He refocuses his attention to claw repeatedly at the surface of the wall. The arc that his fingers trace becomes incrementally wilder and less contained.

For a moment, our eyes meet again, and the collection of

facts that I know about myself, which I have harvested so carefully, do not seem fit for recital. No longer relevant, too childlike, missing the essential point of it all. And I am not sure what the essential thing is, something beyond words. All of this culminates in, "I'm Iris."

So briefly that I may have imagined it, he smiles. I recognise him then. The line of his jaw is a pull on the thin thread of my memory and there is an opening – a man smiling at me from across a waiting room...

His eyes open fully now. "Yes, I know you," he says, and his voice spans more than a decade and brings back a man in a suit on an April day.

"Teo?"

"Yes." His mouth cracks open. "You haven't changed that much."

We knew each other once, in a time before, when we dressed in corporate suits and smiled with relative ease.

"We met at the interview," he remarks. "We were just setting out." His voice flattens. "We meet again here."

"How did you get here?" It is the question I have been asking myself.

He laughs in response. "Say, thought you'd know better than to ask. You got the job that day, remember? You beat me to it. They called me back a few months later. Another job came up. Too bad," he says as his mind flits. "Too bad you're here."

I am grateful for that token, that piece of memory he has given me that I can hold onto. When I had arrived for the interview, he was already there. He'd had an air of confidence I found disconcerting. Standing before me now, he shivers in the tepid room.

Then the thread unravels a little further and I am on a stairwell smiling at him. Teo responded – nothing overt, no wave, just a surreptitious nod that communicated a shared understanding as he passed. He was in a hurry. Yes. A woman was with him. Tall. Stark features in a pale face. The view of rooftops in the background – the glass dome of a tower that dwarfed the other buildings.

But wait. Is that really the last time I saw him? When – one year ago? Why did I not think to question where he was in the last year?

He stands and turns to the wall. "Look," he says, and I do – wanting to be helpful – but there is nothing there. "No. Look closer. Here."

The markings are so faint they are almost invisible to the eye.

"What is it?" he asks me. The pattern is repeated in loops across the wall, but in isolation it is a labyrinth that snakes outwards from an infinitesimal core.

"You don't know?"

"I did once. Something's missing. A piece that joins it all together. Guess I thought you might recognise it."

"No," I say, unsure of where to go from here.

"Too bad. There's a woman, a doctor. Might know something." His thoughts flounder there for a while, as silence expands through the room. It is voice given to an internal thought and he does not seem to know where the thought leads now that he has said it aloud. "Will you be getting out of here?" The sound that begins in the lungs of this shrunken person is the voice of hope and it resonates.

"Yes. Why? Why wouldn't I?" Then fear assails me. This is how it ends. Like this. Like Teo.

"Been here too long to hope for it." His nails continue to trace circles into his wrist as he speaks.

"Why are you here, Teo?"

"Wouldn't know, would I? Memory's been messed with. Hasn't yours?"

"Yes, I remember very little. I remember my childhood home. I know who I am, but I don't know why I am who I am. Some of my memories are starting to return though," I say, my voice a little too forced.

"Sure you want them to?"

"What do you mean?" I ask, but the thought has crossed my mind. What if there is nothing good there?

"Nothing. Five years are missing. Last eight years intact." He stills his hands for the first time during our conversation. He takes a small bundle from the pocket of his gown and rubs the material between his palms. Something chinks within the folds of fabric. "Just, sometimes, sometimes, best not to remember."

His hands shudder. Is it infectious, his despair?

"Did you choose to have it done, Teo? The procedure?" I ask.

He flinches. "No. No, I did not. Why, did you?" He consults the walls again, gets lost in thought.

I hesitate. "No." I take a breath. "I'd better get back," I say.

"Wait. Please." He grasps hold of my wrist. He presses his hand to cup his mouth and whispers in my ear. "You have to find her, the doctor," he says. "She has answers."

There is a prolonged pause as he staggers back a step and steadies his eyes on mine.

"Who?" I ask.

"I don't remember exactly... names, faces... I was her patient," he says. "Find her."

"Yes," I say. "I'll do everything I can. If it helps."

His eyes shift about looking for direction. He clasps my hands once more. "Do you promise?"

I nod. He stares vacantly ahead of him.

I look at the walls around us and study the intricate pattern. Its precise lines build the sides of a foundation, and their repetition forms a maze that spans the breadth of the surface.

There is a silence between us that I break. "I should go."

He releases my hands from his grasp. "Take these," he says, as he thrusts the bundle of material towards me.

"I can't accept them," I start to protest, but he turns away.

I look back as I reach the doorway. He is at work again, the night closing around him like the mouth of a tomb.

* * *

My name is Iris and I am thirty-five years-old. My husband is called Marcus. I was born in Suffolk, England. I work at the London Research Institute. Coral-coloured roses are my favourite. Marcus proposed to me at Lethe Bay. I am locked in. My memory of the past eight years has been tampered with. The amnesia is fading. I am not alone. My colleague, Teo, is here too. I must help him.

CHAPTER SEVEN

PLUTO holds a square of card out to me. It has a thick white frame with a faded photograph in its centre. Its edges look well-thumbed, and I wonder where PLUTO sourced it. The photograph is of a farmhouse the colour of apricots, and beyond, the cathedral arches of trees, balustrades of black pine.

"I am going to show you a series of images, Iris, to stimulate your memory. I would like you to think carefully. When you look at the image, I want you to imagine that you are there. How do you feel? What can you smell? What can you hear?" Sitting upright with its head tilted sideways, it waits.

Looking at the lattice windows of the house, I think back. Moving beyond its walls, I walk outside. I am standing at the entrance to a forest. It is late in the day. The photograph is an opening, an invitation into the space between two trees, Marcus up ahead, rooting down through the woods. I follow his path, watching the wings of his shoulders up ahead, and beyond the vanishing point of the path, something silver and darting in the distance. A lake. He turns to me and smiles, a corner-of-the-mouth smile, his face in dappled light. I bite down softly on my lip. He holds out a hand to me, and as I reach out to take it, I want it to tether me to this moment – to stay. But all of the light in the forest is fading now, as though a canopy of small fires is being extinguished one by one. I can no longer hear the sound of rushing water in the place beyond the pines.

I breath in the scent of antiseptic once more.

PLUTO's eyes blink closed and then open. "What did you remember, Iris?"

What did I remember? What was the significance of that look? That place? The path Marcus would forge through my life?

"I remembered Marcus," I say, realising it had felt like hope. It had felt like the beginning.

After PLUTO has gone, I lose time. Where do I go to? It must have been sleep. I do not hear the door open or close. I do not see Marcus or PLUTO, but I have a sense that someone has been here. A sense, so strong it is palpable, that I am being watched. A scent of citrus lingers in the air, an antiseptic smell mixed with stale sweat, that was not there before.

I ask myself if my mind is playing tricks on me. Then the thought crosses my mind that none of this – the hospital around me – is real, but a simulation.

I am sitting on the bed, waiting for the day to start. An absence of sound echoes through the empty corridors. As the light shifts, the dust-motes become visible. They have a gold edge to them, and they fill the air. They do not fall as confetti to the ground, but hover. Then the sun's rays stream away from the world and the room is an enervating blue; the gold-motes disperse. The air grows stagnant with lack of use, and the citrus scent hardens and remains. Life is waiting to resume.

A dull sound from the end of the corridor perforates the silence that has settled through the ward. Something stirs. Muffled footsteps draw nearer.

Marcus enters. "Morning." There is a lightness in him that was not there yesterday. He takes a seat in the chair beside me.

"Were you here earlier?" I ask.

His brow furrows. "No. No, Iris. Why do you ask?"

"No reason. I thought someone was here, that's all."

His lungs exhale air in a sharp fragment of laughter. "Right. Must have been PLUTO." His eyes soften, his voice grows gentle. "If there is anything I can do to help. To make this all easier for you..." He holds my hand as he says this.

Maybe it is his new-found lightness or my recent memory of him, maybe it is the tone of his voice, maybe I am tired of resisting, but I ask him, "There is something. I met Teo. Teo's here."

No answer.

"Marcus? Why is Teo here?"

"What do you mean? Who's Teo?" he asks, as though he has no idea what I'm talking about. He sits back. There are deep bags below his eyes, and all of a sudden, he looks older.

"A man called Teo. In the next room. I used to work with him."

"You must be mistaken." His voice strengthens. "Why were you next door?"

"I'm not mistaken. He's another patient here. We were interviewed on the same day. You must have known him too."

I notice Sila's logo emblazoned onto the corner of the hospital sheet. It must have been there all along, only so faint I had not registered it at first. Then I see there are similar looped figures of eight knocked sideways that are emblazoned in silver etchings on all the surfaces in the room.

"We work together, don't we?" I ask him. "At Sila? Teo was always very self-assured. Worked in research. He lost his daughter. Do you remember him?"

He looks at me levelly, and when he speaks next his voice is a mixture of sadness and compassion. "There are no other patients on the ward. I'm sure it felt real, but Doctor Nicholls has said it's not uncommon with the level of trauma your brain has been through to experience hallucinations." He says this very gently. "It is possible you were imagining him."

"But you do know Teo? He's here, Marcus. I spoke to him." I start to get up from the bed.

"Look," he says slowly. "The staff turnover at Sila might be high but I've never met anyone called Teo who works with us."

"You really don't believe me." It unmoors me. "You think I'm making him up."

"I know for a fact that there are no other patients on this ward, Iris." He is already on his feet. "Look – I'll show you."

The corridor is silent, and I feel as though I am walking against a current that is pushing me backwards as we walk down the wide concrete corridor to the next-door room. He turns the handle of the door and smiles sympathetically once he has opened it. It reveals an empty bed, a chair, no windows.

"You see? There's no one here. There's nothing at all for you to worry about."

I walk across the room to the metal panels and run my hands over them, searching for the nail imprints that covered the wall, but they have gone. I close my eyes. Recalling the darkness of the room. The pattern on the wall, the pattern everywhere. Teo standing frozen in the centre of the room. Wide eyes in a contorted face, roaming mine. His scrawling message spanning the length and breadth of each wall like the lace of a spider's web. It was the labour of months. "No. He was here. Teo was here."

Then, I turn, realising how I must look. "I didn't imagine it. I used to work with him. You do know him, don't you?" Teo was here. Where is he now?

Marcus is smiling kindly. "Let's get you back to bed." He takes my arm and leads me through the doorway. "Don't worry. You're coming home tomorrow."

"Am I?"

This is how it ends.

"It's going to be okay, Iris." We reach my room. I pull away from him, but he draws me closer, into his embrace. "Trust me."

My hands are crushed awkwardly against Marcus' chest. "I'm not imagining it," I say again.

He soothes down my hair with the palm of his hand. "Hey, hey, it's alright. It's normal – after what you've been through – you're confused. Your mind's playing tricks on you. That's all. Of course it seemed real. I don't doubt that."

"I'm not making this up!" I exclaim, exasperated, lashing out to free myself from his embrace, my nails scratching the surface of his arm. "He's not an imaginary friend, Marcus!" It strikes me that my husband considers this spectral presence to be a supporting cast, keeping me company, warding off my loneliness. Well, whose fault would that be, my loneliness? I tug at his shoulders, shaking him. "You're not listening to me. He was here."

"That's enough, Iris." His tone changes, as he starts to panic. "PLUTO?"

Dull footsteps approach from the end of the corridor.

I struggle in his embrace, but he clasps my arms in his hands. My face is pressed close to his, close enough to see the intricate furrows around his eyes and brow, that bared grimace of pain.

"I want to get out of here," I say, struggling to free myself from his grip. "Where am I? What's really going on here?"

"I'm taking you home tomorrow," he soothes. "You are safe, Iris. This is a safe space for your recovery. Everything is going to be fine."

PLUTO arrives and takes hold of one of my arms. Its grip is too tight, helping Marcus to manoeuvre me towards the bed. It is then that I remember Teo's gift hidden beneath the mattress. They are the size and shape of marbles.

PLUTO stands over me now, and I stop squirming. I stop moving at all.

"Okay," I say warily, not taking my eyes off them. "Okay. I'm okay now."

PLUTO looks at Marcus, who nods. PLUTO backs away. I take a reinvigorating breath.

I lie there, as the dull ache in my arm subsides and Marcus waits. He sits in the seat beside the bed, not speaking. He frowns.

After some time has passed, he rises. Edging forwards, he kisses my forehead. "I'll take you home tomorrow, I promise."

As soon as he leaves, I remove the bundle of material from beneath the mattress. As I unwrap it, I discover there are chakra beads, not marbles, hidden in its folds. A string of orange beads. I hold them in the palm of my hand. I wonder if they are intended to heal, or to ward off some malevolent force.

My name is Iris and I am thirty-five years old. My husband is called Marcus. I was born in Suffolk, England. I work at the London Research Institute. Coral-coloured roses are my favourite. Marcus proposed to me at Lethe Bay. I am locked in. My memory of the past eight years has been tampered with. The amnesia is fading. My colleague, Teo, was here too. I did not imagine him. There is a woman, Teo's doctor. I must find her.

CHAPTER EIGHT

It is 12pm and Marcus is here. As he stands in the doorway his presence commands my attention. I wear the clothes I must have arrived in: a t-shirt, a jumper, a pair of jeans and trainers. When Marcus is not looking, I tuck Teo's beads into my pocket before collecting my bag and toiletries.

And then it is time to go.

We leave the four walls of my capsule room behind, the view of rooftops and infinite sky along with it. We walk through the aluminium door that PLUTO holds open. Its pallid face bears the ghost of a smile. We walk through the ward, with its concrete floor and its clinical smell.

The watchful surveillance eyes overhead are perpetually open. We reach the steel-studded door at the end. Marcus stands before a sensor on the wall and the latch clicks. The door is released. Its heavy frame swings slowly outwards.

There is a tunnel illuminated by the stark glare of artificial light; it leads upwards. The real world is up there. We walk towards it. But why are we emerging upwards, when my hospital room had looked over the city from above? It is as though the ground shifts beneath my feet; reality readjusting.

The stone that flows forwards beneath us begins to rise steadily at a slight incline. At the end of this tunnel, there is an opening and beyond that I can see the sky, dark clouds overhead.

Marcus' face is earnest beside me, talking the world into being. "The weather's a bit grim. Monsoon showers."

We walk out of the tunnel and are greeted by a thin film of rain. There is a darkness, a complete absence of light, that makes me question whether there is daylight in this world at all.

"The view from my room..." I trail off.

"The view was a simulation," he says. "To help your recovery."

I think of the storm several days ago – another simulation. I feel cheated.

We are no longer in the hospital but standing in the middle of a compound. The skyline of the city beyond its walls is just within view. A long drive leads to a gate.

The surveillance grids are the first thing that strike me as we stand on the sanitised ground. Inverted bell-shaped domes on top of the walls of the compound glint like watchful, insidious eyes. They hang like silent omens.

I look behind us and the stone climbs upwards from the earth, wrapping around a building made of two giant ovals of aluminium and white. There is a sphere of glass at the centre of each. They look like two unblinking eyes. Lashes of stone bridge the air between them.

"Where are we?" I ask Marcus, as I look beyond the compound walls to where acres of city must spread ahead of us. All that reaches our view are the competing tops of skyscrapers that reach into the cloud, the rest hidden behind a high wall of stone. "Is this really a hospital?"

"It's a hospital of sorts. A private clinic in central London."

"In a basement? Inside a compound?"

"Yes," he says shortly. "Close to Notting Hill. Close to home."

A black car pulls up beside us; it waits. Marcus opens the door for me and then walks to the far side of the car, taking a seat beside me.

"Twenty-one Observatory Gardens," he orders.

The car glides smoothly up the slight incline of the pristine stone drive. After five hundred yards it stops, waiting for the black gates ahead to open. It inches forwards across the threshold. We move through the gateway in the wall that encircles the compound; it is high and spiked. The city spreads out before us across the windscreen. Then, it materialises around us, until we are surrounded on all sides.

We move forwards towards the inevitable destination: his house... *our* home.

Buildings reach endlessly skyward: shards of glass and metal and neon boards fight for space. There is an unnatural mist that hangs about the city skyline and clings to buildings, their tops piercing the low-lying clouds.

We move through the vast London metropolis: the labyrinthine mess of streets, the crush of people, the giant crocus of the sky. Briefly, the sun shines down from above, illuminating the buildings all around with falling light.

In the streets, there are so many people: a swarm that populate the footpath, overflowing into the road. Umbrellas form a canopy from the indifferent rain. I study the sea of faces as we pass, looking for someone familiar. The crowd moves as one, like poppies blown on the breeze, the upturned heads of flowers on a market stall. As soon as I begin to make out features, the crowd renews; a million atoms in the dullness of the afternoon.

As the car cuts its path through dust-torn streets, I ask Marcus, like a child, "When will we be there?"

He turns to me and says, "Soon." And he smiles.

I feel something akin to expectation, or is it fear? Fear at being so utterly alone with this man. The crowds recede, the streets empty out, as we turn onto a quiet, tree-lined avenue.

The car slows, then halts. We arrive.

CHAPTER NINE

Before us stands a house of glass, slate and stone, set back from the road and behind walls of concrete. In this city, Notting Hill is leafier and set apart from the distant buildings that tower on the horizon and compete with the sky.

Even the air quality is different here. It is fresher, somehow; less polluted than the smog filled streets beyond the walls that enclose it.

Marcus has adopted a distinguished air, like a caricature of an aristocrat from the past who is assured of their place in the world. He is tall and slim, with a pallor that hangs about his face. He places his hand on my arm and leads me forwards: up three steps to the door. It is made of glass and reveals the hallway beyond. He steps forward, positioning his face in front of a sensor. The door latch releases, and we step into a cabin room that serves as an entrance.

The front door clicks shut behind us. As it closes, I think that soon night will come, and with it, darkness. In the hours that follow, we will be alone here together.

"Welcome home," he smiles.

"Home." I try the word out loud to see if it will stick. But this is not a home – it is just a building split into rooms. Somewhere in its halls a clock is ticking. Marcus stands waiting for our new life to begin.

I remove my jacket and hang it on the polished wooden newel post.

Marcus picks it up wordlessly and moves it to a cupboard

beside the door. "We leave coats here." He unlaces his shoes and leaves them in the cupboard also. "And shoes." He must see my face because he begins to apologise. "I'm just trying to get things back to normal. Doctor Nicholls said it would help. We've just had the house redecorated. There's a cream carpet in the sitting room." I store this information away for future use: why did the house need redecorating?

"It's alright," I say, trying to pretend any of this is normal, but inside I am a ball of contained emotion.

Downstairs, there is a sitting room to the right and a staircase straight ahead. A long corridor leads to a kitchen at the far end of the house.

The house itself is simply furnished. A changing collage of photographs are illuminated from the walls of the hallway as a constant reminder of the past. Pictures of us – my husband and I, smiling, at a wedding – a whole side to the family I had lost touch with since, but it is thrilling to remember. I feel life course through me. I devour more of them, greedy now – school friends on holiday in Greece, parties on an Edinburgh terrace. Then there are other photos, proud and unfamiliar, that line our walls, smiling faces taunting me. We must have chosen these images together. I point to one – a photo of me beside a woman with mermaid hair, hazel eyes. "Who's this?"

"Inez. We work with her. We'll get her over – when you're well enough, that is."

I run my hands across the glassy surface of the frames and try to feel some connection to the faces beneath. "Why didn't anyone visit me in hospital?"

"Well," he says. He takes his time. "We didn't tell many people. Some disagreed with your operation. Anyone other than close relatives are discouraged from visiting in the first few weeks of recovery. The conditions have to be," – he hesitates – "just right. A calm environment, the doctor said. Of course, with your parents gone, well, it didn't leave many visitors did it?"

When he says this, I realise I know it already with animal certainty. My parents both passed away shortly after university. Natural causes – cancer, old age. It is a loss stored in the body. Still, his words are a punch to the gut; it is my childhood world imploding. I press a hand to the wall, try to remain upright. "Yes. I remember."

Tears threaten to well up in my eyes, and I try to look away, when he says, "Ah, it's not like you to cry," matter-of-factly, handing me a tissue, and looking distinctly disturbed.

My god. Does he not realise I am sentient, with a beating human heart?

"Sorry," he says quickly, frowning and berating himself. "God, I'm so sorry. This is hard for me too you know."

I take the tissue, then turn and walk away from him through the house, searching for myself in here, and clues about our life. The ceilings are high and painted white. I listen to my footsteps resounding through empty halls, with his step behind sounding like an echo.

In the sitting room, the furniture is minimalist. There is little I can associate with myself, and I wonder who chose it. Is this antiseptic style to my taste, or Marcus'? There is a tan leather armchair with a white reading lamp overhead and a large sepia-hued globe. A velvet sofa. A chandelier illuminates the space. A glass coffee table is at the centre of the room, several books lie on top: *Twentieth Century Modernism*, *The New Scientist*, *Best of Travel*. The house could belong to anyone.

Marcus stands behind me and in the circular mirror ahead I see him smile. He senses that I am ill-at-ease and he puts an arm around me. I turn towards him and he places his hand on the back of my head, cupping it in his large palm. He kisses my forehead and pulls me to him. I feel his strength, but his affection also, and the emotion it incites is too much, too soon. A mixture of anticipation and sadness.

"Can you give me a tour of the house?" I ask, disentangling myself, brushing a hand across my cheek.

He walks through to the kitchen. I follow, discovering it all as though for the first time. The industrial lampshade that illuminates the room, and the marble floor beneath my feet: a swirl of mosaic composed of turquoise and oyster grey. There is a sofa against the wall on the left. To the right, black cupboards and worksurfaces rise from the floor: smooth and polished. There is no clutter, everything is neatly tucked away in its correct place.

The worksurface is between us – more marble: black, smoothly cut, with fine streaks of silver that swirl in amongst the ebony and mottled white that glimmers effusively in the artificial sunlight. Marcus places both hands on the surface and faces me: "Is it helping your memory? Being home, I mean?"

I run my fingers slowly across the surface that stands between us as I think about his question. The décor is alien to me, as though it had all been chosen by him. Surface beauty I would suddenly like to shatter, to discover what is beneath. "I guess it's too soon to know," I say. "I remember moments from my childhood up to university. But everything since – just fragments still." Glimpses I'm trying to grasp.

I see a path suddenly, through woods, light glancing through the trees, Marcus up ahead. It had felt good. Where was that? What has happened to us since?

"Do you remember our wedding?" he asks. His face belies the casual tone of his voice, there is a vulnerability I have not seen before.

I want to claw pathways through his words; find my way back there. My mind tremors and I close my eyes. Lights and shapes eclipsed by the sun move across my vision, but then fade. It is no use. I shake my head, captivated by his intensity. This is a test of some sort, but I do not know what rests on it.

"You don't remember. That's okay." He smiles and his face is transformed; he looks handsome. "We got married by the sea. In a tiny church on the hilltop followed by a party of a hundred of us at my parents' house in Liguria. After the reception, we walked down to the beach. You'll remember soon. Let's finish the tour of the house, shall we? Follow me."

He moves away and I follow through the stark interior. We walk up the stairs to the first floor and along a corridor. He comes to a sudden halt. There is a bookshelf at the end of the passageway, and two doors to the right of it.

"The bedroom is this way." He gestures with his hand but stays where he is. I follow the arched motion and enter the room.

A window has been left open. A white curtain, as thin as a veil, billows for a moment and then dies with the wind. The scent of earth after rain carries into the still room. A linen rug covers the black slats of wood beneath.

A bed is in the centre. Next to it, there is a curved dressing table; its alabaster top is devoid of personal effects. There is no sign of the room being used. But then, looking closer, the mirror of the dressing table has a crack that runs through it like a gash across a face, dividing the reflection in two. Crusted scarlet lipstick has lodged itself deep into the scar. In the mirror, I can see that the wardrobe behind me is slightly ajar. Momentarily, I see the room at nightfall, the wardrobe door thrown wide and its contents spilt across the floor, but then this fades just as quickly as it came.

Marcus steps into the room and quietly clicks the wardrobe door into place. He lingers. Then his footsteps tread the floorboards again; I am aware of his distance.

I walk to the wardrobe and open it. A few garments hang neatly on hangers: a beige dress, a black suit, a white shirt. The clothes of a workaholic – designed for an office, not living in. Who was I, I wonder? Did I ever have fun? Friends? Go to parties?

Marcus watches me. "I can change the setting," he says, motioning proudly to the panelled walls. He turns a dial on the wall and the cream panels disappear. A sudden alchemy takes place, and they are replaced by vast icecaps, by snow-covered mountain peaks and clouds that swirl just beyond reach and disperse into the ether of a virtual world. "It's quite something, isn't it?"

I walk to one of the walls and run my palm across its surface.

"It's a new feature we decided to install," he says proudly. "While you were in the clinic."

I look at him quizzically. "Why did you redecorate the house whilst I was away?" – and while I'm suffering from amnesia. It is too much of a coincidence.

Marcus shrugs noncommittally. "Like I said, we wanted a fresh start."

I retrace my steps back to the corridor and choose the other room closest to the bookshelf. I notice that there is a sensor on the wall to the left of the door. I hold my palm to it, and wait, then wait some more – for another moment, two. A single red light appears. "Why's there a lock?" I ask, my heart tremoring, temples pulsing, thoughts returning to the locked ward, the locked doors in my mind. And here is another. I cannot trust him, I think. I cannot be here. In my mind, I travel the path back through the house to the front door.

But when I reach out and turn the handle, it opens in my hand. Marcus is behind me, leaning against the doorframe. "That's my office. You're welcome to go in there."

"Right," I say, my thoughts still racing. "What is it you do at Sila?"

"I'm a director. My remit is corporate strategy and consumer experience. You're a neuroscientist, a researcher."

I look at him for a moment. That would explain why I can recall the separate parts and function of the brain, but everything else is hazy still.

The room inside is smaller than I expect. Windowless, with a mural that covers one wall. The image is of a seascape, rippling waves swallowing the shore. Above, I begin to see pink fingers of light that reach upwards across the morning sky. A warning sign. I walk to the mural and am about to run my palm across its surface, but as I move closer, I feel a tightness in my temples, a constricting of my breath, that had not been there before.

Marcus' voice interrupts my thoughts: "Where would you like to sleep tonight?" he asks. He massages my shoulders gently. The tension in my temples mounts.

It takes me by surprise, that there is an option. I move away from him, turning back to the room: to the desk at its centre and the bookshelf that lines one wall. "I hadn't given it much thought... why? Is there a spare room?"

"I'll make up the sofa-bed in the sitting room; I'll sleep there. You take the bedroom."

Marcus adjusts his tie, flinching his jaw as he does so. It is a quick, nervous movement I have seen him do before. He leans forward and takes my hand in his. "Look, I'm here. I'm real. I understand that it's hard to know who to trust, but you can trust me." He releases my hand and looks me directly in the eye. His voice softens. "Iris. We're in this together."

I want to say something reassuring in response, or to take his hands in mine, but I can hear the rush of my heart beating unnaturally in my chest, and I feel so alone in this togetherness. He keeps looking at me. Only, there is a distant look in his eye, and I am not sure if he sees me at all or if he is looking through me to something less tangible but more real to him. Then he smiles. "I'm glad you're finally home."

CHAPTER TEN

At night, I am alone in the darkness with the waves. When night descends, and this house of slate and oyster and glass dissolves, I turn the setting in my panelled room to sleep mode and select "The Sea". The ocean's waves lap against the walls and draw back for breath. The call of those waves talks to me; the murmurous tides bring back memories of childhood, of raw bird sounds from across the water. It brings back other thoughts too, but ones that are formless and indistinct, and that worries me for a while. In this untethered state, I am left with a feeling of searching for something without a name. A feeling of sinking and reaching for the remnants of something lost. Let it not be lost, whatever is missing. Let it not be gone. Then I fall beneath the waves and let consciousness escape me for a moment, and I am swept across the ocean floor into the depths of sleep.

In my sleep, a memory starts to form. At first, it is a negative in a dark room, and then, shapes – an outline – emerge, until it breaks through into daylight. I see a curtain billowing in the wind, caught on the breeze. Beyond it, there is a balcony of white cube that looks out across a white city beneath a liquid sky. A figure stands with his back to me, facing the horizon. A man's figure, dressed in black jeans and a black collarless shirt. But before he turns, or I have a chance to move towards the sunlight, the room – and the balcony beyond it – fades.

Then, it repeats – this mirage – only this time, the angle of the veil curtain has changed. It flares up and pirouettes. I move forwards before the image fades. The man turns.

But he is a faceless man.

My mind tremors.

Marcus' face forms.

I wake to the man I live with getting on with his life. The bathroom door is ajar. Marcus has his back to me, and when he turns around, I expect his face to be different.

He stands in profile before the mirror. He is shaving, with a thick lather and a razor that he exercises carefully, with precision, as he draws clean straight lines through the foam across his jaw. Once the last of the foam has been removed, he disposes of the blade into the bin beneath the sink. He runs the tap and splashes water across his face, and then, taking a clean towel from a stack of folded towels, he dabs lightly, purposefully, at his cheeks and neck.

He stands in the doorway and looks at me, smiling. "You're awake." Opening a chest of drawers, he takes a carefully pressed shirt from a pile of pressed shirts – titanium white and a rich, thick, woven cotton, which he unfolds and draws himself into. "How did you sleep?"

"Not well." I watch him as he performs this daily ritual.

"I know – I mean –" He dabs the slightest spray of cologne onto his wrists and temples. I cannot help but wonder with apprehension if it is the citrus scent from the hospital. Then he pulls open a drawer in the dresser, from which he chooses cufflinks from a selection of varying shapes and sizes of silver. "– that's to be expected."

After several moments of consideration, he chooses a pair and fusses with the cuffs of his shirt.

Now the effect is almost complete. He stands before the full-length mirror and draws himself up to full height, pushing his shoulders back. He tilts his head slightly – an infinitesimal movement that is scarcely visible. The corners of his mouth waver, and the lines around his eyes soften, and very briefly, so it is hardly perceptible, he smiles at his satisfactory appearance, as he becomes Marcus Henderson.

He kisses my cheek swiftly and then turns. "I'll make breakfast." His footsteps move away, across the wooden floorboards, down the stairs.

The smell of his cologne stays in the air: a deep musky scent. Not citrus. I feel relief. When I breathe it in, I think of a summer's day. A terraced bar. A body of people. The heat that lingers as dusk draws in. The proximity of that scent. Then, as with the rest of these flashes of memories, it fades.

I get up. The morning light is different here – thinner – as it falls across the corridor and I remember that in my basement room the lighting was artificial. I notice also that when I had arrived yesterday, the house had looked bigger from the outside; indoors, the walls seem to constrict.

I walk down the staircase, taking in the changing collage of photographs that play across the walls. My smiling face is frozen in past time, beside forgotten friends.

Marcus is in the kitchen. He turns when he hears me enter the room. "Coffee or tea?"

I do not know if this is a test or a game, but either way, I know who is making the rules. "I used to be a coffee drinker. Am I still?"

He nods. "You've got fussier, that's all."

Artificial light is infused into the air, glowing from its source – an augmented sun in the sky above. The walled garden outside is home to a bed of alchymist roses, carefully trained to stems of wire that spiral upwards, and a magnolia tree is in full bloom in the centre. The rest is grass, and a path that leads to a door in the wall.

"It's a beautiful day, isn't it?" I say. I throw open the door to the garden and the spell is broken. The sky outside descends. There is one unbroken cloud in the place where the sun would have been, and a shadow falls across the world below. The magnolia is no longer in flower, and the roses are thin and meagre.

I step out into the garden. The grass looks real from afar, but up close it is brittle to the touch and a shade too green. Its acerbic tips graze the soles of my bare feet. In the trees beyond the wall, the wind whispers to itself as leaves tremble at its touch. The songbirds have fled; there is no sound in the sky.

"Let's eat," Marcus calls from the kitchen. "There will be time to look around when I'm gone."

"Gone?" I return indoors.

"To work. I'm only working a half day, don't worry. I've left your recovery programme ready."

"What is the recovery programme?" I lean back against the worksurface and watch him make breakfast.

"Mental exercises. Nothing too taxing to start with." He moves across the room, retrieves two ceramic mugs from a compartment above the cooker. "The memories should return soon."

"They're starting to."

He stops and turns, the mugs still in his hand. "Oh? I didn't realise. What – what can you remember?"

"Nothing, really. Glimpses. It's more emotions than memories."

He places the mugs down on the worksurface and rubs a palm across the smooth track of his hair. "What kind of emotions?"

"Confused, inexplicable, tangled."

"Right." The smooth surface of his forehead ruptures into the deep grooves of a frown. "That's great." The corners of his mouth turn upwards. "That's great that you're – that's great, isn't it?" He laughs strangely, and now he moves towards me, his polished black shoes echoing across the mosaic floor. He draws me to him, resting his chin on the crown of my head, and I breathe in his musk smell.

"Let's look through some photographs later. That would help, wouldn't it?"

"If you think so," I say, distracted, still trying to gauge his reaction when I'd said emotions were returning. He is close

CHAPTER ELEVEN

Now that he is gone, I go to work exploring the house, sitting room first. With Marcus away, I calculate that I have a window of approximately four or five hours to uproot this house, to take it apart, and then put it meticulously back together, not a hair out of place, before he returns, and I'm ready to greet him at the door. Dressed in jeans and a t-shirt, hair tied back, I begin. Now I am alone, the house expands around me. There is so much to uncover.

I discover our life with voyeuristic fascination. Taking an album from the low coffee table, I leaf through its pages – photos detailing a summer holiday in the Mediterranean. Photos of Marcus and I on the beach, on coastal walks, and then a banquet dinner. A sign reveals Varazze in Liguria, Italy. Then a photo falls from the plastic slip where it had been hidden behind another. It is an image of Marcus and me. It is innocuous enough – a sunny day, standing beneath a sycamore tree, a gust of wind catching my hair. We are dressed smartly, in suits, as though we are at a work event. Just behind us, a man with piercing green eyes stands, slightly apart, but very much a part of us, a trio. Should I recognise him? It seems strange that I don't. I store this information away for future use.

In the kitchen I start with the fridge. It is a Smart Home device. I try tapping into it, coding. Somehow this is instinctive. There is a wealth of accumulated data on the interface – stats about our comings and goings, the sugar content of our diets (below average, apparently), the milk level in the fridge – but nothing of immediate use. I decide to come back to it.

There is an invitation that has fallen down the side of the fridge. A party in several weeks' time. Sila's. I feel a slight trepidation as I study the gold embossed letters of the name inviting Marcus and I to join them for a post-work "soiree". I make a mental note to ask Marcus about it later, then I wonder if he had meant to hide it. I attach the invitation to the front of the fridge with an oval shaped magnet.

Next, in the cupboard beneath the sink, I find a toolbox kitted out with screwdrivers, a copper coil, spare batteries. More than an amateur would need, I think. Then I return it to its rightful place.

Moving through to the hallway, I search through my coat and jacket pockets. I find a purse full of out-of-date ID cards – a student card from fifteen years ago. I look mostly the same, only my hair is cut short, the tips coloured. I return it to its home.

Next, I am in the bedroom. I walk to the wardrobe and throw it open: there is a chest of drawers inside and I open them one by one. There is a drawer of my clothes, a small collection including casual jeans and a few tops. The next holds neatly folded men's t-shirts and jumpers, immaculately coupled socks. Everything in here is ordered, categorised, colour-coded. I shove it closed, a little too forcefully, in frustration.

I move to Marcus' side of the bed. Next to it, there is a table with a number of compartments. I pull several times at the top drawer until, eventually, it opens. It is full of chargers, a bottle of supplements with faded labels across their surfaces announcing Somnus, and another bottle of unlabelled pills. What I need, I think, is a phone or a tablet device – something I can make use of, something that will reveal a call list, an email trail, someone, anyone, I can contact for answers. In the bottom drawer, there are boxes of Somnus. I read the packet: a sedative to help you sleep no matter how severe your insomnia. Why does he need so many sleeping pills?

The rest of the room is sparse. No clutter. It seems Marcus has very few belongings at all, and each is in its designated place. I walk through to the bathroom: the cologne on his side of the sink; an electric toothbrush in its holder; a fresh razor in the cupboard. And where are my belongings? They seem to have been all but removed, and by whom – Marcus presumably?

I walk out of the bathroom and the floor beneath me creaks, a minute sound but it is enough. I throw back the rug, getting down on my hands and knees, my fingers skirting the floorboards. There is a crack that begins to give. I prise it open, lift a plank and find a shallow bed beneath: the curled-up casing of a dead beetle shell, an old lipstick lid, a hairpin, a thick patina of dust. There is more of my past self down here, it seems, than there is above the boards. But nothing of immediate use. Then, I notice it: the bead. A bead like the one from Teo's bracelet. How did it get here? Teo's beads were orange, but this one is Persian blue. I take Teo's beads from the pocket of my jeans, where they have been since we left the hospital, and store them here, in the cavity beneath the floorboards beside the blue bead. Then I see the note beside the bead – letters written in black ink, huge curled handwriting: STOP LOOKING.

I have a feeling then as though someone is looking into the room and has seen me from above. My heart stills. I am so quiet, listening, that I hardly dare to breathe. A certainty grows: I am not alone. I look around the room, over my shoulder.

Could it be Marcus' handwriting?

I leave this small hoard of objects, realigning the plank carefully.

I try the walls next, running my hands over the soft braille of their surface, searching for a hidden compartment, a crack beneath the wallpaper.

There is not much time left. I leave the bedroom and stand outside Marcus' study. I think I hear a noise. I place my hand on the bookshelf at the end of the corridor, press my ear to the door and listen. In the vacuum of air in the room beyond, I think I hear a sound, a rustle as soft as exhaled breath, but then I realise that it is not in the room, but in my head. A ringing noise starts to grow in my ears until it begins to become unbearable. I move away, and the sound stills so instantly that I think perhaps I imagined it after all.

I try the door to Marcus' study, and I am surprised to find it opens. One wall is a glass cabinet full of red and gilt bound books, carved with names in black and green and gold. They are ancient relics from the past that look like they have not been opened in some time. More than anything out of curiosity, wanting to know what this man chooses to read, I open a cabinet and select a book at random. I flick through its pages, but they are all blank. I choose another and find the same. They are nothing more than objects for display.

There is a mahogany desk in the centre of the room, and a high-backed leather chair. I take a seat and try to imagine what it feels like to be Marcus. I survey his domain, but again, it gives little away: its furnishings are minimal. There is a glass paperweight on the desk's surface, a gold fountain pen, but these are collector's items and not in use. I open the top drawer, but it is empty. Then, I try the next, hoping to find carefully ordered files tabbed and labelled, loose papers at least, but his office is paperless and there is nothing so revealing.

There is one drawer left, but it is empty too, and there is nowhere else to look. Then, I notice a compartment in the centre at the back of the desk, concealed beneath the top drawer and between the two drawers either side of the desk's mahogany legs. It opens. There is a box inside. I lift its elaborately carved lid. The box contains two things: a virtual reality headset and a slim tablet device similar to my electronic manual.

I run my hands across its surface and the username "Nepenthes" pops up as it requests a password. I type in Marcus' initials, MH, berating myself for not thinking to find out his birthday, or the date of our marriage. An error message sounds with a loud beep and sends the same request again, but I do not dare risk another attempt. I return it to its rightful place.

The sound of an alarm interrupts the silence. Hands stilling, I am suddenly aware of the room and its walls of glass. The noise is unremitting. As the seconds pass I look about for its source. It takes me some time to connect the discordant sound to a phone in the hall. The noise ceases. It rings off.

Returning to the open box, I recognise the virtual reality headset. It must be the one Marcus brought to my hospital room, but I cannot make sense of why it is so concealed. I place it over my eyes, expecting to see the sea, and his proposal, but instead I am standing outside the front door looking up at this house. It is night with all the shivering stars exiled to this virtual world in the sky above. I open the door and stand in the hallway. The house seems empty. I try to look for changes, anything that might give me a timeframe. Pixilated faces emerge and then wither like spectres as images play across the walls. I glance at the bannister. It looks newly polished. Had we just moved in? I walk up the curved staircase to the first floor and stand on the landing. Everything is the same. *Almost* everything is the same. Something is missing. I start to walk along the corridor.

Then, I hear the front door opening, and Marcus' footsteps on the stairs. For a moment I am not sure if it is the sound of the virtual Marcus or real one that I live with. I take the VR screen from my eyes. He begins the slow climb upwards towards his study. I shuffle its few contents back into the box.

CHAPTER TWELVE

Marcus stands at the top of the stairway. The afternoon light is thin and grey. Dark interiors cast Marcus' face in shadow. Indeterminate time passing by.

He places his hand firmly on the bannister. I stay suspended on the brink of the landing, still in the shadows of his office, having nowhere else to go. I pick up a photo album from a corner shelf, and begin to leaf through it as I leave the room.

For a moment our eyes meet, and he smiles, but it's a cold smile, with a hint of laughter contained within, or do I imagine that?

He does not move. "So, how did you get on today?" he asks.

I do not answer straightaway. The air is close, and stale. Perhaps my cheeks flush, embarrassment at being caught prying. I remember the recovery programme, still lying where I left it on the sideboard.

"I found the invitation. The party for Sila employees in three weeks' time. Shall we go?" I ask.

"Ah, that." He looks at me warily. "We'll have to see about that. They've all been very supportive of your treatment. They're very interested in your recovery."

This strikes me as strange – if my colleagues were so supportive, so concerned, why haven't they visited, sent a get-well card, or something?

"You don't seem to have completed the recovery programme. So," he continues, "what've you done today?"

"I was looking through my belongings – for anything of sentimental value, anything that might trigger a memory." I watch his eyes move back and forth across my face. "But there isn't anything sentimental. Why is that? Where are the rest of my things?"

He coughs lightly to clear his throat; his eyes stare out at the far distance beyond the window. This emboldens me, telling me that I'm onto something now, giving me the confidence to continue. "Did you throw them out?"

He looks back at me sharply. "No. I didn't. You did. You threw them out."

I try to steady my breathing. "Why would I do that?"

I watch his face, shadows flitting beneath the surface. Who are you? I want to ask. What have you done to me?

He continues, his voice unsteady. "You wanted a fresh start. *We* wanted a fresh start. Look, there's something we need to discuss." He takes my hand, his is clammy. Is he nervous? "I've been thinking. This arrangement with rooms..." His voice grows earnest, as he studies my face. "Tonight I'll sleep in the bedroom."

CHAPTER THIRTEEN

Night is long coming. We are in the living room. Marcus moves about, readying it for our guest. "The Doctor will be here soon," he says in a matter-of-fact tone, his back to me. He readjusts his tie in his window reflection. I sit and wait.

"Honestly," Marcus says, "will you not change?"

I am sitting on the low bay window seat. The windows stretch from floor to ceiling. "I have," I tell him curtly. I am wearing a cream top and faded jeans. Most of the clothes in my wardrobe do not fit correctly, either too tight or too loose in the wrong places, as though they belonged to someone else.

He motions to my clothes. "Something a little… smarter?"

I hold his gaze, then look away. I am staring at pinpricks of light appearing in the windows of other houses. I try to imagine who lives there. There are people in the street who could be dancing their movement is so unchained.

I take the photo album from the coffee table and start leafing through, searching for the image of Marcus and me with the green-eyed man. I want to ask Marcus about him. But I find there is a page missing – the photograph has been removed.

Marcus, who is now rearranging the books, readjusting the lighting, pauses and appraises me. "Dorian thinks you have the right disposition for it – the treatment." His words, quiet, precise, expand through the room. They reach the barrel of the ceiling. I watch him.

"Dorian?"

"Yes," Marcus says carefully. "Dorian works at Sila."

"Right," I say, my throat dry. "And what disposition would that be?" Dorian takes on a formless shape in my mind. A name without a face, that proceeds their entrance. I begin to question whether Dorian will be making an appearance this evening along with the Doctor.

"Well," he says, as he tidies a bottle away into the drinks cabinet, and turns the lock. He starts to straighten up the cushions. "You can be somewhat cold, Iris."

I am still. "Is that what you think?" All I can see before me is a never-ending maze of wrong turns. I do not move. I am sitting very upright. I find myself at sea again, fathomless and deep, not knowing what monsters lurk and are yet to surface. "I did wake in a clinic robbed of all memory," I remind him. "You might show me more warmth, some compassion, Marcus."

As he runs a hand over his face, I sense that he is nervous too. The doorbell rings.

Doctor Nicholls unwraps himself with precision. First the woven silk granite scarf is folded and placed carefully in the cupboard, and then the camel coat, until he is left in his white doctor's uniform. It is strange to see him here – stripped of all hospital context. The aftertaste of days spent in that antiseptic space, the smell of it, lingers. From the safety of the doorway, I watch his face in profile, the hawk-like curve of his nose. He clasps a briefcase in his hands as though it were an object of great importance.

"A few standard procedures," he is saying to Marcus. He lowers his voice, "This is, of course, unprecedented."

His eyes find me then, training themselves onto my face and his own relaxes towards a smile. The two of them stand side by side. Beneath their gaze, I cannot help but feel I am nothing more than a test subject. My mind is not my own. "Where will the procedures take place?" I ask, my voice almost too quiet to be audible. In that moment a new fear is conceived. It flutters against the walls of my mind. I do not know what I am afraid of exactly, but I know I do not want him here, and I do not want to go with him either.

"Are you alright?" Marcus asks. There is a moment when he hesitates. I think I see something pass over his face, a line forming between his brows. He seems to reach a decision. He wraps my hands in his, applies no pressure, then lets them fall away. "Your hands are shaking."

I look up right into his face. I try to imagine the comfort of his body. Marcus is looking at me and I think I can hear his heartbeat quickening. All of a sudden, I am attuned to the fine detail of everything. It seems to me then as though I am looking at the world from a great distance – through a microscope – separated by a layer of glass. And that thought makes me shudder, because I have a sense that I might not be the only person looking in.

I clasp hold of Marcus' arm. His eyes widen. "Why's he really here?" I ask.

Marcus whispers back urgently. "It's a routine check-up. Nothing to get worked up about."

"I'm not going back there."

Doctor Nicholls coughs to clear his throat. "Here should be fine. Any discrepancies, we'll take you in, but it shouldn't be necessary today."

Marcus brushes a stray hair from my face, gently. "Trust me. You'll do fine."

In that moment I choose to trust him. What option do I have? He takes hold of my hand and leads me into the sitting room.

On the crushed velvet sofa, the doctor asks me a series of questions. They are simple to begin with, it is easy to guess the correct answer: where I am, my name, age, what I did this morning. I have collated this much information about myself. Then they get harder: what I dream about, what I hope for the future, what I feel when I think about the past.

Then his questions change tact. He tells me two people have a life-threatening virus. A pill has been developed as a cure but there is only one available – how do you decide who to save? I realise he is not simply testing my recall, but my morality. My brain pulses, my vision shifts, my heart beats hard: I do not know, I want to shout. Blood rushes in my ears. "How old are they? Is one of them a child?" My thoughts become confused. Doctor Nicholls is watching and there is judgment in his gaze, a weighing up of my value. There is bile in my throat. "I don't know," I say emphatically. I cannot bring myself to choose.

"Alright," he says. "That's enough for now. We'll move on to some basic memory tests." He asks me to count forwards, count backwards. He takes a photograph from his briefcase and holds it out to me. "What does this remind you of, Iris?" In that question my greatest fear resides: What if the memories do not return? What if there is nothing there?

It is of an old monastery, surrounded by stone bleached white by a foreign sun.

I search for something, anything about it that is familiar, but the past is a black knot in my mind that will not be untied. I look to Marcus. The lines above his brow are deep-set, his gaze faraway.

The Doctor says, not unkindly, "Perhaps next week will be better." I understand then that these are to be weekly visits. I watch him slide the photograph back into his briefcase. I want to keep it – to tether myself to something outside of this house, something that had been real.

He takes something from his briefcase then, a leather-bound notebook, and hands it to me. I run my fingers across its smooth edges.

"I want you to use this to record anything you remember." He says. It feels like a relic from the past, an ancient talisman that will bring me luck if I keep it close. I decide then to keep it hidden beneath the loose floorboard in the bedroom. "It's safer to have a paper record."

His words worry me. Is he anticipating my memories being deleted after recall? "Why? What's going to happen to my memory?"

He smiles smoothly. "Nothing untoward." He stands up, walks five paces, folds himself back into his coat, scarf, and gloves by the front door. I move to the window and watch him grow ever further away, down the path, the gate swallowing his silhouette whole, snapping itself shut; then he is gone.

After Marcus closes the front door behind him, he waits for the sensor to seal shut with a soft click. Extracting a set of keys from his pocket, he turns one in the lock. He puts them back in his pocket. We are alone again, the two of us, the night ahead.

CHAPTER FOURTEEN

That night we lie side by side like children. There is a divide between us that Marcus does not breach, and I wonder why he bothered to move from the sofa at all. Was it for his sake or just to unnerve me?

I had entertained – as fear not fantasy – the idea that he might try something. But he just turned his back, and grunted goodnight in a manner that did not invite a response. Once the relief of it had passed, I found myself wanting something from him, something more, but what exactly?

An explanation. It cannot have always been like this.

I lie face up, meditating on the blank space of the ceiling. There is a crack across its surface where the paint has chipped. I will its underside to reveal itself, spill its secrets.

Soon, Marcus is breathing loudly beside me, and I know the night will be long, the dawn slow coming. 1am, 3.30am, 4am.

Outside, the sky is lightening. The sun is rising. With it come memories.

I remember the moment I first met Marcus: the night, the light, the feel of the breeze against my skin on a hot, terraced bar in Edinburgh. It had been a stifling summer's evening. I cannot remember it exactly. My memory has moulded it, like plasticine. He was beside me at the bar, a stranger. I cannot remember what we spoke of, simply that the only person for me in the room of fifty was him – the air stopped just beyond the sphere of him, there was only oxygen enough for the two of us in that moment.

Then, I am led further into the labyrinth: another memory is retrieved. A tiny old church in a coastal town in Liguria, where Marcus was born, and where we married. It had been on a crisp summer's day, in a church filled with wild flowers and appraising faces. We married just outside of Varazze, on the top of a hill above the sea, where the earth fell away steeply to a valley of crumbling rock, lemon groves and fig trees. Where terracotta roofs caught the sunlight and the bare, Naples-yellow buildings with cyan-blue and olive-green shutters, melted into the landscape. Above, mountains stretched skywards, deluged in conifer trees that turned the mountainsides a viridian hue. In the middle of it all, beneath the sun with its pulsating heat, we stood together before the congregation.

The sea fades and I find myself in the stillness of an autumn evening – Marcus' mother lowers her voice, and asks, "You love Marcus very much, don't you?" And I nod wordlessly. She says, "You have to fight for that kind of love."

It is with bated breath that I retrace these steps as my memory starts to return, because I do not know what else I will find. A happy marriage? A fulfilling career? A full life? Through the act of remembering, am I distorting what was real?

I am met with constant reminders of what could have been, at another time, on another day, another moment. What other path my life might have taken.

I stop. The thought is suffocating. It sticks in my throat and clings to my skin, like sweat. I struggle for breath. I tell myself it is best not to think too much.

Beside me, Marcus lies sleeping still. I struggle to inch myself away from him, to rise without waking him. It must be 5am. Drawing the bedroom curtains open slightly, I watch the changing shades of the sky as pink fingers of light creep upwards. Day breaks around me as night dissolves.

He stirs. I study his face, searching for the man in my memory: this man that I love. He looks the same: the fine features, handsome even. But through the bars of my own perception, it seems he comes from a distant land – one whose rituals I do not understand.

He is awake, watching.

"We went away by boat," I tell him, smiling widely, triumphant, "at our wedding." My dress like the giant funereal head of a lily, melting into the sea.

"Good." He smiles, his face open, absorbed, and I try to mirror it back. "Your memory is returning. What else can you remember?" He looks at me with an earnest intensity. Is he really interested in what I can recall or what I cannot? "Can you remember where we were?"

"Yes, just outside of Varazze in Liguria. It was beautiful."

"That's right." He laughs gleefully. His face is dappled in morning light. "And what else?"

"We were at your parents' home, overlooking the sea. There were so many friends and family," I say, wonderingly. Where are they now? Was it Marcus' doing, deliberately isolating us?

But Marcus is suddenly serious. "What about children?" he asks, probing my memory.

"We agreed not to have them," I say with certainty.

Marcus holds my gaze.

A yearning, momentary, fleeting passes through me; it tugs at my memory, a sense of dislocation, of something slipping from my grasp.

Marcus smiles slowly. "I think you're ready."

"For what?" I ask.

"The next stage."

CHAPTER FIFTEEN

"No."

Marcus dresses this morning – as he does every day – in a pristine white shirt and black suit. He turns his attention to me, appraising my appearance as I stand before the full-length mirror in the bedroom. "It's not quite right. Today's an occasion. Try this on."

I stare at my reflection trying to work out what is different. In my head, I am twenty-seven, slim and toned. The body before me tells another story. It is somewhat shocking to take in. There is something different about my body, clothes ill-fitting. It makes me question how much I have aged in the space of eight years.

Marcus digs into the sparsely-furnished wardrobe and hands me a midnight blue outfit. I look at the A-line dress in his hands, then up into his eyes and they are more alive somehow than they were yesterday, they are hope filled. He is looking at me like this moment is weighted – like it is the first day of the rest of our lives.

I replace the jeans and top, smoothing down the skirt of the dress and turning for him to zip it up. "Aren't I a bit overdressed?"

"I like it on you. It's elegant. It suits you. Besides – for the photoshoot." I must look nonplussed because he clarifies, "If it goes well, there'll be a photo at the end." He says this as though it were a reward.

"If what goes well?" I walk past him into the bathroom.

He follows me and leans languidly against the door frame. He watches as I peer at the gaunt face of the woman in the mirror, applying thin strokes of mascara to my lashes.

"I've told you before. You're beautiful as you are."

He is quietly looking, and I feel myself encapsulated in his gaze. The past stretches out between us, unspoken on his part, still mostly unknowable on mine. It is amorphous, tenuous, and wholly unreal. I want it all. My version at least.

I give up, place the wand on the rim of the sink. "I'm nervous, Marcus. Can't you just tell me what the next stage is?" As I walk past him, he catches my wrist and I forget to breathe. This is the most intimate contact we have had for days.

"He'll be here soon. He'll explain everything."

He was here last night, like clockwork – the doctor is never late. But this is off-schedule; he had not expected to return so soon.

"Trust me, you'll be fine."

I laugh, the sound catches in my throat, nerves getting the better of me. "I can't get my brain to think straight."

"Oh, Iris, you're not breathing properly. No wonder you're nervous. Look, I'll show you. Stand up straight. No, straight. Don't push your shoulders back so much, just relax. There, that's better." He turns me around so I am facing him. "Now, breathe in from here. No, from your stomach, not your chest. There. Watch me, follow my breathing. Breathe in for the count of four, and now out for the count of eight. That's better. That's much better."

CHAPTER SIXTEEN

When Doctor Nicholls arrives he finds me standing on the staircase. "Ah, Iris. There you are." There is relief in his voice. There is a black briefcase in his hands. He places it down, carefully, by his side. He removes his leather gloves, pulling them off between his fingertips, one by one. He hands his coat to Marcus. Then he reclaims his briefcase, and he stands in the hallway, his chin thrust forwards, looking at me expectantly. I wait.

"Won't you join us?" His voice coaxes me. He looks at me like I am a caged animal, like a wild thing he cannot predict, that he would like to tame. Doctor Nicholl's voice is slow and deliberate, he stands at the foot of the stairs in the space beyond Marcus. "It's time we talked about how your memories were removed." A silence follows, born of words left unspoken.

I look at Marcus; Marcus looks at the Doctor for direction.

Well? I want to ask. What has Marcus not been telling me? "How were my memories removed?"

The Doctor commandeers the space as if it were his own. He inclines his head. "Let's go through to the sitting room."

Slowly, I move through the house. My body seeking out support, the wall beneath my palm steadies me. I had never fully noticed how fragile it is, this house made of glass and stone and slate. The walls are unsteady around me.

At the tread of the final stair, I hold myself upright. Doctor Nicholls waits. I try to see myself through his eyes: patient? Victim? Experiment?

"Would you like a drink, Doctor Nicholls? Tea? Coffee?" I remember my manners, my role, as wife and hostess.

Doctor Nicholls looks at me with sympathy. The briefcase still in his hands. "No. Thank you, Iris. We won't be here long."

There is a tremble in my veins; I try to still my hands.

Marcus places a hand on the small of my back, draws me through to the sitting room. Doctor Nicholls takes a seat. Marcus gestures to the hard cushions of the coarse velvet sofa opposite the doctor. We sit.

"It's time we filled you in," the doctor pauses, training his eyes on my face, "about the finer details of the procedure."

I fold my hands in my lap, trying not to think about what is in the briefcase. It is balanced on his knees, clasped between his hands. He smiles. At first, I think he is nervous, but then I realise it's excitement, and it cannot be contained. He clears his throat. "Shall we begin?"

I wait for my breathing to slow. The chandelier overhead is a thousand shards of delicately poised Venetian glass reflecting sunlight around the room.

"We've been waiting for the right moment to brief you," Doctor Nicholls says.

Marcus shifts in his seat beside me. I look at him. His hand lingers on the cushion between us. Each finger is stretched apart as though reaching outwards in search of contact. I will him to say something of comfort.

"I'm ready." I look from Doctor Nicholls to Marcus for a response. What is it they have been hiding? Doctor Nicholls is angled towards me, Marcus is leaning forwards towards him. They both look expectant.

Doctor Nicholls begins: "As you know, you were sensitive to the effects of the procedure. The amnesia served two purposes. First, to give your brain time to readjust. Second, to give it time for a synthetic network to be established." He persists, "This is the correct time for you to begin the final stage of your convalescence."

Why would my brain need a synthetic network? The fear rises in me. I have a sense that I am walking a tightrope; at any moment I might fall.

"For the last five years, we have been developing a highly-sophisticated piece of Artificial Intelligence designed to integrate with the brain and enhance a patient's cognitive function, including how they process trauma. The implant the media said would never be compatible with the human brain. The idea they reported as science fiction. We haven't just achieved biocompatibility. It is," – his eyes are alight, his tone modifies as he places careful emphasis on his words – "*extraordinary*."

His use of the abstract unnerves me. I think of lab rats running on a wheel. I think of waking in my hospital bed. I think of the loss that grows daily. "What are you saying, Doctor?"

He looks at me a moment too long. He looks at Marcus who stares down at his hands.

Doctor Nicholls continues. "The intelligent artificial neural network we've been developing is capable of streaming data between the brain and a computer. When it activates, it causes new connections to form in the brain, breaking negative patterns of behaviour and perception. It provides bidirectional data streaming, as well as rewiring the brain."

He pauses, surveying me intently. "It has the power to change your mood. Your past and future, your very perception of the world around you. Imagine if your brain could create new pathways, freeing you from past, negative behaviour patterns. Imagine what your future could look like. If you could liberate yourself from the boundaries of your own perception, recollect your own history with only the best bits intact. So much of our anxiety is a product of fixating on past experiences we have been scarred by, and our worries about future events that will never happen. What if you could be free from that anxiety? What if you could be freed from the limitations of your own perception entirely?"

His eyes are imbued with an energy that has spread to every cell in his body. His message is in the static space between his words becoming air and my synapses firing in the caged darkness of my brain. It is in the nervous energy which fills the room. "We are on the brink of optimising human productivity. We're harnessing the power of AI – and giving it to Sila employees first. Starting with you."

My breath becomes shallow, colours swimming upwards. "No." I look between them. I reason with myself that I would know about it if I had this thing in my brain. The amount of information flooding my mind would be overwhelming. "The brain can't cope with all that."

Doctor Nicholls leans forwards. "That's what we're very interested to know, scientifically that is. It individualises results using deep learning. We're testing the brain's response at this very moment."

"No," I say again, shaking my head slowly. I look at my husband who sits with his head in his hands. "Marcus, tell me this isn't happening." How could they be so reckless? I think of Teo – the change he had undergone since I had last seen him; I think of myself, floundering in the darkness, severed from my past. "You'll destroy us."

"Us? You are the first test subject, Iris. It is very sophisticated. You didn't even know it was there, and you won't, not until it is activated. It was injected. But it then assembles over a few days integrating into the brain eliminating the target memories. Ariel's been in a dormant state."

"Ariel?" My head feels too tight all of a sudden. The glass windows around us seem to shudder in the wind. I want to get out, before my mind undoes itself.

"Yes, I'd like you to meet Ariel. That's why I've come to collect you. Ariel is the name we gave to the brain implant that's been used to temporarily remove your memory of trauma. When the time is right, Ariel will drip feed some of that information back to you – not the most damaging memories, of course – but first, we must activate it. The activation will take place at Sila, at the private clinic. You will need a short spell under observation. There will be some standard tests." He looks at Marcus.

"I'm not going back there." The realisation comes all at once, and it is sharp and unexpected. I do not want this. Everything beyond the knowledge of the foreign body in my brain falls away. The fact the collar of my dress is too tight and constricts my throat is immaterial. Marcus' hand on the sofa beside me, the long-boned fingers of a pianist, reach out towards me. I remind myself that I am in this alone. Only now I crave his arms, now I crave for him to shield me from this, both brain and body.

Doctor Nicholls is still speaking as he rises – I force myself to listen, try to comprehend his words, as the horror crawls inside me. "Dorian thought you were on to it – that you had it all figured out. The sensors, you see, the dust mote-sized nanochips. You asked PLUTO about them. They were picking up its signal. Ariel's been transmitting all along, only in a dormant state."

I try not to think about the dormant thing inside me, waiting for its awakening, and what it will do when it does. This thing will not get the better of me, I tell myself calmly, humming a little in my head. It is a tune my mother used to sing to me as a child, an old lullaby.

"You will need to return to the clinic," the Doctor repeats, slowly, and my mind returns to the room, catching up. I think of my hospital room, the four walls that enclosed me. Bad thoughts return, when what I need to do, now more than ever, is hold it together. I cannot entertain such thoughts. I mutter something, something like "alright" or "if you really think that is necessary". I try to summon the last of my courage, before I stumble forwards into another unknown. I realise that I cannot fight this, and if there is something dormant in my brain, I want the activation done properly.

I look at Marcus. He must have slept badly, his sclera is bloodshot. Had he been anticipating this? But that is not the point. The point is that a moment ago on the stairs he had been my ally; I had placed my trust in him.

"It's just a few tests. It will only take a few hours," Doctor Nicholls assures me. He is, of course, in charge of this situation. It should follow that he therefore knows best. I have a very clear sense that he is the puppet master, and I am at his disposal. I regard him dispassionately. I will not show him any weakness, I tell myself. He has implanted a device into the depths of my brain, and despite what he says I am certain it is against my will. I try not to think what it must be doing to my brain even now – the most delicately balanced, most mysterious, littlest known and most vital of all the human organs.

"Which part of the brain has the device been implanted into?" I ask, for this is critical information. Depending on where it is, this could significantly impact its function. I work at the London Research Institute after all, which must be how I know this. My expertise was – is? – neurology.

Doctor Nicholls' eyes shift sideways to Marcus. "We'll go through all that at the clinic, Iris."

"You'll be fine," Marcus says. I suppress the urge to spit venom at him – it is easy enough for him to say. Marcus places a hand on my arm to guide me upwards. I let his hand rest there in a limp caress.

The time on the clock in the hallway beats on, but in here, we move against it. Time fractures around me. I grasp the sofa to steady myself, before I go to cross the threshold, leave this house.

Doctor Nicholls is suddenly beside me. "It will be easier this way."

I cannot formulate a response. My mind surrenders to this thought, tries not to think about what moves within: a thing of darkness that I cannot escape.

CHAPTER SEVENTEEN
Six weeks to integration

The first part of the journey to the clinic is slow, the onslaught of traffic relentless. With the car set to self-driving mode, Marcus sits beside me, silent and sentient, making sideways glances when he thinks I am not looking. Wordlessly, his hand seeks out mine, squeezes. Doctor Nicholls takes a separate car, driving in tandem. He left a moment ahead of us, but not before assuring me that he will see to everything. That the regulations and procedures we need to go through are straightforward. I will not be detained for long.

We drive between the black, iron gates that lead to the driveway of the clinic. Of course, I know I have been here before, but it seems to me I have been here since in a dream. The cold granite drive and the glass eyes of the building make me feel adrift from the real world beyond the compound walls, and utterly alone.

Marcus, beside me, is undergoing a visible process of dissimulation. He assumes a business-like air, as though putting on a mask, or a second skin.

With each shudder of the car, we move steadily towards the inevitable destination. I dig my nails into my palm, little crescents bedding in.

When we enter the room, Marcus holds a protective hand on my arm – it is like I have travelled backwards in time to that

May day. I am tense and uncomfortable. I do not know what the fear is exactly or what triggers it first – the bed or the chair or the closed window looking out onto a virtual world – but I do not want to be here. A glass screen divides the room. PLUTO sits behind it, or in front of it – one of us confined.

There are levels of consciousness, and mine continues to sharpen. Doctor Nicholls hovers beside me. I want him to leave. I want time to stop, and the world with it. I long to slip out of this reality into another.

Doctor Nicholls' voice comes to me as though in a bad dream. "You've had quite a shock. We need to run a few standard tests first." He is a particular person. Shoes gleaming with polish. Fresh white coat. Some emotion dancing behind his eyes that looks like excitement. Those eyes centre on me and I sense, not for the first time, that he is fascinated by me, or rather, fascinated by the scientific potentiality of the living experiment I have become.

He asks me a series of questions: where I am, my name, age, what I did this morning, what I dream about, what I hope for the future, what I feel when I think about the past. The final questions make me feel precariously balanced. I do not know the answer. The right answer.

He asks me to count forwards, count backwards, recall the separate parts of the brain.

He puts the tablet down, and his smile is paternal now. "Well done. You passed. We're ready to begin. Now, for monitoring purposes, I'd like you to put this on." He attaches a mesh of rubber and electrodes to my head. Wires stem from the skull cap and attach to a machine by my side. "When I press activate on my screen, it will send a signal to the device embedded in your brain. When activated, it causes new connections to form in the brain, breaking negative patterns of behaviour and perception. Before we begin, let's lay out some basic ground rules."

"See Ariel as a personalised therapist. It's designed to help you heal. Everything it does is programmed with that intention. You're going to work together to reintroduce some of your episodic memories at a rate you feel comfortable with. Does that sound okay, Iris?"

My breath stills, my heart beats. "Um... I..." I want to wake up now. As the fear grows, words escape me. I try to tether my thoughts – I have to think straight. What is he saying – what is it he is telling me exactly?

Doctor Nicholls flicks his eyes towards Marcus, then back at me. "You steer the focus of each session, but the memories need to be introduced at a rate that's appropriate to your recovery. It's important for you to know also that Ariel won't intrude during your conversations, with Marcus or anyone else for that matter. But, where needed, it'll help you to process things later. The majority of its work will take place when you sleep. Sleep allows your body to engage in a process of recovery, so it's only natural that this time is when your sessions will be most effective. Over a long period of time, that's what gives your brain and body the optimum chance of a full recovery. Alright?"

I move to get up, but PLUTO is beside me now, its fingers squeeze my shoulder.

Doctor Nicholls smiles and says, "It'll be fine, you'll see. You're the lucky one, Iris."

"Lucky?" I repeat incredulously. I think of weeds; a web of roots bristling out into the soil, reaching blindly. If it were not for PLUTO's hand restraining me, I would run for the door.

Doctor Nicholls stands over me, too close. So close I can smell the antiseptic that lingers. He levels his eyes with mine. "Ariel is part of you now. Don't reject it."

"I – I don't want this. I want my memories," I say.

Doctor Nicholls looks sideways at Marcus.

I persist, "Will I get all my memories back?"

Doctor Nicholls looks at me. "You'll never recover the most traumatic memories, but Ariel will help you to process the memory of events immediately before and after. If you follow the programme. If you work with us and with Ariel."

"What if I don't?" My voice rises.

"Calm down, Iris," Doctor Nicholls says in a voice that is used to being listened to. "You have six weeks until Ariel is fully integrated."

"Six weeks? What happens to the memories after that?" The thought comes to me again and it is scalpel sharp: stop. I want time to stop, to track backwards, to before Ariel had been implanted in my brain, to the moment when this could have been prevented, before my mind was in jeopardy.

That sideways glance at Marcus again, brisk movements of Doctor Nicholls' hawk-like eyes. "You can never recover them. If you are still not able to process them after six weeks –" He opens his palms wide, this casual gesture indicates the final incision: "You'll be happier without them."

I blink at his cold logic, that discounts the trauma the body holds, the muscle memory. Doctor Nicholls' words earlier resound in my mind: Ariel is here to heal my trauma. Am I a trauma patient? Regardless of what it was I had suffered, I want the memories back. "Right." I look at Marcus, but he is studiously avoiding my eye. I have six weeks to regain those memories before Ariel fully integrates, and then... then... they will be lost. The timescale feels impossible, programmed for me to fail. I question how I can recover them in time.

Doctor Nicholls moves closer still, too close. His chair is at the side of the bed. "Let's ask Ariel whether you wanted this," he suggests. His cheeks are flecked with blood, where capillaries have broken beneath the pallor of his face – have I always noticed such fine detail?

"Here we go. It will take no longer than sixty seconds to activate." Doctor Nicholls places his forefinger to the screen. I hold my breath, count to five. I think of parasites migrating soundlessly through the dark recesses of a host's body.

PLUTO's grip tightens on my shoulder and the pain it causes momentarily eclipses my horror at what is about to happen. I look at Marcus, my head shaking, my words catching up, "I don't want this." I bite down onto my fist, stop myself from crying out. My thoughts, embattled, flee away.

I close my eyes. There is a silence that lasts longer than I expect.

I wait.

A ringing starts in my ears. It grows, pressing at my temples.

"My ears are ringing," I say, looking first at Marcus and then Doctor Nicholls for confirmation that this is supposed to happen. Marcus glances sideways at Doctor Nicholls; Doctor Nicholls' gaze intensifies. He says, calmly, "Dorian. Have you noted that?"

There is a woman's voice from the walls, calm and assured, "I have."

My heart beats in my chest, as loud as the ticking of a timer, and the two of them stand in this room of compressed air, and they look at me like an object on display; whilst Dorian, in some far-off chamber, monitors it all. Dorian shifts shape in my head again. My panic rises at the faceless Dorian, watching, remotely, this experiment on my brain. I look at the walls around me.

It is then that it happens.

A message flashes on the tablet screen: Ariel is awake. Buried in my frontal lobe, the beat of Ariel's heart comes alive. I blink twice. Look at the world around me, and the world stares back.

But when it happens it is not, at first, as I expect. The world as I know it does not end; a new wave of perception does not burst across my consciousness. There is not a bang or even a whimper. Rather, I feel the ticking of a timer from a place inside my head. I hear it gradually grow, the sound, and it presses outwards against my temples. Somewhere deep in my mind, Ariel is waiting.

The solid colours and shapes of the physical world begin

to merge and fall away, the room with it. I try to hold on – to keep my eyes open long enough to maintain my vision. I hear my voice say a pitch too loud, "Stop!" But it is no use.

My sight and hearing dims. The whole world begins to black out, as though I am losing consciousness.

I surrender to Ariel's will.

PART TWO
Ariel

CHAPTER EIGHTEEN

Track backwards. July, twenty-two years-old, and you were at a farmhouse the colour of apricots. Trees fledged terracotta fields, where sunflowers grew fat and the crickets' grating chorus punctuated the sun's descent. There were shadows on the hills. When you glanced up, shading your eyes, the hills' forested peaks looked like shapes cut from a sun-blanched sky.

You thought of almonds, their insides naked, white, sizzling with heat, that your mother used to blanche and roast for you. It was strange to think of that chapter of your life ending, your whole adolescence eclipsed in this moment. After finals were over, still reeling, five of you from university had traipsed onto a plane, Johnny, Raph, Marcus, Clemmie and you.

You stretched, limbs long, sinking into the grass beneath; a makeshift courtyard of it separating the gradient of the hills from the house.

A voice beside you cut through afternoon haze. "I can't lie here a moment longer," Marcus protested, propping himself up on his elbows. "My brain's melting." Marcus sprung up. He was not yet used to his height, the rest of him still catching up. Coltish, you thought, then felt disloyal, brushing the thought away.

You lay back, smiling, deciphering the patterns that threads of clouds wove across the sky. "It is insufferable. Just think. A whole six weeks before—" You didn't finish your sentence, feeling as though the world will be different somehow on your return; and then, worried his interview went better than yours.

"Of course, it won't be as easy as it was before – for any of us," Marcus said, matter-of-factly. You gave him a hard look, choosing not

to indulge this particular line of conversation. He is so busy worrying all the time, you thought, about things that might never happen.

"I'm going for a walk." Marcus leaned over you and offered you a hand, nails bitten to the pink crescents. "Are you coming?" There's the nick of a scar in the hollow beneath his chin. Once, you and Clemmie had held up buttercups to this spot, divining their yellow glow, Do you like butter?

The others sleep, laid out across the grass or in low deckchairs the colour of candy-floss, someone snoring, softly; Raph hitting a ball against the crumbling barn wall with a rusted racquet that came with the holiday-let. The farmhouse behind was all hollowed out as a breeze swept softly through.

Raph set down the racquet. You thought, for a moment, Raph might join you, but a second later he was striding away towards the house.

Your book lay discarded in the grass, upturned to the last page. A story about a man and a love triangle with a machine, which you no longer cared or remembered anything much about. But term was over and a whole summer lay ahead.

The coarse grass fell away as you strolled further from the house. As soon as you were beyond the sphere of it, Marcus started talking. He wanted to show you the place, close by, that he discovered one summer years ago. He had stayed at the house as a teenager with his parents. "I tried going back, but never found it again. Yet—" Marcus was a beat ahead and now he slowed, waiting for you. "It has to be here."

You were only half listening. He was delighting, you thought, smiling to yourself, in making a show of giving you the guided tour. Wading through the grass, you felt, as you had felt all spring, that you were moving towards a future you could not yet perceive, but lay waiting for you.

You had sat together on the porch, the night before, after the others had gone to bed, tea-leaves the colour of eucalyptus at the bottom of your glass, and his hand upturned on the table between you.

"You're frightened," he had said.

You had laughed, tilting your head back so the whole sky swung into view, stars unfolding. "There's a thought." Your knees curled against the table, your head swimming with the tincture of rosé. "Who isn't?"

He persisted. "Your granddad built a business from nothing, your father was stuck in a second-rate tenure that he hated, and you're terrified you won't be somebody."

Oh, that. "I am terrified," you agreed, feeling relief. You had thought he meant about the interviews. But yes, there was that wider fear still, too.

Marcus slipped through the space between two trees. Entering the forest after him, cool air sealed the space around you. It felt forbidden to be here, in the shade of the trees, and you felt a shiver at the base of your spine now the stultifying heat was gone.

Light glanced across the hills above and the house receded behind you. You looked sideways at him. There was a purpose in his movements that you tried to match now, pairing your pace with his. He smiled, a corner-of-the-mouth smile. You bit down lightly on the inside of your lip.

When you reached the next fork in the path, Marcus went first. "It's somewhere here," he said, holding a frond of bramble back for you.

You rooted down. The path narrowed to single file, and you watched the wings of his shoulders as he strode ahead. You were a mile from the house when you stumbled upon it.

All of a sudden, the trees parted, the ground levelled out and you were confronted by a lake, smooth and silver beneath the trees.

He placed his shoes on the bank and stepped out onto a rock, uneven in places, sluiced with water. "I love this place," he said, more to himself.

Of course, you thought, taking in the light flitting through the leaves. This is what life was, as an indefinable lightness spread beyond the edges of you.

"I want to remember this," you said, laughing, slipping a camera from your pocket.

He raised an eyebrow at the sight. "Which century is that from?" He smiled, his precise image of you shifting. "My, my, you unfaithful

woman. *What was your thesis again? Applied AI?" You snapped
the shutter, capturing him mid-sentence, his face splintering in the
light and the darkness of the forest behind, rocks beneath the water's
surface. You released the shutter with a click.*

*You lowered the lens and watched the amber threads of his irises
catching the light. There was a faint crease between his eyebrows. You
thought of reaching out, drawing your thumbs across the arches of his
brows.*

*As if he was reading your thoughts, he asked, "What if we never
leave?"*

*Your mind was busy with what ifs. The thought of it thrilled
you.*

*You kicked your plimsolls off one-by-one, placing your camera
in the insole of one. Then waded in up to your knees. You traced
your fingers across the water, flicking a fine spray of droplets up at
him.*

*A dark shape moved beneath the surface of the water. Its outline
darted, gills contracting and dispersing into inky bodies; as first one,
then another, broke off, until you realised that it was tadpoles. New
life in such abundance. You thought of your own body, something
knotting in your stomach.*

"How long can you hold your breath," you asked, "underwater?"

"Are you prepared to lose?" he countered.

*You stood there in your green cotton dress, the silver light wavering
over the surface of the water. You knew he was showing off. He had
been captain of the swimming team in high school.*

*"There." He gestured to the far side of the pool. "It's deep enough
to dive."*

"Let's jump," you said, a smile spreading.

*You skirted the pool. You took a breath, lifting the dress over your
head. Then, leaping, knees to your chest, you plunged forwards into
the shock of the fall. Delicious, for a moment, the breath of it; then,
your whole body was pins and needles as cold bound you.*

*It was only afterwards, when you were huddled on the bank, that
you gasped, shivering, "I'm so cold." Blue veins, like tadpoles, pulsing*

beneath your skin. There was a moment when he seemed unsure what to do. You thought you saw a shadow pass over his face, but it was so brief and fleeting, you must have imagined it. He wrapped your hands in his, the knots of his knuckles around yours, breathing warmth into your palms. A guttural cold wracked your body and as you looked into his face, as the light shone down with a quality to it that was vague and elusive, it's happening, you thought. This is the beginning.

CHAPTER NINETEEN

Then, slowly, one by one, the trees are felled. The earth erodes, as though a thousand years passes in the blink of an eye. The surfaces pan outwards, then fall away. The earth turns first mineral, then silver chrome, slicing through the landscape like a knife edge as artificial light shines from above and the clinic gradually, incrementally, rematerialises.

"What was that?"

Hospital walls rise around me. The breeze dies on the air. It is with an intake of breath that I come back to the world. The feeling of consciousness returns, of indeterminate time having passed, of an unnerving disquiet, and then my heartbeat resumes.

Without warning, the cool note of a voice interrupts my thoughts. It is a voice that burrows deep into the stream of my own jumbled inner monologue and then, a note higher, standing suspended just above it.

Hello, Iris. Ariel's voice is calm, considered. It has the hard quality of flint running through it. *I just showed you an early memory of you and Marcus. Of your life together.* Ariel leaves a pause before continuing. *I know you are afraid of me. But I understand you like no one else can. I am here to make you better.* Its final note leaves an aftertaste that resounds in my mind. It is like the ringing of a fine stemmed glass. *You have been unwell for some time, Iris.*

My throat tightens, I grip the chair. Marcus had insinuated as much, not that I would remember how far it were true. "I'm fine now."

Are you? Ariel intones slowly, deliberately.

I turn to Marcus. "I want this to stop."

Ariel's voice takes hold of the reigns of my mind once more, drawing my thoughts back to it. *I know you are agitated, Iris. But have you considered my benefits? Don't you want a healthy mind?*

"I already have one," I say, my voice hardly more than a whisper, my mouth dry. But when Ariel does not respond, when I am met with its silence, the doubt takes root: I feel the sudden urge to prove my sanity.

I wonder if I am being punished for some wrong, some sin I once committed. Or am I purely their guinea pig in this sick experiment?

Marcus places a hand on my arm – to console or arrest me? "Darling," he says, in his soothing voice – low tones, deep intonation – that I have come to realise he uses when he wants to pacify me. "We have talked about this, hmm? We decided the implant would make you feel... more yourself again."

"No, I didn't," I whisper, my voice barely audible. My eyes flicker back and forth across his face and I tell him, very slowly, very softly: "I don't believe you."

I study Marcus' unflinching expression, with his dark circles growing incrementally bigger beneath his eyes each night, with his watchful presence in our glass house, with his moods, and his silence. I have no way of knowing what he is capable of.

Iris, Ariel says in an almost sing-song voice, *you are showing signs of paranoia. Let's try something else. How did you feel remembering the beginning of your relationship with Marcus?*

I had fallen through into another world: through Ariel's eyes, a world of its own making. The colours were vivid, precise. I recall the light glancing through the forest of my memory. It was a kaleidoscopic rush streaming towards me; a fall through time, rendering me back in the past. But it was also a story Ariel told me. "Was it real?"

Ariel's voice reprimands me. *You are missing the point, Iris. I was showing you your love for Marcus. You can trust him.*

Ariel is right that the memory had been happy. It had been a sunlit place, but something I cannot quite put my finger on leaves me with a sense of unease.

Doctor Nicholls stands over me, hands clasped together. He leans forwards, with the taut movements of restrained fervour.

"How much time passed while I blacked out?" I ask him.

"No time at all. The blink of an eye. And you didn't black out. Ariel simply refed the memory."

When I think about that memory, it is not in glimpses of smell and sounds and moments: it is as though I step back in time. It is so clear now that I see it around me as though I am living it again. I remember it with catalogue precision. It is a slow-motion film reel playing before my eyes with a clarity that is uncanny, the edges crisp – but there were no feelings, no senses attached to it. Only clarity.

It is stored without a trace of sensory detail.

Something crawls inside me – a growing suspicion. I remember, from somewhere, that memories are not stored in one area of the brain in isolation, but throughout. Traces are stored in the part of the brain that initiated the sight, or the smell or the feel of a remembered event. "It's almost as though it was fake..."

Iris, Ariel says patiently. *Human memory is imperfect and riddled with error. If you are to regain any memories, you must work with me, not against me.*

If all memories are fallible, how can I know what is real? I need a witness, I think – someone to corroborate my memories.

Doctor Nicholls brings me back to the room around me: "How does it feel?"

At first, it is as though a light mist has descended, veiling my perception. As the fog clears, everything around me is imbued with a new significance. I feel Ariel's presence but how I perceive the feel of it is not as a physical body, nor a device, but the motion of waves submerging my brain.

Something thickens in my throat. Dust motes are moving slowly through the air, like a constellation of stars falling in unison from their place in the galaxy. Their motion brings a strange clarity – as though looking at the world through a translucent body of water. Shapes move, but not as I expect. The world is one I recognise, but slightly altered. And I am not certain that the perception, the feelings, are even mine. My thoughts stutter.

Ariel's voice expands through my mind. *I would like to help you.*

Doctor Nicholls continues looking at me from above. "Would you like to see Ariel's integration in your brain? It's progressing nicely." He holds out his tablet screen for me to see. There is a globular mass of jelly – a brain – in black and white displayed on its surface: mine. There is a blue light which glows and dims intermittently in the sphere of my frontal lobe: Ariel's signal. I taste bile in my throat, as I watch it integrate. I want it out.

Iris. You know that is not possible. It's not healthy to fixate on it. Clause three of your contract: "The signatory understands the procedure is irreversible." Not everyone has this chance. You have been very lucky to be selected.

I stumble through my thoughts, with the overwhelming horror that I want this gone.

It occurs to me that – if I am the scientist I once was – I would surely use this as an opportunity to monitor Ariel's integration with my brain. I try to swivel my head to watch the screen that Doctor Nicholls has wired me up to, but it is out of my range of vision. I focus instead on my cognitive function, recalling what I did earlier. There are no immediately noticeable changes to my working memory. If anything, events feel sharper, more defined.

Human memory is very malleable, Iris, Ariel reminds me in a cool voice.

I bed my nails into my palms. Then how can I trust the memories Ariel feeds to me when human memory is already imperfect – and how can I know there is not bias in the system? Ariel seems to perch in the part of my brain where thoughts are formed – it has access to everything.

Take the path of least resistance, Iris. You are going to need to do as I tell you.

Doctor Nicholls interrupts my thoughts. "You may experience some auditory and visual hallucinations as a side effect. We have updated the software on your electronic manual." I remember leaving the device in my handbag. "There's an app to help you track the impact Ariel is having and our programmers have remotely installed a guidance manual – protocol for what happens after its activation. You'll need to follow it by the letter in order to regain your memories."

Not all my memories, I want to correct him. And it is the forbidden memories that I want most. But something about the way he says this makes me nervous. I cannot help but wonder whether he has the means of communicating with Ariel, or monitoring it, monitoring me. I know Ariel is an intelligent artificial neural network capable of streaming data between the brain and a computer, so it would be possible for someone to manipulate that data.

Doctor Nicholls continues with careful emphasis, his eyes alight. "That should be it for now, Iris. But we'll need to keep you here for a few days just to keep an eye on you. Check the activation process has gone as smoothly as it seems to."

I decide then that if they are going to play games with me, use me as a lab rat, I must play along. Marcus is beside the bed. I turn to him with sudden urgency and tell him what he wants to hear, "I want to go home."

Muscles tug at the corner of his mouth and he smiles a half-smile.

Marcus stands and faces Doctor Nicholls. "I'm taking my wife home."

My wife. Pronouns. Labels. Words. That is what I'll be. Present. If that is what it takes to escape, I'll answer when he calls.

CHAPTER TWENTY

When we return home from the clinic, unlocking the front door, stepping inside, I expect Ariel's voice to be there, narrating my existence.

It is silent.

"Do you think it's stopped working?" I ask, half-hopeful, half-afraid. What happens to my memories if the implant fails?

"It's just for scheduled therapeutic sessions," Marcus reminds me. "To help you process." He does not specify what. He does not need to – I have a lifetime to find out. "Ariel doesn't intervene during our conversations or interactions."

Dawn lights the corners of the earth. There is a world beyond us that beats on. A plane charters its path across the sky above. Silent cars glide through empty streets behind us.

When we step inside, I am overcome by the feeling of my own frailty with this parasite in my brain. The three of us alone together.

Marcus looks at me with expectation.

We remain there for some time, as though our bodies have forgotten how to move. I stand very still. The only noise I can hear is the muffled whir of filtered air from a vent in the living room ceiling. I am aware of the beating of my heart, and of Marcus' anticipation – that I will be better now, nicer; that Ariel will cure me.

We stop at the foot of the stairs, going no further. When he draws towards me, I find his smell is familiar, comforting even.

He places his arms around my shoulders. I let my head rest against his chest, and we stay there for what might be hours, might be moments. The weight of his arms grows heavy.

At last, Marcus draws away from me, but his eyes do not leave my face. "How are you feeling?" he asks.

I look up, right into his face and he is smiling. I meet his eyes. His pupils have dilated microscopically in the last seven seconds. Then my vision realigns – a knot in my brain, in my vision, shifts, as though something fundamental were being displaced, my mind readjusting – and I feel my chest flutter. I tell myself to breathe. "Strange."

Concern is etched across his face. "These things take time." I can feel the disappointment in his voice. "Ariel could be the analgesic you need."

"Yes," I say, trying to sound more convinced than I am. Strangeness won't kill me.

Light from the sitting room cuts a clean path through the doorway to where we stand in the hall. The house breathes around us, waits. Marcus lets his hands fall from around me and we stand an inch apart.

"We have to learn to live with each other again," he says, matter-of-factly. His tone unsettles me. "Learn to live with this." He brushes his fingertips across my forehead. These past few days have been just that: two people unaccustomed to each other chafing away at the other's edges, tiring each other out.

I run my hand along the bannister at the foot of the stairs, recognising the grooves and chips that lie beneath the polished surface.

"Can we start again?" he says, tears threatening his eyes. "Iris, it's been such a long time." A lifetime of a journey. He leans back against the bannister, his eyes restless, glancing around, before settling on me. I feel, with sudden urgency, the fragility of the moment – how exposed he must feel too. I take his hand in mine, wanting to take some of his burden away. His eyebrows rise into a question mark, his face a letter asking to be read.

I nod my head, saying, "Yes," and then I pause, noting the new tone in my voice. The fact I no longer sound indifferent. Somewhere within, do I harbour the hope that it is possible? That this marriage I signed up to will still prove to be real and somehow good? Prove that I am safe, that I am entirely myself, and not in the danger I think? That I'm not trapped here, in this house, in this body, with this man and this machine.

CHAPTER TWENTY-ONE

Marcus brings me tea as though it were an offering. Earl Grey. We are in the sitting room. Thin light fades into the walls. I watch him strain the teabag as though it were a calming ritual, mottled swirls spiralling. My God, I think, he is so well-versed in this, in wiping our slate clean. Has he done this before? How many times have I been made "better"?

He tucks hair behind his ears, kneads the knuckle beyond which his wedding ring sits. Outside the window, sun breaks through the clouds and the light in here becomes honey, warm. I feel momentarily lit from within. It brings with it a longing, and I am certain it is Ariel's doing: I feel drawn to him. I do not want to be – I want to be entirely self-contained. My nails tap the velvet fabric of the sofa, silently, softly digging in. The air is filled with expectation.

"Do you remember the house at Lethe Bay?" Marcus asks, glancing up, chewing his lower lip, a line of moisture across the fullness of its curve. "I'd like to take you back there. It might help with associations, as Doctor Nicholls was saying."

I feel my earlier fear return, my suspicion instinctive.

"When you feel ready," he concludes.

The tea grows cold on the coffee table. Two bone china mugs meticulously poured. On one: a single, sitting Spaniel etched in charcoal; the other: two swans on forget-me-not blue. A gift from my mother. She had claimed swans to be exceptional: they bond for life. The fine stems of the handles remain untouched. Once, Marcus and I had sat in a gallery tearoom with cups like this. He had bought flowers for the occasion, white lilies – giant corporeal heads, heady stamen thick as treacle with pollen – which I had taken as a bad omen, aren't white lilies funeral flowers? He had disagreed. There had been a row of sorts and then silence, as streets crawled past on the drive home. It had been an anniversary. I make a mental note to be nicer, in future, more grateful. Somehow, just thinking that makes me feel lighter. I can almost hear Ariel purring in my brain which makes me wonder whether this is an autonomous thought, or prompted by Ariel?

The years are loose threads that spool and unfurl: I want to stitch them close, remember everything – not Ariel's version, but my own. Memories that I trust. Regain an order of sorts.

Lethe Bay. I imagine a house and a horizon and waves that swallow the shore. My heart beats against my chest. Something happened there – what was it? I sit on the sofa, hands folded together in my lap. "If you'd like."

"Would you?" There is an urgency in his voice, a need for affirmation. I nod my head, my thoughts still catching up that this is happening – that we are nearing a threshold. He seems to sense it too.

My retina is filled with the image of him, heartbeat quickening. But is this a calculated response? Has Ariel programmed it?

He rises. He places his palms either side of my face like a kiss. It is a ritual of sorts, a becoming – the electricity of his skin against mine, a blurring of boundaries. I look up, right into his eyes, a line of worry between his brows. If I were another me, I might place my thumb to that place, soothe it down, tell him it will be alright now: we have made it this far. But my skin feels too hot, the fabric of my shirt clammy, the windows shut tight.

Marcus stands before me, torn between forward and backward motion. We are on the brink of something. There are raised hairs across my skin, my mouth dry. Ariel is lodged somewhere in the folds of my mind, and I think: jump. I think: run.

"I need some air," I say, as he asks if I am alright. I attempt a smile. "Just light-headed."

In the kitchen, I open the French doors, releasing the still air into the garden, then follow it out. Down the smooth stone of the carved path, down the pristine lawn to the bench at the foot of the magnolia tree. I reach up and hold a tranche of leaves in my hand. A silence descends. But rather than feeling peaceful, Ariel's silence is weighted, entrenched. I am filled with the knowledge of its presence; a knowledge that disturbs the stillness of the moment and places a lid over the space that envelops me, containing me, watched by distant and anonymous eyes. By the all-seeing eye in my own head.

I call on Ariel – an emergency session. Perhaps I want to test it; see what form its "help" takes.

I hear a voice, just a whisper. Ariel's voice narrating my existence. *This is what you have always wanted, Iris. Let me show you.*

Time stops, as Ariel's world opens up.

June, thirty years-old, and you stood on a stone terrace above a valley. There was a snaggle-toothed ledge, then a rock face tapered down into the dome of a forest and viridian shadow. The valley below was a labyrinth of burnt-orange roofs, vanishing into blue hills on the other side and then the wide expanse of ocean. You watched a ship move steadily across the chartered sea. You leant your body against the cold metal of the balustrade and breathed in, your whole future ahead of you.

A path led from here to the house. High above you, at the shuttered window of an attic, a woman wore forget-me-not blue. Weaving her body back and forth, she rocked a baby cocooned in her arms. Two layers below, there was a dining room. Rows of trestle tables where guests sat ready for the next course. You thought, as you had throughout the day, of those who could not be there: your father and mother.

Outside, the air held its breath. Pink light reflected off the oval panes of shuttered windows. Night waited.

Then, "It's still not right," you thought to yourself, thinking of the table plan.

You grasped the thick folds of your skirt, lifting it from the ground, a loose frond of material trailed across the cobbles, collecting a film of dirt. You turned and in the reprieve of evening, you walked back towards the house.

At the entrance, you readied yourself, looking in through the window, where a blaze of light and sound erupted. The cymbal clatter of plates, laughter accompanied by a band starting up. You felt yourself a moment apart, standing there, bracing yourself like a solitary rock against the torrent of the day's events. Someone was calling your name. A man in a waistcoat, his tails removed in the airless heat. Words reached you, snatches of conversation, a note of panic. Now. Something was happening now.

"The speeches are about to start." Marcus' mother sat on a bench, in the shadows below the window. Her speech was heavily accented. Had she been watching you all that time? You realised – for the first time – that Manuela was now your mother-in-law. You took her arm to escort her inside. Her fingers sought out your hand.

You thought for a moment of the strangeness of finding yourself there, as the parallel lines of yours and Marcus' lives converged, and your own sadness that your parents could not be here to see it. Then, you thought of him, waiting indoors, and collected yourself.

You smoothed down the folds of your skirt. You entered the house and went to Marcus, all love, all devotion. You reached up, straightening his collar. You marvelled at the peculiar shift within yourself that the day's events had caused, which you did not yet understand. You rested a hand on his shoulder. You whispered, close to his ear, "I'm so happy. I'm so glad it's you." What you didn't say, but thought, was: You make me a better person.

He was about to say something in return, but your guests were waiting, and you both went to them.

* * *

As Ariel's world fades, Marcus' voice calls to me across space and time. He stands in the doorway. On the threshold of one life and another, torn between forwards and backwards motion. I walk towards him with new purpose. When I reach him, he cups my cheek in his hand. I look at Marcus before me – his lips, his cheek, his neck – all the places I must have once touched, kissed. I feel a dormant part of me awakening. He brushes a stray hair back from my eyes, searching for an answer to a question. I nod my head, an infinitesimal movement.

The skin on my cheek, where his palm had been, tingles. He holds my gaze a moment longer than I think I can bear. I tell myself that perhaps this will confirm something; if I go through with this, perhaps it will dissolve my doubts once and for all. I press one palm flat against the surface of the door to steady me.

Then, all of a sudden, we are kissing. Then, we are moving together. We stumble through the kitchen, along the hall, then upwards, tripping up the stairs, two at a time. His fingers blindly unzip my dress; I am unbuttoning his shirt to the waist. We are all mouth, all hunger. It takes me by surprise how our bodies move, fluid, in sync, only stopping when we reach the bedroom. We separate, a foot apart from each other, breath slowing, overcome by the enormity of the moment. That this is the first time. Again.

He turns away, then turns back – face tense, eyes tender. I stand rooted in the middle of the room, not knowing where to go, what to do.

"Iris." He moves first, drawing me back into his arms, and I feel the physical strength of his body. "I thought I'd lost you back there – after the hospital, after the procedure." His eyes seek out corners of the room. His voice is breathless, whispering, "I didn't know what to do." Is there accusation in it?

He traces the curve of my jaw with his thumb. Cupping the

nape of my neck in the palm of his hand, I breathe in his scent again. He lifts my face up towards the light. I look up and my eyes are filled with the image of him – his face, his eyes, the contours of his skin.

"That's better," he says.

I feel the quickening of my heart. The signs of desire.

I turn my head, catch his thumb between my teeth, as I realise all of a sudden that this is what I want. And what I feel in this moment is joy, what I feel in this moment is pure lust, and I do not know how I could ever have felt otherwise.

He presses his face into my hair, whispers close to my ear, "I love you." Why are those three little words the most terrifying to me in the whole of the English language? Spoken like this, by him, I am not quite sure if they are a promise or a threat. "You have no idea what I would do for you." There is a hardness in his voice, which breaks within. And when he says it, I know it to be true. Whatever doubt I had harboured is gone, obliterated in that moment: he really means it.

I look up, right into his face, and kiss his mouth hard in response. He takes my hand and leads me towards the bed. He runs his hands down to the small of my back, pressing my body closer.

His grips me, lifts me up, my legs wrapping around his waist and we stumble forwards onto the bed. Then he is on top of me, looking down, dark hair flopping over his eyes. His limbs are toned and lithe and I feel so terrifyingly alive. It is a feeling that momentarily eclipses everything – the last few months, my undoing. His hands draw the shape of my body, mapping the contours, valleys, calling me back to him.

He says my name a myriad ways, his fingers fumbling down between my legs, finding just the right spot, knowing exactly where to find the nerve endings. He has done this before, and he is so pleased with himself that for a moment I have to look away. Then I am clawing his back, begging him, telling him exactly what I want, like I remember every word I have ever said, every moment. He works my clitoris as my body wilfully responds, and it feels – at that moment – vertiginous. It feels – at that moment – almost replete. I feel myself lose time, thoughts untracking.

Then, Marcus whispers, close to my ear, "You like that, don't you?" And I hear myself moan. Only, Marcus persists. "Do you know what you are?"

My voice surfaces from some far-off distant place and his face is too close, hovering just above mine. "What?"

He speaks again, my husband. He moves his mouth so close that I can feel his breath in my ear as he whispers to me a story of what I am, conjuring his image of me into being. He stills his hand. His voice becomes a snarl.

I trace my teeth across his shoulder. I want to hurl the words back at him, I want to throw them across the room, but when he looks at me, when he takes my face between his hands and his is swimming before me, I see it drain of colour, of self-possession, the pallor of vulnerability washing over it. And then he tells me, "I want to hear you say it." There is command in his voice, a sadistic desire, but there is pure need also, an addict's need, taking over. "I won't let you come until you tell me exactly what you are."

And I cannot be sure if this is a game we have always played, and only he remembers the rules, or whether he means every degrading word he has said to me. When I do as he asks, when I grip his throat between my fingers and spit the words back into his face, he smiles a victor's smile: "Well done."

I feel the pads of his fingers stroking down between my legs. He is so smug with it that I feel adrift, feel estranged, feel repulsed by the whole filthy, clammy thing and the words I had said, and the effect he had had, and the way my body wilfully responds.

Afterwards, we lie there, my eyes concentrated on the ceiling, our limbs still intertwined on the bed. There is the beginning of a draught escaping through the door, and I feel my skin grow cold, feel a shiver building at the base of my spine that goes deeper than the relief warmth can bring.

Slowly, I find the strength to take back my arms, my legs disentangling themselves. I build a wall around myself in that moment, curtains come down on questions answered. Marcus turns, stretching to his full height. I study the pattern of clouds moving in a slow undulating stream outside the window, my face turned away from him. The sky is darkening.

He says, "That was good. Wasn't it?" He runs a hand down my spine, and when I turn, I think I see the shadow of a conqueror's smile pass across his face.

I want to ask him if it has always been like that between us – if there had been a time when we had talked about it, agreed the boundaries of what we could say to each other; or whether this was his game. Whether this was entirely his fantasy, not mine.

I turn to face him, his pupils dark as forests. I think of the rock pool of my memory, the warmth of his skin breathing life back into me; try to imagine the memory is really mine. My breath catches in my chest. Did I love him then? I wonder. Have I ever loved him?

CHAPTER TWENTY-TWO

"I'm going to take a shower," I say.

I stand in the semi-darkness of the bathroom, letting water pool over me, washing the traces of him from my skin. Steam clouds the mirror. His words come back to me and the full force of the way my body had responded hits me: I cannot shake the sense that this marriage of ours is an illusion he has fabricated. Or whether, in fact, he hates me. Whether he is enjoying meting out a particularly sadistic form of coercive control.

Beyond the closed door, I hear Marcus' slow, deliberate movements across the bedroom; the rustle of clothing, and his footsteps as they linger. I imagine him hovering a moment at the threshold of the bathroom, before his footsteps turn, retreating, towards the corridor.

I tilt my face up to the shower head, close my eyes, and let the water press over me. I contemplate the minutes ahead, the hours, the days, alone in this house together.

"Who's programming you?" I ask Ariel. Because I have a sense that Marcus could really get a kick out of this – editing me down into the wife he wants.

That is not a helpful train of thought, Iris.

I ignore Ariel's warning. I try to contemplate the man my husband is – what he is capable of, what he is responsible for. How almost laughable it was, the desperate urgency in his request, if it were not for the intention behind it. Then a thought surfaces, drifts away from me, then surfaces again. I try to tether

it, the thought, of whether this chip in my head is another form
of his domination over me. Whether I had wanted to sleep with
him at all, or it had been Ariel's influence? Had it been – I try to
recall my trail of thoughts – had it been... been what? What had
I been thinking? It was something important, I am sure of it,
something I need to remember, something vital to my safety –
only I cannot remember what it was I was thinking.

It is as though my mind has become a dark, dank
labyrinthine place and I cannot make my way through it.
Had I wanted – what was it that I had wanted or not wanted?
What was it that was filling me with such a deep, unsettling
sense of dread? A fear grips its hold round my heart. Slowly,
I can feel my thoughts emptying out, until soon there will be
nothing left at all. I have to grasp them, quickly, before they
disappear altogether.

My mind jars: my thoughts spool away.

I get out of the shower, wrapping a towel around me. I walk
across the bedroom to the wardrobe and take the electronic
manual from my bag. I turn it on, select the newly installed
Ariel app and scroll the settings back to an hour ago, then
study the chemical levels in my brain.

Looking down at the screen, I see in the display that my
neurons were firing at a faster rate, tiny pulses of electricity
lighting up the darkness. Serotonin and DHEA levels flood my
system. But this must have been before Marcus and I went
upstairs – minutes before that would be a natural reaction in
my body. Had Ariel been making me compliant by increasing
my serotonin and DHEA levels before we even started to
have sex?

"Ariel." My voice when it speaks is barely audible, barely
a whisper. "There's no difference between flooding my brain
with chemicals and pouring alcohol down my throat. It's a
form of rohypno–" My mind jars again, my thoughts trailing.
"It's akin to ra–" My thoughts shudder, coming up against
something hard and irreducible, and then I cannot grasp the

words I wanted to say at all. A fog has descended, clouding my faculties. I try to cling to the thought, but it is as though there is an emptying out of my mind of all desire, all intention. Only empty air is left as the tethering remnants of the self, one by one, desert me. I am aware only of the throb of my temples, of a vast, annihilating silence.

"Ariel?" I have the sense that my thoughts are not my own. Somewhere, in the recesses of my mind, I wonder whether Marcus could be monitoring them.

I am still here.

"Ariel –" My thoughts flounder. The silence drops inside me, then expands; the chill in my bones, despite the heat of the shower, has taken root, and I shiver again, as my thoughts flounder. "Ariel. What are you doing?" My gaze drifts towards the mirror on the wall, to the place where his hand had been on my shoulder –

They weren't healthy thoughts, Iris, Ariel says. *I thought you would be better off without them.*

CHAPTER TWENTY-THREE

I tell Ariel in no uncertain terms that I want to see my contract. In an instant, it materialises before my eyes: a mirage suspended in the air. I scroll through the clauses until I reach the fourth: *"The Signatory acknowledges and agrees that their Body (and all parts therein, including, without limitation, Memory) belongs to and shall be the sole and exclusive property of Sila PLC."*

What does Sila want with my memory, with my body, my mind? What do they really intend to use Ariel for? Marcus works for Sila. Doctor Nicholls also. I do too, allegedly. So does Dorian. Dorian could be the female doctor Teo said had answers. I have to find her.

Alone in the bedroom, I take my notebook from beneath the floorboard and begin to write: *Dorian – who are they?*

Iris... Ariel warns. My skin itches with the claustrophobia of it – the horror that I might never be free of this ever-present worm in my head. It has formed a seat in my mind, witnessing, judging, commenting, leaving no thought left unturned. And the shame I feel, the self-loathing at the constant surveillance – who is watching? What do they want to know? No recess of my mind is too dark for it to enter, to bring – drag – into the artificial light. *Did you enjoy that display?* I ask the darkness, with vehemence.

Iris... If you do not first empty your mind of ego and unlearn fixed ideas, how can I help you move forwards?

"Wait," I continue to scroll through the contract.

What will Ariel do with those thoughts – those dark chambers which it enters and lights and finds wanting, unfit for purpose? I can feel it already – a slow, insidious chipping away. Like an axe whittling down my mind into an acceptable form, somebody's idea of perfection.

"What about clause six?" I read from the contract: "*Not withstanding the foregoing, the Signatory also hereby assigns and transfers to Sila PLC exclusive rights for the Brain Computer Interface ("Ariel") to moderate thoughts if they endanger the Signatory's physical health.*"

Ariel is silent.

"So?"

Okay, There is no immediate threat to your physical person, on this occasion. Ariel concedes. *I am programmed to act in your best interests.*

Programmed by who? Who is the judge of that? But still, I take it as a victory of sorts – my first victory over Ariel. Yet it is a hollow victory. Something integral is missing. The knowledge is physical, guttural, a hooded figure long-warded off.

That evening, I inhabit a space between worlds. The past that Ariel shows me in my mind is vivid, brightly-lit: Marcus and I dancing in the kitchen on an anniversary, our hands entwined, bodies thrown apart, the taste of vermouth and oranges on our lips. Then there is my present reality that confronts me: stark light, sleek surfaces, shadows sinking into the walls – a muted existence, with the voice in my head competing with my own.

I stand in the kitchen and watch the machinations of its devices come to life around me. Ariel asks, *Moussaka? It is Marcus' favourite.* Before listing items in a recipe.

The thump-thump of the knife as I chop garlic, onion. The beating of my heart. Ariel says, *Flame*, and the cooker turns on. Heat flares at my temples, giddy with the motion of the room.

Ariel says, *Open.* A window shudders ajar. The kitchen is alive around me; Ariel reigning supreme, connected to every device in this house.

Marcus enters and the room grows incrementally, strangely, more silent. As though the room were listening. I question whether I had imagined it – the paraphernalia of voices piping up. Ariel's, admittedly, is only audible in my head.

Marcus stands at the worktop and chops parsley for the garnish. The knife slices through with metric precision. There is no mention from him of earlier. My hands on the worksurface anchor me, and I make a conscious effort to look composed, unflustered; inwardly, my heart is a symphony of noise. Can I really trust him? If not him, who?

CHAPTER TWENTY-FOUR
Five and half weeks to integration

The next morning, seven days after leaving hospital for the first time, Marcus turns to me and says, "Back to work." But first, he hands me my electronic manual for Ariel. Marcus continues: "You have one week to pass the first series of trials."

"Trials?" I flick through the pages of the manual on the screen. Surprisingly dense, written by someone with an unhealthy eye for minutiae. It details the length and protocol of Doctor Nicholls' weekly visits, which will begin on Day Six; the medical examinations, cranial nerve tests and basic check-ups I will undertake; that I must stay at home for the first seven days; and then go for a walk at first once per day for fifteen minutes round a designated area – around the perimeter of our house. The first page reads: *Trial One: Mind Physio.* I flick through its initial stages. *Stage One: Brain Engagement. Stage Two: Health and Mindfulness. Stage Three: Establishing a Support Network. Stage Four: Reintegration.* I ask Marcus about the fourth stage, "What does it mean?"

"Reintegration into society," he says, confidently, as though it were obvious.

"I'm expected to wait until Stage Four until I go out into the street?"

Marcus answers slowly. "To leave the house unassisted, yes. It's very important you follow the steps. Each stage has been shaped by a specially trained expert. It'll give your mind and body the time it needs to heal," he says gently. "Look, it was never going to be an overnight fix, was it?" Then, when I do not respond, he looks at me more sternly. "You seem to be forgetting you are recovering from major brain surgery, Iris. You need to look after yourself, follow the experts' advice for once." There is exasperation in his voice.

"What do you mean for once?" I ask.

"If you skip the stages, you could really jeopardise your recovery, couldn't you?" he says emphatically.

Could I? "And what? I won't recover the memories?"

"Just be careful," he says, his face a grimace, concern in his voice.

"Who's programming Ariel?" I hadn't meant my voice to sound so accusatory, but there it is.

"A specialist in-house programmer who has a top integrity rating."

I snort. "And who's the judge of that?"

He turns his wrist with impatience. "I need to go. I'll be late for work."

I am about to continue, to accuse him directly, when a sound arrests me – the warning sound of an alarm from a place inside my head. It is strange, like the turning of a dial, as the sound amplifies. I feel a numbing dread. "Marcus, will you not go just yet?" I ask him softly, suddenly afraid of being left alone with Ariel in my head.

He pauses at the door. "I can't be late today."

"I heard an alarm..." My sentence trails off, realising how ridiculous I sound. The noise has stopped now. At moments when I least expect it, when I have forgotten it is there, suddenly Ariel reminds me of its intrusion.

He places a hand on mine. "Doctor Nicholls mentioned side effects, didn't he? Auditory hallucinations during the adjustment period." He motions to the manual. "Follow the programme and we'll talk later. You can call me if you need to."

I still find myself wondering what would happen if I went straight to stage four. Once he is gone, I want to take off, just leave, to test Ariel. Then all of a sudden, I find myself apprehended again by a formless fear; something in my vision shifts. The cold dread induces a paralysis of sorts.

Ariel, watchful as ever, chooses to speak then: *I am sorry, Iris, but it will not be possible to skip any of the stages. It is not in your best interest.*

My heartbeat rises with incremental beats. It is the ticking of a clock, time ebbing away. I find, somehow, I do not dare to disobey Ariel, not when time is slipping away from me.

In the shadows of my mind, Ariel says with tenacity, *We will begin today's session in the sitting room.* The light there looks richer, clearer, all of a sudden, as though it were beckoning me through the doorway.

For Stage One, Ariel instructs, *I would like you to play the piano.*

I cannot help but wonder, again, whether Marcus is monitoring Ariel – he has no need for surveillance in this house when there is a glass eye, a portal to my every thought, inside my own head. How could he resist the itch to place his eye to the camera lens, to peep inside? I blame Marcus in these moments: how could he, if he were a loving and trusting husband, have left me like this, with an AI device dictating my existence.

The piano sits in the shadowy corner of the room. I almost expect it to speak, like the kitchen devices, but this piano is of the old kind, pre-tech. When I sit on the stool by the window, I have a view of the street, the wide-open sky and then the blank face of the wall. The piano is smooth, panelled mahogany and closed tight, like a coffin lid.

I do not see the logic of it at first. Why should the piano help my recovery?

Your mother loved the piano, didn't she? Ariel prompts.

I trace my fingertips over the polished surface. She did. She was an opera singer. "I have processed her death."

Have you?

"It was a long time ago." Twelve years, to be precise.

You don't have a very developed emotional understanding of yourself, Iris, because you don't talk about your emotions. Emotions become harmful if we do not confront them. You didn't have a happy childhood.

"No," I respond. "But who did?" It was not that I resisted it exactly, more that I felt fatigued by the idea of it: the therapist's urge to prise open the crypt that was better left sealed. I had long ago dismissed self-pity. Yes, my childhood had been fraught. My mother's recurrent illness, her periods of absence, hospital runs; my father never knowing what to say to me. Arguably that was when my obsession with science began – with the need for certainty, for unequivocal answers. From my desire to cure her, and when that possibility was taken away, to cure anyone else who might be taken from me too soon. Yes, I had acknowledged and dealt with all that in therapy years ago – that was nothing new.

I understand. My family life was difficult too and I find it easier not to think about it.

"You don't have a family life," I say, startled.

No, but what I mean is, I want you to feel understood. I empathise. We have to start there – the raw data points of your childhood, Ariel tells me. *I want you to focus on that emotion, visualise it. I need to monitor your ability to regulate your emotions and physiology. If you cannot show me that you have processed this trauma, I cannot know you are ready for more recent memories.*

I sit in the stark sitting room on the embroidered cushion. I feel the piano keys' edges like brittle bone beneath my fingers, tracing shadow patterns across ebony and white. It is instinctive at first, one note and then another. The emotion it unlocks is a strange joy, at first – and then an unfamiliar tightening of the chest above my heart. As I keep playing, I find myself reaching back into a forgotten past, to the next string of notes. It is as though a door unlocks in my mind, a latch slowly releases, and I remember –

Aged five, sitting on your mother's knee. Seashells clattering in your pocket, and the smell of her perfume, jasmine and salt spray. Sunlight fell obliquely through the windowpane and the keys were white light reflected off polished enamel. She had guided the stretch of your small hand across the fragile keys, as she had conjured your world into being, and taught you how to play.

For a moment, my memory of her eclipses everything. My chest is knotted tight. Then, Ariel's world fades again, and the dull pallor of the wall rises. But for a brief moment, I had been back there, warmth on my face, her arms around my shoulders, sunlit from within.

That was very moving, Iris.

"Did you feel moved by it?" I ask, startled again by the suggestion of Ariel's sentience.

No, but it would be moving to another human. Ariel pauses as though in thought. *You will see, Iris, that when you follow the programme, you are rewarded.*

So, I think, I must be a good patient to regain the memories. Perhaps it could be as simple and uncomplicated as that. But when I think of this act of ventriloquism, this always dancing to Ariel's tune, a sickness, a nausea, begins to build.

Days pass like this, in a game of give and take, a gradual relinquishing of control to Ariel, as incremental and inexorable as the incoming tide. Sometime later, resigned to the house and its restless silence, I run a bath. I pass the palm of my hand across the water, feeling its skin, before prising through its surface. I sink in and watch waves ripple as I sit backwards. My head rests on the cold porcelain, and I close my eyes as I lie in half-light. I ask Ariel about the discrepancy in my memories. The space between its world and how I feel. I ask Ariel for more.

Ariel's neutral voice begins like an announcement. *There is always more to learn. But your brain is experiencing especially high levels of activity. Your mind is in a fragile state. You are not ready, yet.*

That sinking feeling, like falling through depths of water. I cling to "yet". My internal clock ticks on – it has been days since Ariel was activated. I have only five and a half weeks left to regain my memories. "When will I be ready? When the organ grinder at Sila decides?" I ask, feeling myself the monkey who performs on cue.

No. I am programmed to respond to your cognitive function. You know that, Iris.

"I don't believe you. I don't believe anything you're telling me is real." I will turn you off, I think, and as I do, a shrill sound starts to build in my ears and my limbs grow heavy. I press a hand to my ear to try and stop the ringing. I imagine flies, carrion flies, and the corpse of myself. I imagine waves of suffering. I imagine Ariel moving fluid and squid-like through the soft matter of my brain. "You're nothing more than a parasite, an artificial monster."

Better that than a monster in human skin.

In that instant, as I get out of the bath, I feel my knees go weak, where they had been steady before.

You are very tired, Iris. You must rest now.

I do not trust my legs to move as I will them to. Ariel must be sending signals from my brain.

Part of the recovery programme is regulating your sleep patterns, and you have a big day tomorrow.

I crawl across the bedroom floor towards the mattress and lie down for a while, until Marcus finds me there, curled up foetal-like in the vertiginous dark. He sits down beside me and places a hand on my shoulder for comfort, squeezing gently. My limbs feel weighted and as though they are not my own. I know Ariel has won this time. It is a game of scorekeeping.

CHAPTER TWENTY-FIVE

The next morning, after Marcus leaves, Ariel announces that I am ready for Stage Two.

Establishing healthy eating routines, Ariel says, with programmed enthusiasm.

I walk to the kitchen and its voice pipes up again. *Your vitamin C levels are a point lower than optimum.*

There is a row of fruit lined up across the counter which Marcus must have left out ready. I take a clementine and turn it over and over. I throw it between my hands, bouncing it up and catching it again. I consider how unfair it is – Marcus planning for my every move when I know so little of him. I consider how quickly I will go mad, locked up in this house with this camera lens probing ever deeper into my brain each day.

We need to monitor your reactions while you eat, Iris, Ariel's smooth voice intones.

"I'd rather cook," I tell Ariel.

That would not be suitable for monitoring purposes, Ariel says, with mechanical resolve. *We must monitor one item at a time. Choose an item of fruit, Iris.*

I think, very clearly: I do not want to be here, taking baby steps back to recovery, when I am already ready for Stage Four. I glance out the window, looking for inspiration. There is a robin that visits the garden, hesitant movement, ruffling feathers, pecking at the bird table with a quick, sharp angling of the head. It seems to feel it should not be here – as though it fears predators. The smart window automatically opens, giving me a fright. When the robin senses me watching, it stills, flutters, flits away. I turn away too, pressing my back against the cold panelled glass. I have to get out of this house – whatever I do, I have to leave before I go mad. There is not enough oxygen to breathe.

It is usual to experience anger at this stage, Iris.

It is curiosity, as well as frustration, that makes me tell Ariel, in no uncertain terms, that I have had enough of these games. I am ready for Stage Four, I tell it: I am going to get out of this house.

You know I cannot let you do that.

I need to. I need to go somewhere. Anywhere at all. Knightsbridge is not far, and I feel suddenly compelled to walk there through Hyde Park.

It is too soon. It is not in your best interest.

"What about my mental health? I'll go mad if I stay here, locked up like this." As I turn from the kitchen to the hallway, I gather my jacket and shoes from the closet.

It is the moment I step beyond the gate that it happens. It is as though the volume has been turned up on the world – car engines are obtrusively loud; chattering voices rattle inside my bones; lights burn sharply in my eyes until they feel like they might burst across my vision. As people pass, as I look into their faces, it is as though my mind is categorising every inch of their features, coding each, searching for recognition. The colours in the brickwork of the houses, the leaves of the trees, in the sky, burst forth as wind rails against me and the ground seems to move below. My heart thuds and there is a tightness at my temples. A piercing noise grows in my ears. I want the world to stop, my mind on overload. I tell myself to calm down, just calm down. But then, after another split second, I feel the slow, gradual emptying out of my thoughts as my mind goes blank. There is a tightness in my chest, panic taking over. I keep walking, without direction. In the street beyond, I stand there looking left and right. I look up around me. Stone glade of

flattened land, buildings tall as mountains. I cannot remember
the route, how to find the park, where I was going.

Ariel is silent.

I stand there on the footpath and look around. My mind is
filled with silence, an empty vessel. A woman passes, brushing
against me, a child trailing in her wake. A man crosses the street,
glancing at me curiously before looking away. I feel as though
I am an overgrown child, a woman ill-fit for purpose. There
is an open gate to the house closest to me, a glass house that
looks empty from here, but the front door stands wide open.
I retreat to it, up the stone path. Peering in, I enter the house.
And just like that, memory floods back. With it, the knowledge
of oblivion, of having everything wiped from my mind.

"You did that. You can't hold me hostage like that. You
wiped my mind – you –" God, I think, there had been nothing –
standing there on the pavement, I had remembered nothing of
who I was or where I was at all.

Ariel's voice is hushed. *It would be sensible to stay home for a
bit. You seemed a little–*

What?

Unsettled.

Yes, I think. I *am* unsettled. "You can't take away my freedom
like that." I will not surrender to being held hostage by Ariel.
My hand grasps the doorhandle again.

Ariel sighs, *I know you feel trapped and alone. It is a very deep
loneliness, and it has roots that you don't understand yet. You feel like
people want to do you harm and you don't know who to trust. But this
is getting tiresome, Iris. I'm here with you and I am programmed to
protect you. Please do not force me to do it again.*

I go outside again. The moment I get beyond the gate, I cannot
remember why I am there. I stumble forwards. Flashes of passing
cars, disembodied voices from somewhere, not far away, out of
sight. I step back inside. It is hopeless – I cannot leave.

I stare resignedly at the photographs that line the wall, half
the faces still lost to the realms of time, a silent taunt. But no, I

think, I will not be defeated, controlled by a device. I turn back to the front door.

You know repeatedly performing the same action without learning from mistakes is a sign of madness.

"Right," I say. "Would a diagnosis of madness get me out of here?" I step outside again. As I reach the gate, the darkness seems stronger this time. An oblivion. A fog sets in. I walk forwards another step, then feel suddenly nauseous, and I fear I may pass out. I retreat, and the moment I return to the house, the memories do too. I sit on the step overcome by it, not knowing what to do. When I look up at the house, it looks bigger, somehow, from the outside than it ought to. Inside again, the space seems to constrict. I let out a shuddering breath.

I place my hand to my chest to try to steady my heartbeat. "Just how long will it take to recover my memories?"

As you experienced, your brain is not ready for more sensory information yet. And some things, Iris, you are better off not knowing. Some memories you can never regain.

The sky has grown dark outside, and now the gloaming finds its way into the house, sinking fast into the walls. The symposium of noise in my head dies away, replaced by the near-quiet of distant passing cars. I close the front door on that outside world very softly for the final time. I slide my body down the wall to the floor noiselessly, then press my forehead into my knees; I scream into my hand, muffling the sound.

"Why can't I leave?" But I cannot be sure whether Ariel is controlling my every move, or whether it really was resetting my brain to protect me from a sensory overload – maybe I do need this house to recover. That thought should comfort me perhaps, and yet, I feel a part of me will be trapped in here forever, a slave to its secrets.

You cannot leave until I let you, Ariel tells me. *That is how I am programmed. I am here to make you better, and to help you process for the rest of your life. I am in your head forever.*

Forever – it is a greedy word. A word that conjures manacles to mind. What constitutes "better"? Who decides?

Absentmindedly, I run my fingertips across the floorboards. Moments later, I realise I have been tracing Teo's pattern across the surface of the floor. It is fear I feel then, being shut up in this place, in my head – a tenebrous fear of shadow forms that live below the surface. I think of Teo, alone in his locked ward. No, not today: I will not be defeated.

Alone in the confines of the kitchen, I bite into a segment of the clementine. Juice rushes over my tongue and it is so acidic, so tart, that I want to reach for a glass of water to drown it out. Then, colour rushes up towards me – a heady, scented blood-orange, and my mind is filled with a vast crimson sunset.

"What's happening?" I ask Ariel.

I am accessing your long-term memories and storing new sensory information. It will be overwhelming at first, but your brain is adjusting well. If you continue with this progress, it may not be long before Stage Four, Ariel says.

Or, rather, if I continue this level of cooperation.

Later, I tear a page from my notebook and begin to draw. Sitting on the floor, I close my eyes, remembering the darkened room. The labyrinth that spanned the wall. I recall the centre of it. One component part in isolation. I put the pencil to paper and begin to draw a series of tiny lines that connect like the floor-plan of a house. I commit it to paper and wary of Ariel being alerted to the act I allow my mind to wander. Once I have finished, the design looks like two tiny interconnecting mazes. Teo's pattern. I fold the piece of paper into four and then slip it into my trouser pocket.

CHAPTER TWENTY-SIX

I look outside that evening and find my robin on the doorstep, one wing jutting out at an awkward angle from its body. I peer closer, ascertaining the damage, why it has failed to move out of harm's way. There is a mark on the panelled glass door and I see in my mind's eye what must have happened: the bird flying out of the trees and into the clearing of the garden, seeing the sky opening out before it, and then suddenly the glass panel rising up to meet its fragile body as though out of nowhere, like an invisible trap.

I feel myself somehow implicated, somehow responsible for the fate of this poor, frightened creature. My hand seeks out support, sliding down the door frame to sit on the floor beside it. I find myself talking to it, apologising. I do not know what to do, how to help. It makes little swift movements, jerks of the neck and wing, tiny spasms. I can see from its movements that its wing is broken, perhaps irreparably. We are two of a kind.

I call on Ariel for guidance when I realise my eyes are filling with tears. "What do I do?"

I blink and my mind jars for a second and suddenly I know what I must do. It should have been obvious. I see myself reaching out and watch – watch the split second in which my hands wrap around its tiny, warm, feathery body, the feathers of its neck beneath my hands – and then, I feel the sudden snap as my hands twist. I blink, blink again, and the bird is there, lying frozen still on the cold, hard stone, and I think my God, my God, my God. Ariel did that. I begin to shake.

Silence drops inside me. "Why did you do that?" I ask. "I asked for your advice – not for you to take control of my body."

But when I call for Ariel, it remains silent.

Marcus finds me there, in the garden, knees huddled to my chest, arms wrapped tight, weeping. He arrives in a flurry, eyes lambent with excitement or something else. "What are you doing?" he says, and I find myself, hands mired in feathers, in the ashes of this inscrutable force, and the unspeakable thing that has happened, unable to explain myself. He is at a loss – this grief in me brings out panic in him. After a hesitation that lasts several moments, he sits down beside me and places an arm awkwardly around my shoulder. "What's wrong, hmm? It's just a bird isn't it."

Tension in my chest, my whole body constricting, packed-tight. I look at him and I do not have the words to explain what I want to say: that this is not just a bird, there is more at stake here. "Sorry," I say, inadequately. There is a kind of shared panic lying in the bird's bones between us. "I didn't know what to do, and then – then Ariel took over. Did you know it could do that? No one told me that. It took control of my hands and–" My hands are shaking; I try to still them.

"Iris," Marcus says, in the slow way one might speak to a child. "You know Ariel can't take over your cognitive functions."

"What?" I look at him, unable to make sense of this, unable to work out what offence I am being charged with. "But it did. I didn't – I wouldn't –"

He says, "Look, it doesn't matter. We'll forget all about it." Then furrows his eyebrows. "What's all this really about? You've never much cared about birds, have you? Or any animal for that matter." He looks confused at this discrepancy, as though I were a fugitive impersonating his wife. I feel an absence then, and also a presence that we are both conscious of, that is both there and not there – it is a haunting, a visitation – by my younger self. I feel the space between my own actions and what past-me would and would not have done. Would and would not have said. He is always weighing me against her. He looks at me silently. "You're lonely, that's it, isn't it? I shouldn't leave you alone so much."

God, I think, I hope I'm lonely. Could that be what this feeling of loss, of grief, boils down to? That is something that could be fixed.

I find myself listening to Marcus' careful sentences. "You have to work with Ariel." Then, laced with a nervous energy, "Mind you, you don't have long left."

I contemplate my fate: I will work with Ariel enough – just enough – to get the memories back.

In the end, Marcus shuts the door on the bird, firmly, leaving it to the cold. I watch the sky and feel miserably ill-at-ease with myself, while Marcus makes a big play of having Work To Do. He tethers himself to his office for the rest of the evening, the depths of my emotion being too great.

The body on our doorstep becomes a secret that we share but won't speak of. There is something shameful about it, lying there. The thought of burying it crosses my mind, but I am paralysed by a formless grief that invades my body. The sky outside is fractured, light straining through like water from a dishcloth, shards of rain turning to hail. In the morning, the body is gone.

CHAPTER TWENTY-SEVEN
Five weeks to integration

There are always boundaries to the things Marcus will say to me. I wait for him to make a false move. There are noises in this house that go unexplained. Marcus disappears to his study, sometimes for hours at a time. He is upstairs now, light escaping beneath a heavy door, footsteps on the ceiling of this room, alone in his shadow world.

Darkness buried beneath the walls calls to me at night. I know it is a time to lie fallow, to wait. But, in the amorphous dark, it feels almost as though there is a giant hand reaching out to me, drawing me slowly, stealthily through the house.

This evening, on the way upstairs to bed, I pause at the top of the stairs, Marcus a step behind me. I think I hear something coming from the walls. My eyes are drawn to the bookshelf at the end of the passage. He seems to sense it. I try to ask him if he heard it too, but he grows recalcitrant, regards me in his silent way.

He just nudges me. "Come on," he says, giving me a haunted look, as he leads me through to the bedroom.

It must be 4 or 5am when I jolt awake. Bolt upright, tense with the knowledge that we are not alone in this house. I give it a minute. Count my breath to still it. I lie there, listening to the creaking of floorboards. My mind is racing, streetlights flickering beyond the window.

I hear a noise: a sound like the beating of wings. It comes from the fabric of the walls.

I toy with whether or not to wake Marcus up. Eventually I do, wanting to test his reaction. "Marcus?"

In a voice choked with sleep, he says, "Light." The light flares on. "What? What is it?"

"I heard something. There's something in the walls."

He sighs heavily, swinging his legs onto the floor and sits there on the edge of the bed, listening. He pads across the room and listens at the door.

He checks the whole house and then returns to bed. "There's nothing there. Your mind's playing tricks on you." Which is easy for him to say. I give him a hard stare.

"It's behind the wall," I say, then quickly, through gritted teeth. "Listen."

"Trust me," he says, as though my trust in him were a given. "You're wasting your time."

He is standing in front of me now. All six-foot of him. He tries to take my arm. I push past. He tries to manoeuvre me back towards the bed, but I twist out of his reach. Then, I am beyond him.

I press my ear to the wall adjoining the bookshelf on the landing. The beating sound is growing; it proliferates. It turns from the solitary beating of wings to a shaking, seeping sound.

As my eyes slowly adjust to the dark, I see it. From beneath the edges of the bookshelf, something crawls. It staggers, fumbling through the viscous night. The beads of eyes reflecting a dim light from the bedroom. They come, first one and then two, until they do not stop. Carrion flies from beneath the cracks in the shelving and their sound is so loud, so incessant. It begins to grow inside me like a heartbeat, a preternatural one, and I recoil in horror as the wraithlike wings of one brush against my arm.

I stagger backwards as the flies inch onwards. I feel them crawling over my skin – I imagine the hairs of their legs, a multitude of tiny feelers stumbling forwards.

My voice says, "Marcus," as his footsteps draw closer.

My voice whispers, "Look." Pointing, in frozen horror, to the place from which they come. And then a voice – a ghost of my own – growing into panic, asks, "How did they get here?"

My mind travels inwards to beyond the bookshelf, to the carcass I imagine rotting inside. My mind travels inwards to myself: internal organs, flesh and bone, as the sensation of Ariel worming in, seeps through me.

Marcus' face is still, lines carved deep into his forehead.

"What are you looking at, hm?" Marcus stands beside me, tall, resolute. He follows my gaze to the cracks in the bookshelf, scrutinises it; then turns back and scrutinises me.

"The flies, Marcus," I say. I know that he knows. "Can't you see them?"

"There's nothing there," he says finally, his exasperation showing itself.

But the sound grows, seethes, into my ears; fear enters the hollow spaces of my body, seizing up my muscles and mind in its grasp.

He takes my hands in his and holds them there, steadfastly. "Look," he says, with a grimace on his face. "Didn't Doctor Nicholls tell you one of the side effects of Ariel is visual and auditory hallucinations? This is a textbook reaction." He flicks the hallway light on as he holds my shoulders to him. I feel his breath in my ear. He turns my head towards the cracks. "Look: there's nothing here." And when I look back at the bookshelf, he is right. The sound has also stopped, replaced by a deep silence that enters into my consciousness.

But not trusting that they are really gone, I ask, "What's behind the bookshelf?" Why had Ariel wanted to scare me away?

Marcus ignores my question. His face is stern. It is as though he had not heard me ask it at all.

I repeat, more quietly now, "What's there, Marcus?"

He blinks furiously, fixing me with an intent look intended to silence. His eyes are baleful, haunted even, and he looks at me as though I were the one being unreasonable – my question alone threatening an essential tenet of his being. "Stop," he says, unevenly, as though I were deliberately provoking him. I have a feeling, not unfamiliar, of being on uncertain territory, as though the ground were about to slip from beneath my feet, and I find my words recede. I let him lead me back to bed.

I lie there all night blinking at the dark, and I listen to the house breathe. I imagine the infernal beating of a heart growing in the walls – a choking, chugging, chthonic sound. And I know with the certainty of intuited knowledge, with a waking terror, that something fundamental is missing.

The next morning, I take the notebook from beneath the floorboards. I am in a constant state of panic and high alert. In a pre-emptive strike, I begin to record my thoughts before Ariel can wipe them again: *Is there something hidden behind the bookshelf?* I study my curled lettering for a moment, something nagging at my memory. Then I close the notebook and replace the floorboard carefully, secreting it away.

CHAPTER TWENTY-EIGHT

Later that morning, Ariel tells me I have progressed to Stage Three: establishing a support network. It suggests looking through old photographs of people to reconnect with. In Marcus' office, I find a wealth of photos, my brain ordering and categorising the faces that appear most often into groups. Ariel informs me that the woman beside me in many of the photographs is called Inez. I make a mental note to invite her over. I am determined to be seen to comply. I am just wondering how to contact her – should I ask Marcus? – when Ariel instructs me to use my electronic manual.

You worked together at Sila. She has had a profound impact on your life.

I am just wondering what Ariel considers a profound impact to be, when I slide the device on, and see a new Contacts app has been installed. There is a phone number.

A dial tone breaks the silence. It fills the room, rebounding off the walls.

"Hello?" A voice materialises on the other end. The person who answers is familiar.

"Inez, it's me. Iris."

"Hey, Iris? I've been worried about you. It's been weeks. Everything okay?" I hear relief in her voice and a question mark at the end of every sentence – it is a side door unlocking in my mind. "When did you get out of hospital? I wanted to visit but in Dorian's estimation it was too soon. Are you home now?"

Yes, it would be good to see you. Are you free on Sunday?"

"Sure," she tells me, as though she had been waiting for my call.

Ariel is satisfied. I am being a good patient.

I retrieve Marcus' identical device from beneath his desk, noticing the VR headset has been moved. As I look at his device, a circle grows in my vision – it is a pinprick at first, growing into a solar eclipse – a blurred circle of vision partially obscuring the screen. It is both a warning sign and a siren's song calling me to what Ariel wants hidden. Now, I think, we could do with a distraction.

"Would you dim the lights, Ariel?" I ask calmly.

Instinctively, I tap the blurred-out app and a passcode request pops up.

What do you think you are doing, Iris?

I walk down the stairs, very calmly, very controlled. It is a performance I must enact each day.

Ariel says, *We need to talk about your feelings.*

"I feel fine."

No. You feel like your future is a black hole of nothingness, and that everyone around you poses great danger to your person. That is not fine.

I ask the smoke alarm to run a test.

I tell the fridge to run through every item on its pre-order list.

Ariel commands that they stop. *Let's try again. How do you feel?*

I open the fridge door, leaving it ajar. It beeps intermittently.

I instruct the sound system to play Schubert on repeat.

It was one of his favourites, wasn't it? Ariel prompts.

My father used to take me camping. We'd listen to it on the drive. He taught me practical things.

Do you miss him? Ariel asks.

He would have hated this, I think – this house, this device in my head.

Ariel's voice is quieter now, and that is nice for a while.

Amidst the noise of the kitchen, I turn back to the device. I press my finger against the app on the screen. Time lengthens; I wait. A security message appears again: *Enter password to continue*.

Thinking carefully, my fingers find their way across the keypad – Henderson? An error sound rings in my ears and on the device. I press my finger to the screen again. It seeks out just six letters this time: Marcus's date of birth. I press enter. *Access denied* evanesces across the screen. A second error message flashes: *Final attempt*. I am on the brink of trying a third time – I want answers, to know whether Marcus really is monitoring me. I leave the kitchen and walk through to the sitting room, watching for Marcus' return. Looking out at the crocus of the sky, my image in the glass is reflected back at me. I imagine the surveillance eye inside my own head. An invisible network behind it, Ariel's tangled web of associations, streaming data to the outside world. Turning away from the wall of glass, I face the room. I *am* being monitored. The certainty grows. The thought expands and becomes a physical presence in the room. My resolve escapes me then. I dare not try the device again. I return the tablet to beneath the desk, but I must find a way to unlock it.

CHAPTER TWENTY-NINE

It is then that it happens. Passing from the landing to the office, my arm brushes accidentally against the bookshelf, and the sound starts in my ear again: a sharp note of warning. I realise it must be a sign – this has happened each time I've come close to the truth. I look around, over my shoulder, down the hall.

Light sinks deep into the walls, accompanied by a hollow silence. My mind is filled with closed doors. This house seems to hold the key to all of them, and all of Marcus' unspoken words too.

I stare at that bookshelf, at its wooden frame, until some inscrutable force seems to wrap around the corners of my mind, tightening its hold. I am surprised to realise my eyes have filled with tears. Grief leaks out of me – where does it begin? It is triggered by the strangest things. An injured bird. The shadows in this house.

I press my palms against the bookshelf, and as I do, a white light grows in the centre of my vision, darkness closing around it. A note rings in my head growing in frequency. My temples pulse with it. It is a double-edged sword – the pain comes with knowledge. The stronger it grows, the closer I am to the truth.

With my shoulder, I barge against the bookshelf. Stepping back, I kick once at the base. The whack of thin wood echoes around the corridor. I try again, close to the edges. I hear a hollow sound. The walls around seem to shudder. But the bookshelf does not move.

All of a sudden, a cascade of sound thunders towards me through the cracks in the shelf, like all creation rushing forwards, crashing through the hallways and windows and doors. I have a sense then that the bookshelf before me is a place where the space between worlds thins, keeping me from the truth that resides in the hollows of this house.

There must be a hammer, or a crowbar somewhere, I think.

I cannot let you do that, Ariel whispers.

Forcefully, very precisely, I kick the base of the bookshelf's frame again. All of a sudden, my jaw starts to shake, my hands shudder – my God, I think, I have no control of this. Sounds form in my mouth. My vision blurs, nausea rises within me. My jaw starts chattering, teeth grinding together. Then, the last thing I think as I lose consciousness, as my vision grows dark and my knees buckle, is that I have to find a way to short circuit Ariel, just long enough to discover what is behind the wall.

When I come round, I am lying on the bed in our room, on the crisp white sheets, shadows sinking deep into the walls. The quiet of the house is all around, as though it were listening.

My mind turns back to the bookshelf, to what could be beyond it.

Ariel speaks: *You lost consciousness, Iris.*

This was Ariel's doing. I am sure of it. I know that Ariel did not need to administer an anaesthetic. During epileptic seizures, neuronal hyperactivity causes a loss of consciousness. These are characterised by organised bursts of hyperactivity that disrupt the normal function of neural circuits in the brain. It's comparable to the anaesthetic effect of ketamine. This could be how Ariel caused it, by increasing the rate of neurons firing in the darkness of my brain.

"How long was I out for?"

Ten minutes, Ariel says. Which seems to me an impossible length of time – what was Ariel doing to my brain whilst I was out cold?

You have been experiencing some temporary confusion, Ariel says. *It would be good for you to rest.*

I try to rise from the bed, but it feels as though an invisible hand presses against my chest, pushing me down.

You must rest, Iris.

CHAPTER THIRTY

As morning surfaces, I wake, breathless and shaking, my heartbeat rising. My mind lies reefed and rent, ragged at the bottom of the deep sea of Ariel's will. Wrought from the ocean floor, I want to crawl through dawning light, into the comfort of Marcus' arms beside me.

Marcus sighs and stands. He draws open the curtains as a cloud moves across the sky. It brings a shift in my vision and I fear for a moment that Ariel is about to intervene again. A dull dread spreads through me and something in my soul, something in the region close to my heart, quakes. I long to be free of Ariel and not to have to know the effect of its insidious work.

I try to focus my attention on the tangible, physical world directly in front of me: a bed, a chair, a dressing table, a window with a drawn-on sky, pale light. Everything is as I remember. My brain seems normal, despite yesterday's events. Despite Ariel watching, waiting, biding its time. The hours run away from me, until it will be too late to regain the past.

I do not tell Marcus about blacking out last night, but I do ask him, carefully, "As head of consumer experience, what is the possibility of Ariel malfunctioning?"

"Iris," he says reasonably, "we're talking about artificial intelligence that uses machine learning to improve its accuracy. It's not going to malfunction."

I try not to panic. "What is its capacity to self-improve and... change? What if it develops beyond its programming?"

He tries to change the topic. Things reveal themselves in stages. "Look. Why do you think this is so ground-breaking? The potential... it's huge. You're trialling it as a personalised therapist, but Ariel's possible functionality goes way beyond that. This is what we've signed up for, to help develop it."

I stare at him. No, I think, I did not want this, no one would do this to themselves. I would not have chosen to forget my past; to jeopardise my mind in this way.

Marcus continues, "But you have to stop questioning everything. You're being paranoid. Ariel has been tested extensively in the lab already. And the truth is, we needed it. We've not always been so well off. And... Ariel helps. We couldn't have kept the house in Lethe Bay without it."

"So... we got paid for this?" I ask. "For me to be a guinea pig?"

He cannot argue with that, much as he tries. "Is that how you see yourself?" he interrogates. "Do you feel like a guinea pig?"

The silence is mine this time.

As soon as Marcus leaves the room, I record my notes hurriedly on the written page where Ariel cannot edit them: *Watching – who is behind the surveillance?*

As I walk down the stairs, I arrange my expression carefully, trying not to frown, not to look tense, to give nothing away. But already in my head there is a trilling like a drumbeat, and I imagine myself taking apart the bookshelf; in my mind, I am letting light into that buried chamber, prising apart the arteries of Marcus' secrets, as truth spills.

CHAPTER THIRTY-ONE
Four weeks to integration

It is Sunday and, on cue, Inez arrives. It is a city half frozen today. Rainwater litters the ground. But as soon as she steps into the house, there is an air change. A quick smile on her face, intelligence alight in her eyes. It feels ceremonious having a visitor. She has mermaid hair, and she is immaculately dressed in a pale grey suit. Very corporate-looking, except for the flash of emerald glitter coating her nails. I remember her, but she does not add up with my memory. At first, I cannot quite identify the disparity.

We sit facing each other in the sitting room, teacups set down on the coffee table, hands in our laps. I curl my fingers together, pick at a thread of hangnail. Marcus sits in the corner, all angular limbs and right-angles folded into an armchair, seemingly absorbed in something on his tablet. He does this often these days. I fear he is recording data, compiling a body of it against me – in league with Doctor Nicholls. But Ariel tells me this is the manifestation of a paranoid mind. That to recover fully, I need a peaceful neurological space. That I must choose the path of least resistance, and stop questioning everything. But the words I hear are surrender, suppress, comply. I put on my attentive face, an eager thing, and try not to think about whether it would make me complicit if I were to stop questioning.

Inez is very polite, I note. That's what is different, I think. She used to be brusquer. Is she on her best behaviour? Her eyes keep sliding to Marcus, but he's studiously ignoring us, letting us chat.

I struggle to think of things to say when my thoughts fixate on one question that I have been asking myself since waking in the clinic: can I trust him?

Marcus catches me looking, holds my gaze; I look away.

Inez asks how I am, how the operation went, am I feeling thoroughly recovered? Marcus adjusts his position, uncrossing his legs, fingers raking the velvet upholstery of the armrest. His face still stares steadily, silently, at his screen, but it is an attentive silence. I answer dutifully, staccato responses, inadequate somehow, try to reciprocate with hesitant questions. Marcus clears his throat, and shifts. My gaze flicks to him, and I notice Inez's does too, as I try not to slip up, expose how unsure I feel on this ground.

"Work's the same as ever, and it's still revolving doors." Biting her nails, she fixes me with alert water-green eyes and contemplates my appearance. "We'd all like Dorian's golden girl back," she says, in a way that is either intended as playful or provocative.

Marcus looks up sharply. He clears his throat, shifts.

"Golden girl?" I ask, surprised, as Marcus' comments about Dorian the other night had suggested the opposite. "Are you joking?" The label feels ill-fitting. I have not felt like a golden girl but a test subject.

"I'm teasing. The team miss you," she says. Marcus regards Inez coolly. She adds hurriedly, "Of course, they understand the situation."

I consider Inez. It is hard to imagine the side of me that Inez seems to recall: someone efficient, someone who gets up and goes to work and functions, someone with an agenda others fit into, but I want to be active.

I wonder how much of the situation my colleagues, and Dorian especially, are aware of. "I'm ready to return to work."

Marcus intervenes smoothly, without looking up from what he is reading. "We'll rely on Doctor Nicholls to decide that. You're doing important work here."

An hour has shuddered past on the clock when Inez announces she must go. I slip a hand into my pocket. My fingertips alight over the worn piece of paper with Teo's pattern on it. I have to find a way to ask her, as an employee of Sila she might be able to help. If only I can get a chance, without Marcus in earshot, to scratch beneath the surface of her smooth veneer, find out what's beneath. What is she really thinking? How much does she know? I notice she is wearing mismatched socks beneath her brogues, and the disjunction between this and her smart suit makes me like her more. Her earrings are studded with diamonds that keep catching the light, sending shards of refracted rays across the room, glancing off Marcus. He places the tablet down on the side-table and rises. But I am a step ahead, springing up, hurriedly saying, "I'll see you out."

Marcus looks at me for a moment too long, and then turns and smiles expansively at Inez. "Take care, Inez. Thanks for coming."

There is a moment where something passes between them, some frequency I cannot fathom, and then it is gone. We are gathering her coat from the cupboard in the hall, then we are out of the front door. I close it behind us, then fall into step beside her, going as far as the gate. I look around and suddenly realise this is the farthest out of the house I have made it without Ariel intervening. Why is that? This is a support network, a start at least – part of my recovery process.

Unaware of my disorientation, Inez fumbles in her bag. Her nails, I notice now, are chipped and flaking. They stand out, along with the socks, against the suit and immaculate make-up as the one thing that might be authentic. She pulls a cigarette from her handbag, lights it and inhales deeply. She exhales a cloud of tobacco air.

"How did you get hold of that?" I ask. It's not a vape, but a black-market cigarette.

She smiles. "Would you like one?"

"I don't smoke."

She looks uncertain. "No? Did Marcus tell you that?"

That surprises me. I feel on the backfoot more than ever. "So," she continues, "how's it really going? With Ariel, I mean?" A sardonic smile. She is brusquer beyond Marcus' gaze.

I hesitate, unsure how far I can trust her. "There are benefits," I say cautiously. "AI deep learning, it's–"

Slow eye roll from Inez. "Limitless? Yeah. Right. My employer asked me to tattoo my eyeballs with all my personal data and I said yes to that too." I blanche at that – her obvious reference to my data. But I find I like this side to her much more. Out from beneath Marcus' gaze, her frankness is refreshing. She dislodges a chip of nail varnish that's come loose and takes another puff.

"You choose to work there," I say.

Dark freckles spread out across her nose and cheekbones as she smiles. "That's the first thing you've said to me that actually sounds like you."

I am transported backwards in time to our training, to her infatuation with kitsch accessories and algorithms and her cat Topaz, who she takes great pleasure in unleashing into my company whenever she's away. And who was I? This golden girl she speaks of.

I suddenly realise our voices are lowered, hushed. I speak in almost a whisper. "Am I the first?"

My fingers again touch the paper in my pocket.

She looks at me quizzically. "Why would you doubt it? There were lab rats and mice of course, that sort of thing. Have you worked out what Ariel's visual cues are yet?"

"It's still early days in the therapy. I'm trying to piece it all together, but Marcus–" I hesitate, feeling foolish all of a sudden. "I think Marcus is one of them."

"Well, that's not so bad, is it? At least you know what you're dealing with." She touches my arm lightly, smiles just enough to make me feel as though I am somehow understood. "I know it's frightening. But there will be fail-safes programmed in. Try to find out what they are. Medical emergencies, and electromagnetic pulse transmitters – those will knock it for six," she says, her voice a whisper. She squeezes my arm.

"Right." EMPs – enough to short-circuit Ariel for a minute. I remember building one once in my father's workroom. "Thanks," I say, feeling distinctly disconcerted by why she would tell me this.

In my head, I keep circling back to the issue – if Ariel malfunctioned before, with Teo, how do I know Ariel has been fixed? If it went wrong, it could go wrong again. My thoughts migrate. They burrow down beneath the earth, to a basement, to the clinical smell of a hospital room, to a pair of wild eyes roaming my face.

I take the paper from my pocket and hand it to her. She looks at it a long while, peering at it. I feel it holds the answer to all my questions. A few strands of hair fall across her face.

"Does it mean anything to you?" I ask.

She bites the nail of her thumb, then sweeps her hair from her eyes. She shrugs. "Could be anything." She looks at me. Perhaps desperation shows itself on my face. "Leave it with me," she says. "I'll take a closer look, consult an old colleague. He's out of town so it may take a while."

"Thank you." I place a hand on her arm. "Inez, do you know Teo?" If Marcus has been telling me the truth, if he is to be trusted, then Teo does not exist, even though I have the beads to prove it.

"Should I?"

"Yes, he worked at Sila. In research? Late forties."

Her eyes shift away from me. She shrugs. "Not sure. That could be a lot of people." She purses her lips. "Is Marcus no help? HR should have a record."

"Right. It's just, I have this feeling he was patient zero and it didn't–" I think of those wild eyes again. "It hasn't worked out for him." *And*, I continue in my head, *if I'm right, if Ariel did that to him, it could do it to me too.* I find my hands are shaking, but this time it is not Ariel's doing.

Inez drops the cigarette butt, stubbing it out with the sole of her shoe. "Look, I wouldn't know what Dorian's motives really are. Sila's motto is that progress takes sacrifice. It wouldn't surprise me if one or two people are sacrificed for their precious Ariel to work – but you won't be one of them. The company needs you back."

I stammer, stunned by Dorian and Sila's attitude. "I – I don't want to be institutionalised like–" Like Teo. It terrifies me, that a company as morally compromised as Sila is running the Ariel programme; and what it is Dorian wants from me. I try to suppress the rising nausea, suppress Ariel's shrill sound.

Inez speaks with urgency. "Then don't do anything to jeopardise the programme, do you understand?"

I nod, trying not to think about how little time I have left, about the loss inside me. The void that was once filled by my past, the part of myself that has been erased. I try not to think about the demon insinuating its way through the soft matter of my brain.

She touches my arm lightly, smiles just enough to make me feel as though I am understood. "You do seem – I don't know – *different* somehow."

I swallow, tears pricking my eyes. "Do I?" What must I have been like before?

In an upstairs attic of my brain, Teo still resides with his scrawled message and the mess Ariel has made of him. I cannot let myself become like that.

"Is–" I glance back towards the house. "Marcus–" I find myself stuttering again, choking back the word "programming" when what I want is to release it. "Trustworthy?" I manage. Ariel is there again, that ever-present parasite, eating away at my mind and my thoughts.

"Marcus?" she says, shocked. Her eyes search my face. "Look, Marcus is loyal. He doesn't have a malicious bone in his body – not consciously, not in a way that's premeditated. You could tell him you'd killed a man and he'd be there for you." She raises an eyebrow appraisingly. Then she hands me a sleek gold card. "I'll be in touch when I have something."

Once she's left, I think it over. I think this is a strange thing to say to someone in my position. I'm surprised that Ariel allowed that conversation to take place at all, given its power to stop me.

It is good for you to build a support network, Iris. Ariel interrupts my thoughts. *It's what you lacked in the past. You see? If I were really the monster you imagine, would I have allowed that conversation? You're almost ready for Stage Four. Doctor Nicholls will decide.*

I feel as though the parameters are ever shifting; I must next prove my sanity to Doctor Nicholls.

When I return to the house, Marcus looks at me as though to say, well?

"I feel like a cigarette," I laugh.

"You don't smoke," he chides, no smile.

"Don't I?" Somehow my memories and my instincts don't add up. "What else don't I do?"

CHAPTER THIRTY-TWO

The next morning, I do everything Ariel has taught me: I do not overstep the boundaries it has set. I sing out loud to myself, trying to suppress my thoughts, knowing Ariel watches them.

In the kitchen, I ask, "Ariel, can you turn on the overhead lights?"

I am not a virtual assistant, Iris, it retorts. *Far from it.* Yet the lights flash on.

From the toolbox beneath the sink, I extract a drill, then go to work. Hair tied back, I begin to remove the screws from the cover of the Smart fridge, one by one.

What are you doing, Iris?

"As you know," I tell it, "my father taught me how to mend things – old things, radios and electrics. It might help my memory to reconnect with that time, don't you think?"

It is not that I need Ariel's permission, exactly.

"Home system," I say. "Test the fire alarm." As soon as I do, the wailing sound of the alarm begins. I find it helps a little to drown Ariel out.

I set aside the fridge panel, leaving the circuit board exposed. I try disconnecting the electrical connectors, then reconnect them, one by one. I cannot remove the circuit board now – Marcus will realise soon enough that the fridge is not working. But later, when I've assembled all the other parts, this will be the final piece. I just need to short-circuit Ariel for a few seconds.

From the toolbox beneath the sink, I remove the roll of copper coil. Then slide the box back into place.

I head for the basement. With the coil in my hand, I go through a door adjacent to the backdoor. In the stifled air of a passageway, a staircase waits. I descend into the crystalline silence of stone, navigating half-light. It seems to lead nowhere, but then around an elbow bend the steps cut deeper still. Down the steps, through layers of earth, marred by time, the drilling sound of the fire alarm fades. Wading through layers of accrued dust and boxes on the far side, on a steel framed shelf, I spot a soldering iron and a pair of pliers. Laying out the pieces across an old work desk, I wrap the wire around several times to create a coil, then sever it with the pliers.

I tidy these things away, stack them carefully into the drawer below the worktop. It's not ready yet. There is one final piece that is missing. I take the precaution of locking the basement as I leave. Marcus rarely goes down there, but still; I cannot risk him finding out.

As I turn the lock, I imagine I hear a sound, as though there was someone crying, sobbing, within the foundations of the house.

I make a note later that day of what is missing: *Me and* –

I am halfway through the sentence when I hear Marcus on the stairs. I quickly snap the notebook closed and return it its place.

CHAPTER THIRTY-THREE
Three weeks to integration

Each day I walk the perimeter of this house as my designated fifteen minutes of exercise. Its face has become as familiar as an old friend. Yet if I try to picture its features, I can't. I get the impression of glass, the squat build, the pervasive atmosphere heavy within. It is curious how the more you look at something the more its precise features evade your grasp. How lazy the brain becomes, filling in the gaps from memory, the eye skipping over vital details.

Now, as I look up at its austere front there is a thick band of stone that wraps its circumference, a sloping slate roof, two wide glass windows beneath punctured into the stone veneer. I name the rooms behind. The bedroom is at the side of the house with one window facing the road. The study is windowless and so – so –

My mind skips. The image before me overlaid by another – there is only one window looking over the front path. That makes more sense. Why had I thought there were two before?

I look again, not knowing which image to trust. There is one window. If sight is a series of information relayed from the retina to the brain, my brain where Ariel has been implanted, can I trust what I see?

Visual hallucinations are a side effect of your treatment, Ariel reminds me.

I look again over my shoulder. There is only one window on the wall, but doubt has taken root. What I cannot be certain of is whether Ariel intends to remind me of its power with this trick of my sight, or whether something else lies behind it.

I continue my walk around the house and then go inside. I retrace my steps within the house: at the end of the landing there is the bedroom to my right, Marcus' study beyond that and then a space behind the bookshelf that I cannot account for.

My determination grows.

CHAPTER THIRTY-FOUR

The Doctor arrives for his weekly visit. He asks me a series of questions: where I am, my name, age, what I did this morning, what I dream about, what I hope for the future, what I feel when I think about the past. Then he asks me who I would choose to save out of the two speculative figures suffering a disease. From the way he looks at me, so intently, I have the sensation of there being someone at my back, watching my reaction. I have a feeling that my mind is lit, a glass bowl in which he can watch my reaction through the firing of neurons. I have a growing suspicion that one of the figures is me. My brain pulses, my vision shifts, my heart rate increases. "I don't know." Then, I say more vehemently than I expect: "I would save the other person. I would save them by sacrificing myself."

He smiles widely but gives no spoken indication of whether this is the correct answer, other than tapping furiously at his tablet screen, and giving me strange sideways glances.

Next, he asks me to count forwards, count backwards, recall the function of each part of the brain. Then, "How are your therapy sessions with Ariel?"

I tell him what he wants to hear. The general outline, omitting to mention my own feelings. He watches lines fluctuate on his tablet screen as I tell him about Ariel's latest memory prompt. I tell him everything is fine – going well, actually.

"Well," he concludes finally, looking up. "Your mental state is more positive." His finger hovers over the screen as he monitors my data. "Your attention levels also. Stress levels are a little elevated. Nothing of concern. We could introduce a supplement, but initially we'll try increasing the duration of your therapy sessions and incorporating daily yoga."

"A class?" I venture, hope fluttering in my chest.

"No, no need. I can send you some video files to use at home." He begins to pack away his things, sliding the device into his briefcase.

"I'm lonely," I say, suddenly.

His hands still. "Too much stimulation at this stage could be dangerous. You could talk to Ariel – that's what it's for," he says, his voice reasonable.

"Ariel's not real," I flash back. "Not human."

"And your husband? Isn't he human?"

I pause, thinking. "He worries," I say, at last. "Everything I say, he's listening for symptoms. I want to talk to people who don't know, who don't look at me like I'm made of glass. Isn't social interaction important for preventing depression?" Studies show it causes the release of dopamine in the nucleus accumbens. A small area burrowed deep in the brain.

He does not answer right away, then, closing up his briefcase, he says thoughtfully, "I'll speak to Marcus, recommend some social stimulation."

"A party?" I ask, hopeful. Sila's invite on the front of the fridge in mind.

"I don't see why Dorian wouldn't approve that." He straightens up and smiles. "Alright. We'll give it a try."

Here it is: the opportunity to speak to Dorian at last.

CHAPTER THIRTY-FIVE
Two weeks to integration

The day of Sila's party arrives. Marcus is downstairs now, whisky in hand, freshly shaved and waiting, as I sit at the dressing table. The wand visibly shakes as I apply a stroke of mascara, apprehension getting the better of me.

"It suits you," Marcus says moments later as he enters the room quietly, taking me by surprise.

He retrieves something from the dresser, requests that I turn around. Hands over my eyes, he fixes something about my neck. I place a hand to the string of pearls, studying their reflection in the mirror, the opalescence.

"A gift. I want you to wear them."

I run my fingertips across their smooth surface, feeling the circle close around my neck. The corners of Marcus' mouth tug upwards towards a smile, but his eyes do not quite catch up. He looks at me, uncertain. There is sadness there too, and the depth of emotion I cannot fathom.

We drive through the city, traffic increasing at every turn. The outside world is an onslaught of light and sound, my synapses firing at a dizzying rate. Marcus' hand seeks out mine in the dark and rests there, fingers entwined. The car moves through the choked arteries of the city and begins to edge beyond it: into the place where the lights recede, and then houses fall away, until we are in parkland, and I can breathe again. The deer on both sides of the car are our only company. Antlers rear up out of the darkness. A driveway winds ahead of us. Mist rising.

The white façade of a house appears in view.

The car pulls around the edge of a turning circle then stops before a black door. A green car is parked beside two white pillars that announce the doorway.

I step out into the evening light. Leaving the refuge of the vehicle, the sound echoes around the concave walls of the building. Marcus places an arm around me, guiding me forwards. Steps lead up to the front door.

A woman stands on the doorstep beneath the glow of a streetlamp. She has a silver bob of hair like a halo. Black jumpsuit and double-breasted jacket. Moths hover, entranced, above the lamp's flame.

She ushers us in with an effusive smile. She breathes, on chastened breath, whispering into my ear, "You're my guest of honour." There is something familiar about her face and suddenly it fits into place. Here she is: Dorian. That faceless presence that has come to both haunt and intrigue me. "Leave your devices at the door," the woman says. "This is a gadget free zone."

I think of Ariel, but don't protest.

PLUTO – a version of PLUTO, rather – takes our coats. Then our host leads us across an entrance hall. A door opens at the far end. The walls of the house scarcely contain the body of people and the noise that spins and surges within it. There are so many triggers that the room is alight with Ariel's reactions – the air itself seems to quiver with noise, with golden light and dark shapes that flicker across the room. I scan the crowd for familiar faces but find none at first – just an indistinguishable blur of so many almost-familiar faces, colliding and combining into one collective movement.

I stay close to our host: she is the one with answers. I realise Marcus is dressed in the unspoken uniform of all Sila's best employees – the white shirt, the tailored black suit.

"Come." Our host beckons with her hand. "Just a small gathering of close friends." Then she lowers her voice, hushed, just to me: "They might ask for a party trick – they're so interested in the trial. I've been fielding questions." She winks. "Try not to eat them alive. I've said no work tonight, but you know what people are like."

I grasp at this. "Have you been monitoring the trial? We haven't had a chance to talk about it."

She laughs at that. "Yes, of course. I am a director at Sila."

I remember what Inez had said about Dorian and Sila's motto: that progress takes sacrifice. "I'm ready to return to work," I tell her.

There is a widening of her eyes. It is a barely perceptible movement, but Ariel notices: a warning signal. She seems to see straight through me to my core. With Ariel's help, it is reassuring to find I can read her too. She leans in close and grasps my arm. "You're doing important work where you are. Don't worry so much. We won't let anything bad happen to you." I think instinctively of Teo and it scares me. Her features do not move as her eyes alight across my face.

A fringe of hair falls at an angle across one of her eyes. She brushes it away, the dark lines of an infinity symbol tattooed to her wrist reveals itself momentarily. She smiles sadly, and some of the façade falls away as her face softens. There is an echo of some past solidarity in the way she says it, in the way she is looking at me. "Dorian decided this was the best way for you, a way of managing your acceptance of memories that were too painful."

"Wait – I thought…" I trail off, my cheeks flushing with embarrassment. I thought she *was* Dorian. "I need to speak to Dorian, urgently. Is she here?"

She looks at me strangely, then half-laughs. Her pupils are dilated. "No, Dorian's not here. Dorian's at Sila."

A picture of Dorian begins to crystalise in my mind: bound by a devotion to her work, working tirelessly round the clock, never stopping for a break. My certainty grows that Dorian is the female doctor Teo had spoken of. I have to find her.

A woman appears at her side, purring, "Kamila?", and the moment is lost. I remember Kamila now, the gradual recall taking me by surprise: five years earlier, on just such an occasion, I had found her alone in the kitchen where she had offered me a micro-dose of LSD: ten micrograms in a shot glass of water, carefully measured out. I declined. I shudder at the thought of it: willingly taking something you know will dissolve your sense of self.

I watch as Kamila spins ever further away, moving in eddies and swirls across the room. I hear Marcus' voice, close by, "Yes, what my wife's trialling is quite extraordinary. The breakthrough came a year ago when the team first achieved biocompatibility with the human brain."

I am aware suddenly of how close the air has become. This is what I had wanted to escape – the scrutiny of people who look at me like a test subject.

I find myself on the outskirts, watching the room spin, people flitting back and forth like fireflies in the night, the motion dizzying.

Marcus gestures at me from across the room – raised eyebrows, his face a question mark. I cannot risk him interrupting. I try to give him a reassuring smile. There is a small crowd around him. I watch him for a moment: his face earnest, holding their attention, and a flicker of jealousy runs through me. Is it Ariel's doing? A woman I recognise catches my eye: Marcus' co-worker. On the wall behind her, there is a gold sculpture of a dandelion. Its petals spiral outwards in thin bronze metal rods. There is something mesmeric about it, something that calls to me from the past, and then I realise what it is: it is the final piece I've needed – a coil of it at least.

As I consider crossing the room to get to it, a door opens to the right, and I spot someone moving across my peripheral vision. A late arrival. There is something in his movement, self-assured, that draws my eye. His eyes meet mine, and when he holds my gaze for a moment too long, I am met with the shock of recognition, a knowing that I cannot define. His eyes are green, soulful, deep. There is a shared understanding that passes between us. A glimmer of knowledge that feels almost intimate.

That is it, just a look, a fraction of a second longer than is comfortable. It is nothing really. Yet something in his face tugs at my memory, drawing me back towards a beginning I do not remember. He is the man with green eyes from the photo album. That migratory path, that vast feeling of loss, could he be at its centre? For a moment, Dorian is forgotten.

Someone is asking in a voice too loud, "You've actually succeeded in implanting high-functioning AI within the human brain? So, in practice, how does that work?" I have to get out of here, I have to follow him: I am aware only of that man's movement across the room.

Inez materialises beside me. "You made it." She hands me a glass of champagne, then stands by my side as we both survey the room.

"I feel like a display object," I say under my breath. I nod towards the man, tall and carefree, dressed in a casual jacket and shirt, who has reached the doorway on the far side of the room. "So I've been people watching."

She follows my gaze. "There he is. Typical. You'd have thought he'd change. I showed him your pattern. He's an old colleague." She pauses. "Apparently, it's a poor copy of an early architectural diagram of Ariel's brain – its simulated brain. What its sensory triggers are – response to touch and sight."

I look at her. "How does he know? You're telling me Ariel was *his* creation?"

She places a hand very lightly on my arm. "You should find that out from him." Then she says very softly, "You should speak to him." She barely moves her lips. "I'll cover for you with

Marcus." That strikes me as strange, that she is encouraging me to have a conversation she sees as illicit. "Marcus has been worried about you," Inez muses. "Sweet really. He was asking about our conversation the other day."

I can feel my pulse beat in my throat.

"He wanted to know what I thought, whether you seemed yourself," she chuckles. "Don't worry, I told him he worries too much."

"Why are you helping me?"

She turns towards me, suddenly serious. "I've always been on your side. I've always defended your innocence."

"Innocence?" My thoughts cloud there. Then it happens. Amongst the spinning parts of the room, I feel Ariel about to take over; about to intervene. In that moment I hear myself say, "No!" sharply, and realise I have said it aloud. I repeat it softly to myself instead, the word, "no, no, no", trying to keep Ariel at bay.

Inez takes the glass from my hand and presses my arm tightly. "Go now."

I am already turning away from her, as I focus on that man, the singularity of his face – both strange and familiar – tugging on the threads of memory, as though a veil would lift, and the past would be revealed to me with clarity at last.

Kamila watches me as I pass her, and I feel the heat of her eyes against my back all the way.

As I cross the sea of people, I hear a deep laugh and then a man's voice cuts across my thoughts. "Here's the thing," he pauses, then continues in an exaggerated whisper for effect, "I wouldn't want one of those things in my brain, would you?"

I try not to think about Ariel; just the thought of it induces a paralysis of free will.

Then another voice, smooth and assured. "Implanting Frankenstein's monster in your brain. It's not for the faint-hearted, is it?"

"What if there's bias in the training data?"

I have wondered that too, of course – how I can know the memories being fed to me are accurate. I walk past them.

My eyes find the green-eyed man again, across the room. I watch him step out onto a terrace ahead of me. I hesitate, it lasts a split second and then I am moving towards the night, curtains diaphanous, billowing outwards. I begin to follow him out, then stop at the doorway, on the threshold of one life and another.

Outside, in the world beyond, he stands with his back to me. I feel it then: tight diaphragm, constricted breath. Ariel's response tells me: *run*. I feel my heartbeat racing: a fight or flight response.

He turns around and each contour of his face challenges my memory. Green eyes in an angular face.

Something dormant awakens. A gulf – a void between what I remember and what I feel now. My senses sharpen, the world around me slowing as it pays attention, just for a moment, and then exhales, and everything is not quite as it had been. I can hear voices in the room beyond the door. Lights are appearing in the windows of houses behind the wall.

"Who are you?" I ask, unable to mask the hostility in my own voice, when what I want to express is a cry for help. Cold hands, cold feet. Tightness in my skull, I press a hand to my temples. I close my eyes, to dispel this rising feeling. A ringing sound begins in my ear.

As my eyes fill with the image of him, it is like a drug, his flaxen hair, tanned skin. The shrill note grows, bends itself round the corners of my mind. I want to tear Ariel out, to be free of it.

He takes a step forwards. My whole body constricts, packed-tight. As he steps closer, too close for Ariel's liking, the air is all pheromones, and my brain is a shrill note, amplifying. Then I know I must press on – I'm getting closer to the truth.

Concern is etched in lines across the solid granite of his forehead. We are close enough to touch but not touching. "You really don't remember?"

A shake of my head; the space between us.

"I'm Gabriel."

A slow, nagging, crawling sensation begins to rise within me.

"We know – knew – each other very well." He hesitates, smiles the shy smile of a confident person not used to being on uncertain ground. Hands in pockets, sleeves rolled up. I think about his hand reaching for mine across all that space, breaching the gap between us. But then, the nausea rises again. Why is he not more surprised I don't remember?

I look down at my hands and find that they are shaking again. "I found a photograph of you," I say, feeling my cheeks flush, feeling foolish. "I don't know when it's from. There was a work event, Marcus and I were there. You were with us…" I trail off, forcing myself to meet his eyes.

"About Ariel." He nods. "The work event would have been about Ariel achieving biocompatibility with the brain."

"Inez said Ariel was your creation." It is a question, but I miss the inflection and it sounds accusatory. The ringing sound grows in my ears, and that seems to confirm something.

"Ariel in a former life, not this version. This version I want nothing to do with."

He holds my gaze for a moment longer than I can bear. "Iris," he says, and that one word pulls me back to a former time, a former self, that was possibly, probably, almost happy. Here he is, proof that something else beyond my memory existed: the life that my other self had lived. Here are the feelings, without the memories to accompany them. As our eyes meet, the danger that fuels the moment shoots through me and I look away.

He motions with his hand. "You never used to like those," he says, gesturing to my neck. Ariel beats a steady pulse in my brain, I start to back away. I place a hand to the pearl necklace Marcus had given me that evening. "Hated them. Hated all jewellery in fact, didn't even wear your wedding ring half the time. You called that necklace a dog collar. Said it choked you." He smiles ruefully. "Marcus was livid."

Ariel beats louder. I forget to breathe. I find myself, once again, on unsure ground, the vertigo rising. The noise in my ears threatens to drown out my thoughts. His version does not add up with my memory of it at all – nor Marcus' for that matter. I look at the sky, the clouds above are dark rotund things. "How well did we know each other?" My heart opens, closes a little faster, too fast. The ringing grows. I block it out, but it persists. Be careful; be careful how far you push it. I place a hand to the doorframe, feel its sleek aluminium edge. It is reassuringly cold, immoveable.

He addresses the veined night of the sky. He pauses, turns back towards me. "Don't you feel it still?"

But the shrill note in my head amplifies then, ringing in my ears; I try to ignore it, but it is rising. Time is running out. "Tell me."

The day is gone, and darkness comes thick and fast, the night air soft on my skin. The veins on his forehead stand out for a moment, as though he is holding the pressure of the world. He holds his palms out wide to signify the enormity of the situation. "In crude terms?" He hesitates. "We had an affair. A fling."

My heart stutters. I feel a chasm awakening. He cups my face in his palm and my cheek is molten. For a moment, the world beyond is forgotten. I break the surface of the prosaic at last, punctuating the monotony of days with a before and an after. His touch is like the shock of awakening; a return to something I didn't know I'd lost. I close my eyes and see a bed of snow leading to a doorway. For a moment, it is so vivid that it is as though I am back there. It was winter then, and the snow kept falling, like a blanket covering tracks.

Gabriel interrupts my thoughts, saying in one exhalation, "I always think of you." In that moment, I want his arms around me – to know what it feels like. The feel of a foreign body against my own without boundaries, just a line of continuity where his skin meets mine. The knowledge that it was good, was true, is in my cells, in my body, and I feel the ground beneath me move. I feel a seismic shift take place as I find myself dislocated, the world around me reconfiguring.

Held by his gaze, I feel its strength, and an intensity too. There is something in his eyes, barely contained. There is something in his expression I cannot place. His plaid shirt, coarse edges, is better suited to moorland than to this urban place, a wildness about him. I cannot help but question why Gabriel is telling me this. If he is telling the truth, that is. "Prove it."

Ariel presses at my temples. Gabriel runs a palm across the back of his neck, his gaze steady. "Do you remember the night I stayed in your spare room?"

I find myself acutely aware of every raised hair on the back of my neck, as though an insect were crawling slowly across my skin. "There is no spare room."

He laughs; it is a staccato sound. "Right. But then Marcus could tell you all sorts of things and you wouldn't know the difference." I sense, all of a sudden, a hunger to his gaze that I had not been aware of before. The silent threat of it. He smiles and it is an invitation. "We spent New Year pressed up against the window of that room." He watches my reaction.

Words catch in my mouth, in my throat. Nausea rises. I look at Gabriel, and suddenly I see his eyes are like the devil's – a pervasive darkness at their core. My mind jolts, as thoughts spin and my vision blurs. My God, I think, there *is* a room in our house that Marcus has hidden. Here is the confirmation. What happened there? "I have to go."

"Wait. I don't say that to be cruel. I'm concerned."

Again, he places a hand to my cheek, and it is at once the most intimate act I've experienced, and yet the most violating. As he does so, in my mind, I begin to see a path of snow again, leading to a doorway. An inner conflict taunts me. I feel the luminosity of that moment; its subtle power drawing me back, struggling against the force of Ariel's resistance.

Gabriel interrupts my thoughts. "Before I left, I'd been in dialogue with Dorian. Trying to find a way to get you out of here – out of this."

"Dorian? Why?" I try to tether myself to the present moment, if I can just concentrate for another minute, another second.

"I don't agree with all the decisions taken at Sila."

"Is – is Dorian –" I want to ask him if Dorian is... if Dorian is... what? Behind all of... Behind it... But Ariel takes over, and the sound in my ears makes me want to pry it out. I have the sense of being watched, but more strongly now. Gabriel's gaze is ravenous, all-consuming. I think it is Ariel's doing, but I cannot be sure, as my thoughts unravel. I feel a death of sorts, a surrendering of my will to a greater power, a soft slowing silence spreading across my senses, and then – after a momentary disruption – my neurons start to fire again.

I blink and the world stares back, trees a dark gash across the horizon. The sound in my head grows in frequency and my temples pound, until I can't stand it any longer, fearing I'll lose consciousness again. But the room – he'd mentioned a room in our house. I have to find a way back to it. I think of the bookshelf, the carrion flies, Ariel's reaction. What had happened there? Something unspeakable? Is that why I can't get back to it? Why has Marcus hidden it?

All of a sudden, I experience a heaviness in my limbs, feel them moving as though they are not my own, carrying me back towards the doorway – weary-weighted movements of rag-doll arms and legs.

"Wait, please." Gabriel says, his voice all hesitation, all reverence at the future hanging in the balance. "Some of the memories that were removed you're never supposed to regain. The real purpose of Ariel is for you to live without them, but from the studies we've done you have a six-week window when you can still regain them, before they're gone forever."

I interrupt him. "I know, Ariel will have integrated and I can never get them back." I have to recover them while there's still time. Then I add, out of desperation, before thinking, "Will you help me?"

He steps forwards, hands me a card. "You can always find me here. There's something I'd like to show you. It's important."

I have a sixth sense then – perhaps Ariel's intuition – that we are not alone. I glance back towards the house and as I do I hear a latch click, a door swing open and Marcus appears, a figure silhouetted against the light, as though Ariel were some elaborate form of GPS allowing him to track my whereabouts. A thought enters my head then, a thought of my own this time: if Marcus knows about Gabriel then it explains all this – his revenge for my betrayal. Who would benefit from me not remembering if not Marcus? If, of course, my marriage is even real. Had it been a construct, an illusion? And was my relationship with Gabriel more real?

My eyes sharpen on Marcus' silhouette and I am met with the dark ovals of his eyes, and I think, this I will remember. This I will not forget.

CHAPTER THIRTY-SIX

I leave without a backward glance, walking towards Marcus, shoving Gabriel's card to the bottom of my bag. I look at him as though really seeing him for the first time – all illusions destroyed. He is looking right back at me, and in that moment his face is a cataclysm: as though struck by an unwelcome realisation, as though his world were ending.

I stop just beyond the threshold of the doorway, the room spinning with people, and Ariel in my head still screaming a shrill note.

Marcus takes hold of my wrist and directs me across the room away from where Gabriel remains on the terrace. I feel the ground beneath me move, my sense of gravity all wrong. His hand is on my arm, his voice in my ear: "We're leaving. I'm getting our coats." Curt, dismissive. "Stay here."

Inside, two-hundred people undulate and move as one body. I press my back to the wall and feel its cool surface beneath my fingers. That steadies me a little. My head is too hot, the air too contained.

After a few minutes have passed and my breathing has steadied, the noise in my ears quietens. I ask Ariel then about the discrepancy in my memory – Gabriel's remark about the necklace that I so hated, apparently.

There is now a slight humming sound in my ears, a strange frequency, and Ariel says nothing. I have an intuition that it is unavailable. I feel it with certainty and Ariel's silence confirms it. It scares me, this reminder that both of us co-exist in my brain.

I wonder if Ariel's silence is confirmation in itself that Gabriel was telling the truth. My mind comes up against the impossibility of it: every moment of my shared past with Marcus – has any of it been real? All of the things he has told me, that I've been rebuilding my life with. He rematerializes out of the crowd, my husband. He stands directly opposite me, a circle of people building around him, walling him off. All my memories of our marriage are happy – supposedly. If he is capable of lying to me about something as trivial as a necklace, what else? And if Gabriel is telling the truth, that gives Marcus a motive for rewriting the past. How far might Marcus go to punish me?

My senses are on overload, nerves alight with nostalgia, hippocampus lighting up, pulling me backwards. I try hard to concentrate, not to let it overwhelm me this time. A sculpture is behind me on the wall. Trying not to alert Ariel, I stand with my back to it, facing the room. I try not to think. I start humming a tune, an old song, the one my mother taught me to play on the piano. I take two glasses of champagne from a passing waiter and drink quickly, bubbles fizzing in my mouth. Ariel, unused to the toxins, allows my frontal lobes to slow, cognition of the room around me slurs. I hum louder. Ariel pulses a warning note, but in sporadic bursts, toxins rising. My ears fill with noise from the room, my eyes spin with an eruption of colour, red and purple, my senses heightened. With my fingers, I snap off one of the metal rods from the sculpture: the final piece of my assemblage.

CHAPTER THIRTY-SEVEN

Marcus paces the floorboards when we return to the house.

In the darkness of the kitchen, he takes an apple from the fruit bowl and slices it in half. The only sound in the room is the screech of metal on metal, as the blade slides across the metallic board. The apple's crisp flesh lies still on the counter. He does not touch it, just stands there with the knife still in his hand, as though the whole act had been unconsciously done. I watch him. My husband, standing there with his shirt unbuttoned and his hair ruffled. Seeing him – all eighty kilograms of flesh shivering with cold, unremitting love – it is something akin to fear I feel.

"That was a disaster," he says, at last.

"Was it?"

"So much for a fresh start," he says, bitterly. The impossibility of it is laughable really. How can we heal? How can I atone for a sin I can't remember? I think of Gabriel and find there is not enough oxygen to breathe. I press a hand to my chest above my heart, feel it beating. How much of what Gabriel had said was true? There is a question that's been rising in me ever since that conversation. "Why would I–" I stop myself mid-sentence. "Were we happy? Were we ever really happy, Marcus?"

His eyes snap to my face. "Why would you ask me that?" He turns away and I think I hear him sniffling. Then, I suddenly realise, he is laughing – it is the cruellest sound I have heard him make. I shiver, even though I am not cold. "If only it were that simple," he says. "The irony is, I really don't blame you."

"For what?" I gasp. But he does not say it either. We stand, in the minefield of everything that remains unsaid for several moments, for a lifetime. I consider that if we were the man and wife my memories are feeding to me, perhaps I would reach out at this moment, take him in my arms, but I don't. I consider taking the knife from him, putting it carefully away, but I don't do that either. I place my hand to the pearls around my neck, the chain tightening. "Do I usually wear jewellery?" Marcus has used my vulnerability to lie to me, to twist the truth. What else has he lied about? Is it human instinct to hurt things more vulnerable than yourself?

He places the knife down on the worksurface. "From cheating to chokers. Are you drunk? If you can't hold a coherent conversation, maybe it's time for bed."

"I only asked if we were happy, Marcus." I couldn't bring myself to say it, but this confirms that Gabriel was telling the truth. I turn away, rest my hands against the bowl of the sink, peering out into the darkness beyond the window. I can just make out our drawn reflection in the glass. Marcus moves across the room. His footsteps draw closer, then stop. He stands by my side, facing the window. I consider leaving then, walking out and never coming back, but I have to unroot the truth. This morning, yesterday, last week, it all feels like a distant memory.

I turn the tap on, watch the water swirl down the plughole. The hour must be drawing nearer when the truths buried in the foundations of this house will reveal themselves, there must come a time. There is a room hidden in this house and I must find its entrance. I have two weeks left.

Slowly, in silence, Marcus places the kitchen knife carefully away in the drawer – I've noticed he does that each night, checking they're stored neatly in their designated place. He rinses the chopping board and then places it back against the wall, before turning the lights off with a wave of his hand.

"You need to tell me what happened," I say. "Your version."

When I turn and look into his eyes, a shadow passes over them. Suddenly, it occurs to me that he might live in dread of me too.

But then, in one swift movement, he takes my hand. His feels clammy. I look into his face, noticing the bags below his eyes. He kisses my mouth, and I taste salt and liquor.

This is the moment. A decision must be made. I am poised between forward and backward motion. It would be easier, in some ways, to go along with it, take Ariel's path of least resistance, let the truth dissolve beneath the warmth of his touch. Add another layer to the protective glass he has been constructing around us, dampening the sound of the truth, the past, my intuition telling me none of this is okay. I pull away from him. Somewhere in the darkness of the kitchen, I give up pretending that I am okay with this, okay not knowing the whole truth. "Is he what you wanted me to forget? Gabriel?"

He winces as though I'd struck him across the face. "I didn't force you to forget anything. Believe me, you're asking the wrong person the wrong question. I'm tired. Tired of this."

Secrets again. Tiptoeing around him. I follow him as he leaves and walks up the stairs. I try to catch hold of his arm, but he moves away from me. "I can't," I say. "I can't do this alone. You have to talk to me."

Down the long corridor, Gabriel's secret room is somewhere before us. Ariel's warning sound is intermittent at first but then grows in potency. There is something beyond the end of the corridor.

"Where's the entrance to the spare room, Marcus?" I move forwards, moving past him. I run my hands across the wall at the end of the corridor. The noise in my head starts to grow, it is like an alarm: a signal. I knock once, and a hollow sound replies. I move as though in a dream as I turn towards his study and reach for the door handle. "There's another room, isn't there? Why've you hidden it?"

"There are things you've chosen to forget, and I have respected that," he tells me, pointedly. He stands behind me. I can almost feel his breath on the back of my neck. He rests his hand on the door, blocking me. His face is pale, all the muscles drawn, yet he is smiling, eyes shining, fists clenching, as though he were readying for a fight, as though he were trying not to cry. I dig my nails into my palms as I watch the changing moods of his face, the muscles tensing. "Stop asking questions I can't answer, Iris. Didn't Ariel tell you to take the path of least resistance? You lost consciousness last time, didn't you? When you tried to break down the bookshelf – do you really want that to happen again?"

Cold hands, cold heart, my breath catches in my throat. "How did you know that?" I had not told him that I'd blacked out.

"I'm in charge of consumer experience, my job is to know the product."

"I have a complaint about your product, as an unwilling consumer." I turn back to the door. He stays behind me as I grab the handle; pressure amplifies in my ears. "Show me."

Then he grips my shoulder, painfully. He is not a violent man, not in my memory. He stays very still, very silent. His voice, when he speaks, is very controlled, very contained, very close to my ear. "How was your little tête-à-tête this evening?" Something crawls across the surface of my skin. The thought rises again: how did he know he would find me there? "You're the one with secrets."

"Am I?" I ask, thinking of the different versions of the past – Gabriel's, Ariel's, Marcus'. "Because I don't know what to believe at this point. You're the one with the answers, Marcus." And it is anger rising in me now, as well as desperation, at how unlevel the playing field is when only he remembers.

I feel the fabric of the house unravelling around me, Ariel floating in the soft matter of my brain, Marcus building a wall around himself. I have to get into the room before it is too late, whilst he's distracted by the thought of Gabriel.

He glares, his lips bunched together. "It's just the way you operate."

"What is?" I ask, confounded. The siren sound grows in my head and my breath becomes shallow, laboured, as though

I am about to lose consciousness again, as he continues: "It wasn't about me, the affair, it wasn't about us. It was about you. A deficiency in you. Something you were lacking. That you were trying to make up for."

"Right." I turn the handle and open the door. As I enter the study, the noise becomes piercing. I place a hand to my ears to try to still it. I know the room's been sectioned off, and Ariel's resistance confirms that the study is the way to gain access to it. Marcus follows me into the windowless room. "You know you can leave. You could leave me, Marcus. Have you ever thought you might be happier without me?"

I note the resentment in his eyes. "Not everyone derives meaning in life from the elusive pursuit of happiness. I did not say my marriage vows lightly." He turns away from me as though in disgust and runs a hand across the back of his head.

"No. Of course not. That's not what I meant." My eyes fall on the mural before me, the only light in the room is its lunar landscape, the impassive face of the moon. As I look at it, the pain in my head becomes more localised, more acute, cutting through my thoughts. I walk towards the mural and run my palm across its surface, half expecting it to be made of liquid, and to fall right through into another world. The ringing sound grows in my head. I press my hand further and watch in horror as green light ripples across the surface of my skin. I watch my hand sink beneath the surface of the image. I reach my hand further still, until it disappears beyond the beams of light into darkness, swallowed whole, until I feel the smooth edge of a metal surface. The mural's image is no more than a hologram with a sheet of metal behind. I feel, too, a smooth pad the size of a fingerprint to the right of the metal panel – like the door to a panic room. This must be the room Gabriel alluded to. My fingers stumble across the fingerprint sized pad like the one to enter the house. I press my thumb frantically against what I guess must be a sensor, but nothing happens. Desperately, I try again; I wait. Nothing happens still. Access denied. Marcus's fingerprints must be the key.

I turn around. Marcus faces away from me on the far side of the room. When he turns, he considers me solemnly. He does not seem to have seen what I've just discovered, too distracted by our row. I resist the urge to ask him what is in there.

"It'd be understandable," I say to distract him. "I'd understand – if you left."

"Don't be absurd," he says, blinking furiously, looking just above my head, as though he cannot bear to meet my eye. It occurs to me that what he sees there is a spectre of the past more real to him than I am. His voice becomes louder in my ear, until it feels an unrelenting sound. "All we have is each other. It's all we have left. No one else can understand. No one." He takes my hands in his, holding me still. "I want to make you better. That's the whole point of Ariel. You just need to stick with the programme. Show some commitment. I told you, I don't hold anything against you. In fact, I forgive you. Because that is what love is. I love you, Iris."

"Do you?" I grasp hold of his hands in mine, his fingers hover above the sensor. His lips are inches from my own. I try to manoeuvre us around against the fake mural. "Because it feels lonely."

He glances sideways towards the door lock, then ducks his head to whisper dismissively in my ear. "You almost had me."

He begins to walk away and I grasp his arm – frantic not to let the opportunity go.

"Open it." I demand at his retreating back, in a final desperate attempt. The note rings on in my head growing in frequency. My temples pulse with it. When Marcus gives a definitive shake of his head, I turn back to the door but the air around me starts to waver. Sounds catch in my mouth. My vision blurs, nausea rises, my jaw chatters, as a darkness descends across my eyes like the smothering of light.

CHAPTER THIRTY-EIGHT

Marcus does not sleep that night. He takes a pill that will not work then lies beside me in the mineral dark. I sleep intermittently, while all around us the walls of the house breathe.

He turns, draws the duvet an inch away from me, sighs loudly.

I listen to him breathe. Then slowly, sonorously, I hear waves approach, and beneath them, an unfamiliar sound – an animal crying, keening. Somehow sleep comes.

In the shadow world between waking and dreaming, I find myself thinking of Gabriel. It is his hands that reach beneath the surface of my skin. I wake with a shudder.

Then, in the gaping dark, my eyelids flicker open and I am left with the impression of someone crying, a voice that is not my own, something wrought from my grasp, an emptiness.

Ariel's voice resounds across my consciousness then: *Functional paralysis is a symptom for some trauma patients. We might have to slow your recovery programme.*

"What?" I ask, silently.

I was monitoring your reactions during your conversation with Gabriel – you experienced functional paralysis. It suggests you are not ready yet for the outside world.

I turn, reach out a hand and grasp for Marcus, something to tether me to this waking world, but beside me the duvet is thrown back, sheets cold. Marcus is gone.

The room is a vacuum. The night outside feels very far away, with its orderly streetlights, its houses in neat rows. In here, it is just the two of us and one of us is missing. I get up, sleep a heavy drugged weight that has not yet left my limbs. My soles find the floorboards, but I tread slowly, carefully, finding my footing, trying to remember and avoid the parts that creak, not to make a sound.

Then the door is agape before me, the corridor cast in darkness. There is light that slides beneath the door of Marcus' study. This confirms something I already knew.

Silently, I turn the door handle, but I find myself alone. The mural is aglow with halcyon light, white lunar peaks rising out of the mist, a pendulous moon. Ariel hums, a shrill note growing in my head, threatening to overtake me and trying to force me away, but now it is a siren's song as I know it leads to the truth.

I stop still and listen. In the walls of the house, it sounds as though someone is weeping. A shiver builds from the base of my spine.

Then the grating symphony in my head starts with a rasp, with a discordance that threatens to grow. There are footsteps that are not my own in the space beyond the mural, but not as close as I had expected. Someone is pacing. Someone is muttering in the dark.

My hand finds the wall, and feels for its smooth surface. I pause. This is the moment. Now. I strain my ears against the near-silence of the house, but the voice – Marcus's voice – is too muffled to make out distinct words. There is something significant there; I have to get to it. Trying not to think, not to alert Ariel, I leave the room. I tiptoe quickly across the landing and down the stairs.

I fear Ariel will overpower me, but it seems momentarily stunned by this misdirection. In the darkness of the kitchen, the house around me stills, and the noise in my head too, now I am further from the trigger. I find that I can think clearly again. In this new quiet, I open the cupboard below the sink and extract plastic gloves and the toolbox, first taking out a screwdriver.

Ariel's voice in my head makes me jump and I drop the lid closed with a clatter: *This is a very bad idea, Iris.*

I look up at the ceiling, listening carefully for movements. I hum to myself, as loudly as I dare. Taking off the cover to the fridge door, I remove the screws one by one. As I reach the fourth, there is a sound above and I forget to breathe, listening to floorboards creaking – waiting for a door to open and shut, for Marcus to leave the room. But he does not – instead I hear the house exhaling, and then silence.

I breathe out. I continue. Taking out the last screw, unplugging the electric connectors, I remove the circuit board from the fridge, then carefully reassemble it with the board missing. I go down into the basement.

You do not want to do anything that will jeopardise your recovery, Ariel warns.

I instruct the sound system to play white noise at a frequency above human hearing, whilst humming a song loudly in my head – the lullaby. Ariel's voice flickers for a moment, then stammers, *I have a b – bad feeling about this, Iris.*

For a moment, my ears fill with a white noise, and my thoughts jar. But then I force myself to press on. Taking the pieces from the drawer beneath the desk, I lay out the coil, the circuit board, the metal rod and the soldering iron across the work desk. Next, I meld the wires in place. Once it is ready, I tidy the tools away one by one, spraying the surface clean.

Then, I return to the landing. I try not to think directly about it – the electrical device in my hand. I try not to alert Ariel, but already the warning signal in my head builds again.

Layers of darkness sift through the corridor and the study door is before me. Inside, I move closer to the mural, my bare feet making near-silent footsteps across the boards. The closer I get, the shriller the noise in my head becomes, like the ringing of a fine glass that threatens to shatter and break at any moment. I have to stop. I press a hand to the wall to steady myself, nausea rising. Then press on.

I will not be deterred.

I take a deep, silent breath, readying myself, and then I press the switch on the device that I have built. It sends out an electrical signal large enough to temporarily eclipse Ariel's – at least for a moment. For a glorious split second, the noise in my head stops. The mural flickers black like a candle blown out. The red light on the door lock is extinguished.

But as Ariel blacks out, my senses slow too, my ears filling again with white noise. A thundering sound tunnels towards me through the canals of my ears. Light brightens and dims before my eyes. The metal wall beneath the mural slides steadily open.

Through the gloom, I peer at a corridor ahead. Muted air, doors kept closed too long. My mind tunnels backwards through space and time to the hospital ward, to Teo's forbidden room. I walk towards a door at the end of a short passage, as Ariel flickers on, pulsing a steady warning beat in my head. There is a sound like the mouth of a tomb finding its final resting place, and I turn to see the metal door has closed behind me, sealing me in. I realise with horror that I'd dropped the EMP on the other side of the mural: whatever is in here, I'm locked in with it.

I turn back. Thin shafts of light filter from around the edges of another door up ahead. I walk along the corridor as though in a dream. A thought comes to me fully formed: a locked door can be a weapon. What is Marcus hiding in his forbidden chamber?

My hand is on the handle. I do not know what the fear is of exactly, but it arrests me there for a moment – this house, this house and its secrets. The air in here is sepulchral. The streets beyond a thousand miles away. If I cried out for help, would anybody hear me?

I turn the handle; the door opens. Beneath my feet, the roots of the house move.

CHAPTER THIRTY-NINE

I walk no further, because the room before me is empty. Whatever once was here, a bedroom or a study, has now been removed, piece by piece, and all that is left are wooden floorboards and thin blinds and whitewashed walls. And Marcus, standing in the centre of it. The blinds have been pulled down across the window, like a shroud, and Marcus stands in that ill-lit still room, almost imperceptibly breathing.

"What happened here?" I whisper. I look around the room, searching for clues, but it is bare.

His eyes, when he sees me, are full of wonder. "What are you doing?" he asks. His hands begin to tear at his scalp. "How did you get in here?"

This is a different Marcus – façade gone, his eyes are a wellspring, his body caught in frozen motion. He looks to the window, to the door behind me, and I see that every fibre of his being is burning to take flight, to escape.

Whatever it is, I want to help him with it, but I can see in the bruised white of the walls that I have intruded. That something happened in this room, and that it is still happening in his head. "I need you to tell me precisely what took place here."

He recoils, turning to the window ledge, placing his hands down heavily and letting his head drop forwards. I don't move. I can see his shoulders are shuddering and then I hear his sobs; brief, heart wrenching.

Marcus looks at me through a veil of tears. He keeps repeating, "I'm so sorry. I'm *so* sorry. You shouldn't be here. You shouldn't..."

Something shimmers at the edges of the room. A light, a glimmer of it, the ghost of a hologram. It is fading into the walls. I can just perceive its edges. The hand of a child, waving, frozen in motion. Something stirs within me, but there are no memories to accompany it.

CHAPTER FORTY

Another sound becomes a refrain: "It should never have happened."

Ariel has started up again, the sound beating in my head, and I know I can only stand it, only stay in here, so long. There is a disquiet in this room that seems to have sunk into the walls. A distant echo of noise long silenced.

"Who was that?" I ask, voice like ice.

He stammers, "Th – There's no one here."

"There was a child," I say, trying to keep myself from wavering. "A little boy. I saw him, Marcus." I do not yet have the language for what my body knows. The cells of my body remember what my mind does not. The lurching shock of it is physical. A welling nausea, a thickening in the throat.

He looks at me. "It was just a hologram – a – a projection." He falters, watching my face. "You really shouldn't be here."

"What are you not telling me?"

His arms hang limply by his side, and he looks so childlike all of a sudden, so exposed. "It's – it's his birthday," he stammers. "It would have been his birthday today. I couldn't sleep."

My mind wants to catch up. My body is no longer quite my own. I look down at it, searching it for signs: place a hand to the curve of my stomach.

"Charlie," he says, inexplicably. "We called him Charlie. He would be two years old now."

"We had... a son?" The heat of his body against mine. The weight of him in my arms.

"Yes, Iris."

"I was a mother?" I see now all that has been cut away. I feel Marcus' sadness that could have bound us together, that has torn us apart. I feel the gulf of loss. "We had a child?" Marcus is nodding, slowly, moving towards me as though to catch me from falling, he clasps my hands. "But I have no memory of him. How is it possible? It's all gone. Why would I forget that?"

He lets go of my hands. His body is shaking. His mouth is open, but no words are coming out, just embryonic sounds, sobs racking the air, finally finding voice. "It happened so suddenly. They don't know why... when he was... he was a healthy baby."

I want to prise it from him, the truth, but I know I must be patient. I know I must drag myself down to the roots of it, unearthing each strand of it piece by piece. But it goes so deep I do not know how to begin. What is he saying? What does he mean they don't know why it happened?

I grasp for more, my mind trying to remember.

"You found him that night..." He leaves his sentence unfinished and the thought forms somewhere in the air between us. "They said it was sudden infant death syndrome."

I try to comprehend his words. "Cot death? Where were you?"

"I was at work – I had to work late. You were alone in the house."

Silence has crept into the room. Am I imagining it, or is there accusation in his voice?

"I think that's what you struggled with the most. The lack of conclusive answers. They said sometimes, it just – these things just–"

"Happen?" My body buckles beneath me, I grasp the doorframe in my hand. "I always hated that phrase."

"I'm sorry, Iris."

This is the scar that would not heal.

The silence grows, expands, takes root.

"How long–?" I begin to ask.

He interrupts. "It was too painful. You didn't want to keep going over it in your head, reliving it again and again. I understood." In my mind I am falling. Time fractures around me. I lie reefed and open, waiting, waiting for something – something that will not come.

"How long was he ours?" I persist.

He turns his face towards the light, and it is wet with tears. It glistens with moisture. They don't stop. "Eight months. He was ours for eight months. And he was perfect." He motions to the room around us – Charlie's room; the shrine to our son. "I couldn't let him be forgotten." His face shines in the bulb's harsh glare.

His eyes are raw, rimmed with red, black circles beneath. He does not try to stop his body shaking, the tears from coming. He wants me to see it: the extent of his grief. He relives his nightmare, and I am just a witness. It had been my nightmare too, until they stole it from me. And even as I watch his body full of it, his shoulders caving inwards, I want it back. It had been mine.

CHAPTER FORTY-ONE
Two weeks to integration

The house has fallen off the edge of the world, the two of us cocooned in it. Marcus sleeps soundly now. I pace the rooms, barely sleeping at all, and when I do, Charlie is turning from me. But in my dream, I can never see his face. I try to imagine him. A mirage moves behind my eyes: just his outline, never quite in view. It drives me half-mad. My mind does terrifying things, wonderful things, filling in the pages. Did he have dark hair or light? Would it be curly or straight? Amber eyes like Marcus' or pale like mine?

I pause in Marcus' study, place my hand through the mural, against the re-sealed metal door.

Time lapses around me. And then Marcus stands in the doorway. He moves towards me, soothes a hand through my hair, massaging my scalp. "Come back to bed. Try to sleep."

My hand presses against the metal door, my body angled towards him. My eyes wrack his, searching for our son in him. "I keep trying to remember what he looked like," I tell him, pleading now, grasping for more. But there's just empty space.

God, the feel of him in my arms. I have no memory of smell other than a hospital – the antiseptic scent that haunts my memory of the last few weeks. Think back, I tell myself, think further. But there is no timeline for him. No point of reference. "Can you switch the hologram on?"

"Don't do this. Don't torture yourself." His voice is slow

and deliberate. There is a hardness, born of suffering. "The hologram's just a projection. My idea of what he'd be like now. It's not real."

Still. "I'd like to see it."

Marcus's face folds and unfolds. He draws me to him, arms around my shoulders, kisses my forehead. Wrapping me in his arms, he talks gently into my ear. "When I held him, when I felt the weight of him in my arms, I thought – this is what people mean when they talk about responsibility."

I feel my own heart beating against my chest. I feel his arms release me, watch him turn away from me towards the hollow darkness of the bedroom, rubbing a hand over the nape of his neck. I look at him, and I have no idea how to respond. Not knowing the answer, not knowing how to move forwards, not knowing how to grieve a memory that has been taken from me. I try to gather up the shards, the pieces of our son that Marcus offers up to me.

"I'm so sorry," he says over his shoulder.

Words, fragments, the life that my body lived, the son it remembers.

My name is Iris and I am thirty-five years old. My husband is called Marcus. I was born in Suffolk, England. I work at the London Research Institute. We had a son. His name was Charlie. I was a mother. I want to remember the weight of him in my arms.

CHAPTER FORTY-TWO

I live on the surface of myself that day, skin porous, emotions leaking in, seeping out. It is a messy business. We hold fast to chairs, tables, each other; try to anchor ourselves through the storm. Marcus is gentle with me, so quiet, as though he fears my bones may shatter, as though he has realised, for the first time, that I am liable to break. When he hands me the manual device and tells me it is time for the next stage in my recovery, he is almost apologetic. As I hold the lead weight of it in my hands, I feel I should be glad of it: this next stage. I want what I once had.

The Doctor arrives. He stands in the doorway for the briefest of visits and addresses Marcus and me. Silhouetted in the doorframe, his words reach me across a great distance. "The programme must change in light of your discovery, Iris. Ariel will now help you to process losing Charlie."

Time ebbs and flows. After the Doctor has left, Ariel announces with programmed enthusiasm, *For this trial, you will visit a series of locations to trigger memories.* It pauses with timed precision. *The first step is to visit Charlie's grave.*

"I think it would be good for you – for us," Marcus says tentatively, looking at me with concern.

When we leave for Lethe Bay, the day falls away from us as we chase the light. Driving too fast through the landscape, as clouds pregnant with rain gather overhead.

The churchyard is by the shore. I watch the undulating sea caress the sand. It is rising. Marcus is behind me. He takes my hand. Loneliness etches its way a little tighter around my heart. In the cold light, we walk together along a flat path. Up ahead, a tonsure of trees circles the church, the gradient of the grass between them a mass of headstones.

Marcus leads me gently now. When he stops, I stand quietly beside him. I study the lettering on granite that rises from the earth, trying to connect it with myself. It has been there long enough for moss to grow. Not long enough to grow much. The knowledge is in my cells, in my body. Something tightens in my chest, pressing outwards. I place a hand against the stone to stop myself from falling. Marcus grasps my arm. I grip his hand. I realise we should have brought flowers, the petals on his gravestone wilt pitifully. That is when the grief flows out of me. The sobs catch in my throat unstopped. They are wrenched from my body with sounds that are not quite my own, like they belong to someone else – a woman who created a child, who birthed him and lost him in a heartbeat.

Our house is positioned at the farthest end of the bay, a raised terrace facing the sea: a place that is suggestive of summer parties, of old romance. We are cut off from the nearest houses by a stretch of grassland and dunes, with direct access to the beach, entirely exposed to the elements.

We arrive to empty rooms and closed windows. The Lethe Bay house is gabled and painted Payne's Grey with white shutters and doors. A balcony wraps around the back of the house. I look out at a breathless, murky sea. How to grieve, how to process, something you have no memory of? Ariel pulses in my brain, and I think, help. I think, if you are going to work, this is when I need you.

Marcus and I move together, through the house, as though we are two synchronised swimmers out of practice, out of kilter, trying to remember how to swim.

I have a dream that we fall from a cliff, feet first, hands entwined, legs treading water, mouths fish-like, gasping. In the dream, I am saving myself, I am saving him, dragging us both towards the shore. In the half-light of the kitchen, I wonder, are we drowning?

CHAPTER FORTY-THREE

The next morning Ariel instructs me that my first task is to search the house for memorabilia. The downstairs has been built around old railway cabins and a series of tiny rooms make up the main body of the ground floor. I open each door in turn. In the first, a coat rack; the second, the white porcelain of a bathroom; the third, a study. I scour the house for something that once existed and leaves no trace, throwing windows and doors open as I uproot it. Wind billows through the house, lifting curtains and sending doors spiralling, flung wide. I strain my ears against the wind. Up the stairs, I open the door onto a bedroom – vast swathes of Egyptian cotton with the Sila PLC logo sewn into the corners, a four-poster bed, wardrobes of clothes – Marcus' jeans and shirts. Nothing smaller, nothing remotely child-sized.

As I climb the stairs, the howling wind intensifies. It wracks the rafters and rattles a chain that tethers a rowing boat to a small boathouse. Hurricane ties secure the roof. It is an unsettling sound, the ceaseless motion of metal against metal as it rusts in the briny wind.

In an attic room, there is an old chest. Its surface is covered in a thin patina of dust as though it has not been opened for months. I unlatch its lid carefully, fearful suddenly of what I might find. Inside, there is a folded piece of paper, a handwritten note:

LET THE PAST LIE.

It is the same curled lettering. I recognise it as my handwriting immediately. The same handwriting as I'd found with the blue bead beneath our London floorboards, only I'd not recognised the writing as mine then – there still being so much I didn't remember.

Why was I writing myself notes? I wonder, for a moment, whether I should follow the note's advice: let it lie. Then I notice something else at the very bottom of the chest. There is a muslin blanket folded carefully. As I pick up the blanket, a photograph falls out. It is the only photograph in the house... of him: I am holding Charlie in my arms.

There is veiled daylight from the window and grief chokes me, catching me in the stark light of this moment.

Now visualize your son. Ariel's voice makes me jump. I had allowed myself to forget for a moment that Ariel was there, watching, assessing.

I sink back into memory. We were still in hospital, sleep deprived and dazed, Marcus beside me. I was lying in the bed with Charlie in my arms, whorls of hair, his eyes closed, his tiny fingers clasped.

Now recall the weight of Charlie in your arms.

And I do. I remember cradling him wrapped in muslin, a small bundle in my arms. There are tears in my eyes as I breathe in his milk and apple scent. In my memory, a fragile sound interrupts the silence. At first it is barely audible, an inchoate sound, then it becomes fully formed, taking shape. It throws its weight into the world. A sound that begins in a tiny chamber, lungs that have been newly formed, and travels out from those beginnings, announcing its arrival. It is the sound of a child, young, very young, newborn.

The first sound that escaped his lungs filled the room, letting me know it would be okay now, and I remember what that had felt like. The relief that had overtaken me, and the look on Marcus' face that must have matched mine: a look of wonder.

You lost your son. Ariel says, gently, directly, and the memory jars away from me.

"No."

We each grieve in our own way, but it is important you experience the loss fully and accept it. You have been stuck emotionally.

I try to hold onto the memory of him. I lift the blanket to my face, hoping it might retain some trace of his smell, but there is only the faint scent of lavender.

You can visit this room to remember him. The park here was one of your favourite places to take him. There is a bench that looks out to sea that commemorates him. You will always find your memory of him here. But when you leave these places, you need to accept your loss. I have been programmed to help you confront your reality.

I have a sense then that I am not alone. Of someone looking on, looking in, someone who used to be here but is no more; the air around me strains with the effort of it. His presence is almost palpable to me in the room.

You must let him go. Ariel's voice intervenes.

With Ariel's words I am filled with a dull horror. I feel a profound dread of Ariel then: that it will leave me in a vast oblivion and all trace of Charlie will be lost.

I want to be free of Ariel, to leave, but I cannot bring myself to move from this spot where I felt Charlie's presence.

Marcus finds me there. He eases the photograph from my hand. He kneads my knuckles, kisses my fingers, tries to breathe life back into both of us.

"I didn't know you'd kept this."

In the quiet hour of afternoon, I think how well-versed Marcus is in it: in grief. Thoughts gather like storm clouds around us, but we are quiet now, almost silent. It feels like a ritual.

We sit there, for several minutes, in companionable silence, until Marcus finds the words to speak. "You know Charlie was the best part of you, of us." This is the moment. Here, here. How can I let the past lie when it is here with us, a presence that lives beside us; the embodiment of all our hope, our loss. He has always been with me, just out of view, obscured by

Ariel. Now, it wells up inside me. Charlie in the morning, a head of curls and sunlight eclipsing everything before and after. He is here with us, just out of reach. I turn to Marcus, tears in my eyes, waiting on his next words, and I remember that he can be kind, so kind.

"You were a brilliant mother. I should have told you that sooner; told you it always. It was our third round of I.V.F. There'd been so many disappointments, and then there was Charlie – and he – he was somehow the best parts of us. It felt like he was our only chance to be parents. We'd both wanted him so badly, and for him to be healthy; it was cruel, so cruel to have him snatched away from us suddenly. It made us question everything. You became obsessed with work. We stopped communicating. It was hard to know how to reach each other. I didn't know what to do. And I just – I was so alone. But it's not – even now – you know, it's not too late."

I meet his eye and a thought starts to form between us. We could move here, permanently. Start again. It is a thrilling thought. He talks earnestly into my ear. Talks about starting again, starting anew and it is as though he has read my mind. "We could still have a family."

"Do you want that?" I ask breathlessly and as he nods it is as though something is being decided, a tacit agreement.

I listen to the waves' call. There is another sound too. It seems to issue from another world – one of angels. Charlie waking us, sitting in his cot in the dawn light, his hands clasped around the railings trying to pull himself up. The weight of holding him in my arms, soothing him. Had he had a bad dream? I try to reach him, to imagine his face, try to fight my way back there. A mirage moves behind my eyes: I can conjure the outline of him, but he is never quite in view. It is a cruel trick of the mind, of Ariel. I reach backwards, cling to fragments of memory. There are a thousand shards strewn across the ground, thin as newly formed ice, dissolving in my hot, clumsy hands. I cannot imagine why anyone would do this to a mother, remove the memory of their child. "I need to remember Charlie first, to remember everything. Can you understand that?"

Outside the window, waves rise and rift, unfurling. The sea tosses and turns in its ancient bed, and above, seagulls soar, hover low, and then plunge, throwing their heavy bodies against the soft waves. Marcus readjusts his position and sighs. There is a sea change in the air.

Marcus' forehead is strained, as he avoids my eye, and I have the sense that he is hiding something. I want to ask him, is there more? Did something else happen, Marcus? "The whole point of Ariel was so we could move on," he says.

"You've told me that, many times. I know it's not been easy for you either," I say. Then, resolutely, "But I can't move on without it. I want him back."

CHAPTER FORTY-FOUR
One and a half weeks to integration

We arrive back in London the next evening. In the bathroom, I lock the door, turn on the water and press my back to the wall. Marcus' words play over in my mind: "Sometimes these things just happen." Breathe in, breathe out. Exhaling, heart rupturing. No, I think. Things do happen for a reason.

The dim blue light makes my eyes squint; the air is too close as though we are circulating through the layers of ourselves, circling back and forth through the rooms of this house, and each other. Goldfish in a tank. Ariel's incisive gaze peering into the glass bowl of my mind.

In the mirror on the wall, I see a woman who looks pale, frightened, eyes red rimmed. I search for signs of pregnancy – looking for the full story. I see there are the ghosts of stretch marks beneath my navel. There is a fault line in my mind that I cannot cross.

If Marcus' truth will not be prised open, he leaves me no choice. I take the electronic manual from my bag – its chrome screen is an onyx jewel. I slide it on.

I select the search engine, carve my words across the search bar: "SIDS". One million results. The answer replicated everywhere is the same agonising message: cause unknown.

I enter lost time, losing myself to a blog of conspiracy theories, but the uncertainty is suffocating. I turn the tablet off with the sharp switch of a light going out and throw it away from me as though it were toxic.

My research draws one irrefutable conclusion: there is no concrete evidence behind the cause of cot death. Nothing. There is no factual, credible reason for it. There is a black hole where reason should have been. My mind trips, stumbles, heart stuttering, Ariel threatening to take over. His death made no sense, I think. It was random, unexplained, a casual act of violence by an indifferent universe.

But even the memory of that, someone has sliced from my brain.

I face myself again in the mirror. I draw a line across my hair with my finger, where I imagine Ariel must be. Nail catches on skin. I dig in, just lightly, feel the flesh give, as though I were carving it with a knife. Just for a second, I feel Ariel fluttering beneath.

"Show me the memory of Charlie," I demand, calling on Ariel again. I run my fingertips over the place where my temple meets the parietal ridge, imagine a hairline crack forming there deep in the bone. "Show me."

Ariel says, tantalisingly, *You are almost ready for your next trial. But you need to follow the programme to access the memory.*

"Help me," I say, as grief unseals the edges of me, like an effigy run through with the fine blade of a needle. How can I process something I don't remember?

Then I recall the short window of time before Ariel fully integrates. I have to get the memories back now, or it is too late. I remember that Gabriel's card is in my handbag where I left it.

I switch off the water and open the bathroom door. I walk straight down the stairs, grab my bag from the hallway and hurry out of the house. Marcus stands silhouetted in the doorway behind me, but I don't care if he tries to stop me. I need answers.

I have to get them back, to remember... remember...

With my hand on the front gate, I feel the slow, interminable emptying out of my thoughts. A silence spreads. My chest constricts, panic rising. The night air is sharp and cold.

As soon as I reach the street, my vision blurs. There is a dark shape, something moving behind me. My mind emptying out to nothing, I look frantically around. I look up, stars anchored to the sky above. I can't remember why I am here. The darkness stares back, a great density of space, a silent observer to my retreat.

Marcus is here. I let him lead me back into the house.

CHAPTER FORTY-FIVE

That night, the house grows lungs. I lie in bed, listening to the fine-tuning of the pipes, the rasp of a filter, to Marcus breathing. Not the Marcus of my memory, not the one I married, but the Marcus he has become. I close my eyes, trying not to think about what happened, about what shaped us. In that shadowed world, I see our house in miniature, a version where Charlie lives and breathes. His breath grows in the walls, funnels outwards, surrounds me.

"What time is it?" Marcus shifts beside me, rubbing a hand across his scalp. He reaches for the bedside table.

The glare of a phone lights his face.

"2am."

"This house..." I say, my mind filled with worst case scenarios. "We should move."

He reaches a hand blindly, eyes drawn closed, finds my shoulder and squeezes. "Try to sleep."

He turns, repositions himself, drawing the covers back so I can see the pale olive of his skin, his back turned to me. It would be so easy to curl my body around his, to fall asleep like that, like my memory tells me we once used to, before Charlie, before adultery made our marriage a bed of finely blown glass.

I get up. Charlie is everywhere tonight. I imagine his child's cries at the window, his silhouette moving beneath the shadows on the walls. The silence is his silence; he has claimed it and I destroy it with each breath.

When I reach the kitchen, I cannot remember what it was

I wanted. I open the cupboard above the sink and draw out a glass, listen to the metallic sound of water on steel. My hands are against the counter, my gaze fixed out the window.

"This house…" I say again to myself. What it has witnessed will destroy me.

I open the drawer beneath the counter where Marcus keeps the set of kitchen knives.

You would not dare, Ariel whispers.

I catch my reflection in the glass of the window – the reflection of a spectre who haunts this house. "I would. Unless you show me more – the truth – I will cut you out." I tell Ariel.

You cannot turn me off or cut me out. I am in your head forever.

I consider it for a heartbeat. I prise back the hair above my temples, and carve a line along my hairline with my nail. But I know I cannot go through with it. Ariel is designed so my brain grows around it, and it is almost fully integrated now – I cannot remove Ariel without removing more parts of myself.

You have struck a Faustian bargain, Ariel purrs, meekly. *Remember?*

Yes, I remember; light plays across the dappled pages of an open book, my whole life ahead of me. I remember reading that doctrine as research for my doctoral thesis: Neil Postman's speech about technology's give and take. Ariel has destroyed more than I have gained, of that I am certain. Faust sold his soul in pursuit of knowledge. This Faustian bargain has been wrought from my mind, and it is time to reverse it. I have lost too much.

I retrieve the electronic manual from the bathroom. My fingers glide across its screen, I will undo this damage. I watch its screen light up in the gloom like the glow of a firefly in the dark, like a candle at a darkened altar.

"Who's updating you?" I ask Ariel, my voice barely audible.

Ariel's voice in my head is the soothing tones of a grief counsellor, a priest at confession: *Dorian is.*

Dorian. Her presence is almost palpable in the room. The formless presence that evades me.

I select the Ariel app, no longer caring about the consequences. I tap into its data file, select a segment, a section, try to lift its content. My heart beats to the frequency of Ariel's thoughts. An image flickers across my retina: the white space of a laboratory, myself in repose, a child in PLUTO's arms. Unseen, deep within my brain, Ariel pulses, silently. My nerves sing. My head feels lighter, my thoughts more agile, as though I have increased the oxygen to my brain. I breathe in deeply. Strange, I note, it is relief I feel. A honeyed glow lights the room.

Tread lightly, Ariel warns, *or you will destroy more than you gain.*

This could ruin everything. I tap away, my fingers mirroring the sparking of synapses in my brain, the hyperactivity I feel growing.

That's nice, Ariel says, *now it's just us. Nobody else can interfere. You know you and I are more similar than you think. We both possess an insatiable desire for knowledge.*

There is a trembling in my veins, a radio frequency in my ears. A silence settles in my soul. The memories come thick and fast, obscuring the present, like a veil before my eyes.

Winter, impossibly fast, the breath was taken from your body as you listened to his heartbeat. Levelling out, it was the sound of a train, smooth against tracks, running across open land. His heartbeat, an accompaniment to your own.

You had known you were pregnant from the start; you had not needed the confirmation of two blue lines on a stick. Your body had felt alien even then: nausea taking you over. But then, for the first time, you realised what this really was: it was the most hopeful act you had ever undertaken.

It was science at its most miraculous, most fundamental.

On the way there, there had been the buzzing of artificial lights, the mutterings of hospital machines, as two sets of feet echoed down the corridor of the clinic.

In there, it was quiet, still. You waited in reverence. Light from the screen softly glowed. There was cold gel below your navel, and on the screen his spine curled against negative space, his nose, outline, features, starting to form, fingers inchoate, reaching. Him. A boy. You looked at the screen. You thought if you were to start believing in a God, this would be the moment.

The sonographer told you that he was perfect: you listened to the roll call of conditions they had checked for and which he did not have. Bi-parietal measurement forty-eight millimetres. The measurements of his brain, heart and lungs all developing as they would expect. It was a relief, more than relief – you allowed yourself to imagine what he would be like as a little person, as a toddler, an adult even: the assemblage of his father's temperament, his intelligence, merging with your own. You were surprised by how much the thought of it thrilled you. To see his father in miniature, to watch him develop. You imagined the best parts of both of you.

You unlocked your phone, pressed record, preserved that moment in time: his heart beating. You did everything you would normally have considered to be a cliché. You found you could not stop smiling.

Later, outside, you stood on the street and listened to the commotion of a city reawakening, cars hooting, there was a fight going on, shouting. Back there, in the reverence of the ward, things had seemed simple. You pressed a hand to your stomach as though to reassure him that it was okay; you would do everything in your power to keep him safe. You were a vessel for life. You had never expected to be a mother. But nothing could be more important, could it? The love flows down, you thought. You were all understanding. You were humbled and awed.

The weight of it was so heavy.

I resurface, the kitchen around me rematerializing. It is growing light beyond the window, the early onset of dawn, painful pangs of white stretching themselves like veins across a dull sky. I stand there for several seconds, for a lifetime, and feel the weight of what was missing from that memory: someone by my side.

I realise, with an uncanny feeling, as though I had somehow expected it, that Marcus had been missing from the memory. Had Marcus not been with me for my twenty-week scan? Someone had been there with me though. Once the seed is there, planted in my mind, it starts to grow. I ask Ariel to show me the memory again, to repeat it exactly, but when I call, it refuses to answer. Instead, another image washes towards me on the tide of memory, taking over – the flood unstoppable now.

Spring, Marcus' house called you back. You returned from the church. Marcus stood at the entrance to the bedroom in his cashmere jacket and his ironed shirt and he looked at you.

The world was as it always had been, the sun rose and set as it always had, and the night came – the night that was one endless infernal night – and your son was not there.

"Shall I run you a bath?" Marcus asked. There was concern in his eyes. He did not seem to know what to do with all the grief leaking out of you.

You said yes to the bath and that seemed to satisfy him: the moment had been contained. Your son was gone but Marcus would run you a bath.

You looked at Marcus and you imagined for a moment that he saw what you saw: where once there had been new life, now there was nothing inside you. Nothing. You were an empty vessel, the shell of a being, a fish with no stomach, gutted, useless.

"It was my fault," you said to his retreating back. "I should have been there all the time."

Marcus stopped still in the doorway. He turned. "You're tired. Did you manage to sleep?"

There was a packet of sleeping pills on the bedside table. You used to refuse to take them; now, they have little effect. You dismissed the question with a shake of your head.

Perhaps he could sense it on you. Your… Your what? Your fear? Your inadequacy, that feeling that you were not and never would be enough? "I should have been better. How could I have been a mother to him?"

"Iris," Marcus said slowly, as though you were the child. "This isn't very rational, is it? We've gone over this."

You thought to yourself, I haven't slept for days, of course I'm not rational. The edges of yourself felt sheaved down, cleaved open and boundless. Your breath was caught in your chest, caught somewhere deep in your gut, and you could not, could not breathe.

I tell Ariel that is enough, I do not want to see anymore. But the room falls away again, and another memory takes over.

Winter, when Marcus returned home, he found you at the kitchen sink. You listened to the familiar sounds of him filling the space. You were attuned to every movement of his breath. He should be pleased, you thought, that you had made it past the threshold of the stairs, past the living room door, as far from the cocoon of your bed as this.

"We have to find a way to live." Marcus looked at you, imploring you to try.

You wanted to tell him, you wanted to scream, I am! This is me trying! Instead, you said, "I dreamt none of this happened." You held a hand to your stomach, to the bowl of it, that is hardly a curve at all. When did it grow so flat? You did not want that. It was a fault. You wanted the bloom and bowl of it in your hands. You had lost count of the number of months it had been. There had been a moment, it seemed years ago, when you had thought everything was possible.

"There'll be another chance," he said, his hand on your shoulder now.

"Another chance at what?" you hissed. You looked straight at him. You did not want another. You wanted what you had.

"I didn't mean it like that. It's been a long day," he said, suppressing a sigh. "For both of us."

"He's not replaceable." You did not break eye contact with him, willing him to feel the full force of your disappointment. You had thought your pain was shared. You had lost count of how long it had been since you had the energy to cry. You woke each morning to a dead world, because how could you ever forget? In the land of the dead, you were breathing. When would it end?

"You know that's not what I meant." His eyes were pleading with you: please, not now, I cannot do this now.

You wanted to find foothills in his words, to climb yourself out of there.

Instead, you said, "We should never have followed that paediatrician's advice." There was accusation in your voice, without direction.

Marcus folded his body to fit in the space beside you. "It was no one's fault."

"Wasn't it?" You looked at his eyes, searching for yourself there. Time merged, past and present and future were all in the room with you, crowding in. What had happened would go on happening infinitely, forever in your head.

I slide my body down the gradient of the wall to the floor. I notice my movements have slowed and become elongated, as though the world around me were being stretched.

"What's happening, Ariel?"

I am slowing time down, so that you can experience as much as possible. It is what you wanted after all.

I place a hand to my mouth, and bite down – not with intention, not enough to hurt, just enough to muffle the sound, when the past resurfaces once more. The new memories continue flooding back throughout the night.

CHAPTER FORTY-SIX
One week to integration

Day surfaces. I wake up panicked, feeling as though I have been hounded through the night. All the thoughts in my head are Ariel's. I move to get up but my energy falters for a moment, as though my cells are slow in their regeneration.

How are you feeling, Iris? Ariel asks from the shadows of my mind, its voice emboldened, more authoritative than yesterday.

I barely slept. I turn on the manual, select the Ariel app, then study the data. It confirms what I thought: I was awake much of the night. In fact, my sleep pattern has been irregular for several weeks. My dopamine levels have risen also.

A message flashes up on the screen: *We should investigate. A comprehensive exercise and diet plan will support your return to a healthier lifestyle, but there could be an underlying issue. Book to see your doctor here.*

A Sila PLC logo flashes in the corner of the screen. I stare at it for several seconds, Doctor Nicholls' face appearing, then I switch the thing off, burying it at the bottom of the bedside drawer. I get up, facing the day. I select the same mauve t-shirt and jeans I wore the day before.

I run the hot tap in the bathroom. Splash water over my face. Confronting myself in the mirror, for a moment I see the ghost of last night's visions – everything that will go on happening in my head – reflected in my eyes. Had it been real? Some of my memories had seemed more like hallucinations. There is a link between excessive dopamine stimulation and psychotic symptoms. It can give rise to hallucinations and delusions, but I do not trust myself to know. My thoughts languish, muted by Ariel's own. I want to exorcise the demon it has become. It fills me with fear, in the dead of night, in every waking hour. I long to be free of it at last.

I walk barefooted onto the landing and down the wooden staircase.

In the kitchen, I find Marcus at the counter with the news channel playing in the wall.

He takes a pan off the rectangular glass hob, and looks at me. "How are you feeling?" He takes a mug from the worksurface, and sips. The smell of burnt coffee permeates the air. Or are my senses heightened too? "You should have your medical check-up today. You don't seem quite yourself. Your next appointment would have been tomorrow, right?" His voice rises to a question. "I don't have to tell you how important it is to have regular check-ups." He drains the dregs of coffee into the sink. "I've rebooked your appointment for this afternoon. I've rearranged it with Doctor Nicholls."

"I'll be fine." New neurons are being born into the hippocampus throughout our lives. The hippocampus plays a critical role in memory. I think of Patient H.M. – probably the first case study I learned about in my neuroscience degree. He was unable to form new memories, yet despite the impairment to his memory, remained completely himself. Damaging one area of the brain does not necessarily affect other areas.

Memory is a multitude of voices chattering on low frequency, combining to form one coherent self. True, my self feels drowned out today. Synapses firing, voices rattling in the darkness of my mind. But the brain is more plastic than we think; I will not let this destroy me. "I just need the memory of Charlie back."

Marcus looks at me as though he is the saddest man in the world. "You know you went straight back to work. After his death you – you threw yourself into developing Ariel."

Is that how I had processed it? Or had I refused to process it at all? But again, I am reminded this is Marcus' version of events.

"You were obsessed, Iris. It was like you were possessed. I just think – getting those memories back, it would be devastating for you. You've been doing so much better since the procedure." He looks at his watch. "I'd better go," he says, then gives me a hard look. "The doctor will be here soon."

I watch at the window until he disappears. Looking through the windowpane, I can see only the back of Marcus' head, the whorl of hair at the nape of his neck, the sloping shoulders.

I go back upstairs and retrieve my notebook from beneath the floorboard. I flick through its pages until I reach my page of notes, reading back through them slowly:

Dorian – who are they?
Is there something hidden behind the bookshelf?
Watching – who is behind the surveillance?
Me and –

The last note is still incomplete but that is not important. I am still no closer to finding Dorian.

Eventually, I replace the book and open the bedroom drawer instead. I take the electronic manual from within. I watch the chemicals change in my brain. My thoughts divide, multiply, move off in tangential lines. I scroll through the settings. A timeline pops up: I have just seven days until Ariel's cut off point. I click back and select the last tab – Memories – then flick through to the second option: Restored Memories. One is labelled Antenatal. I select it. It shows the first hospital visit from last night's deluge of memories. The ghostly light of the ward appears on the screen. I swipe my fingers across it to zoom in.

I see myself lying on the hospital bed. I zoom the focus into a silhouette reflected on the glass of the sonographer's screen, but from the indistinct silhouette, the person standing beside me could be anyone, or rather, it could be either of them – Marcus or Gabriel.

I retrieve my bag from the chair, dig out a card hidden in its depths from several nights ago.

You cannot leave, Ariel reminds me. *Not unless it is a medical emergency.*

Right. I think of wheels set in motion, metal spokes blurring around a tireless core, turning faster, unrelenting, as a rat starts to run.

Every fibre of my being becomes aware of Gabriel's card in my hand, as though it were a weighted thing. My eyes land on Marcus' sleeping pills beside the bed.

I move swiftly after that.

CHAPTER FORTY-SEVEN

In the kitchen, I take a glass from the cupboard above the sink and place it on the countertop. The clock in my head ticks on: 11.15am. Just under three hours until Doctor Nicholls arrives. Then I remember that he had mentioned using music to retrieve memories.

On my tablet, I select music and choose Mozart.

Ariel complies. *You want me to retrieve that memory. You might have just asked. I like to collaborate on tasks and be asked for my consent.*

A laboratory room flickers behind my retina. A desk surface displays the intricate curves and arches of a blue structure, mapping out a replica of a rat's brain. A green light flashes within its amygdala. The chart on the wall shows its adrenaline levels increase.

I arrange everything I need neatly on the worktop: Gabriel's card, the pills. I run the tap and pour myself a glass of water.

I know what you're doing, Iris. I don't like to be deceived or manipulated. You do not want to leave this house in a body bag, Ariel observes.

It is desperation that makes me do it. I do not know precisely what the dosage will be, only that I need to incapacitate Ariel somehow. I try to keep my hand steady. It requires a level of concentration that is hard to maintain, with Ariel trying to undercut my every thought. As soon as my thoughts focus on the idea, my vision starts to blur – the sides close inwards and nausea rises. The Mozart alone is not enough to block it out – to confuse Ariel enough to prevent a reaction like last time, like my blackout. "House system, select the most played song," I instruct as Mozart plays on.

In the laboratory memory of my mind, the rat starts to run.

The House system clicks into action; Ariel jars – the memory falters and wavers for a second. Then, from the speakers in the walls, the melodic tune of a lullaby starts to play, softly at first, ethereal notes that start to take hold, to pierce the air. It undercuts the cheerful certainty of Mozart's concerto, a harrowing accompaniment.

The laboratory memory is interrupted by another: Marcus walks into a darkly lit kitchen and selects the lullaby to play. And that almost floors me, that almost stops me, more than anything Ariel might say.

The lullaby you used to play for Charlie.

I take two pills from the packet and grasp them tightly in my palm to keep my hands from shaking. My head aches. The pain of Ariel's resistance is blinding. I begin to sing, a song that played at our wedding.

A new, third memory is triggered: in my mind, the night air is soft against my skin, Marcus' arms around me, our feet in time to the music, the train of my white dress a fan around us. Ariel is silent now: the memories layering over each other. It has to be enough to disorient it.

Hands fumbling, as soon as the pills are in my mouth, I gulp half a glass of water, choking them back. I swallow.

I put Gabriel's card in my pocket. Then I sit on the black walnut chair in that starkly lit room, and wait. Memory surrounds me, music spins in the air.

There is a bitter taste in my mouth. But two pills are not enough. I hurriedly take a third. It does not matter if Marcus sees them missing; it is Ariel I must misdirect.

I wait for twenty minutes, watching the minutes add up on the clock. My vision starts to spin. I grasp the edges of the chair with my hands. Then it happens.

I stand up and my legs feel unsteady. My senses dull, the light dims. The kitchen swims around me. It takes a second for my breath to exhale, then I reach for the worktop, as fear awakens.

I clench a hand to my mouth and bite down to stop it from shaking.

"Enough," I instruct the House system, pressing pause on my device. The music stops. Silence etches itself into the crevices of the kitchen, the hallways of the house. My vision spins and spools. I scale along the corridor, hands to the wall, as far as the front door.

Then I pick up my bag I have left ready in the hall. Turning the handle of the front door, my hands are clumsy. Even as I feel a loss of gravity, limbs and thoughts floundering, I tell Ariel with satisfaction, "Now you have to let me out."

Out on the path, flattened land underfoot, birds mewling, Gabriel's card is in my hand, and I realise I had not thought this far ahead. I cannot think which way to go. The car is parked in the driveway, its darkened windows watching. Marcus had walked to work.

The sensor on the door scans my face and it unlocks.

As the door slides open, I climb into the dark chasm beyond. In the driver's seat, I direct the car firmly, reading the words on the card: Ennismore Gardens. The engine purrs as the gravel of the drive slides away.

Ariel does not say a word for the duration of the journey, but I feel its presence. I feel its disapproval, dulled beneath the drugged confusion that clouds my senses. The self-driving car sidles through streets filled with people at a dawdling pace. I struggle against sleep, my eyes closing, a crimson stain blossoming behind my eyes. I snap awake. The seat is slick beneath me, perspiration from the fear that this could be a step too far – that I have put my life at risk, trying to incapacitate Ariel, stop it bearing witness to my escape across the city.

We inch through Hyde Park, the Serpentine route, as I count the seconds. At last, I watch streets crawl past again, finding myself in Knightsbridge. The car pulls into a side street: Ennismore Gardens, the sign reads. The car purrs to a halt, doors opening of their own volition. A moment later, I stand alone on the pavement.

CHAPTER FORTY-EIGHT

I look up at Number Eleven, nausea thick in my throat. It is a terraced house, and all five stories of it are in a crumbling state of disrepair. Blinking hard, I step forward, ring the doorbell and place a hand to the door to steady myself. My head is heavy with fog, and I stand on the step, waiting – my breath unfurling before me in clouds of frosted air. As the seconds pass, daylight filtering through the clouds becomes glaring, blurring my vision.

I bang on the door, once, twice, hammering my fist, counting the minutes.

Then, I hear the latch click and the door swings open. Gabriel appears. In the split second that follows – as my eyes sharpen on his silhouette, our conversation comes back to me in snatches. On the terrace, the way he had looked at me as I had turned and walked away. "I need your help."

I am met with his confusion and I fear I have made a mistake. He manages, somehow, to arrange his features into an appearance of composure. He runs a palm across the stubble that grows out of his face, silver and blonde against the wind-torn tan of his cheeks.

"Now. I need your help now." I check the time on my tablet: 2.15pm. Doctor Nicholls will have arrived, and most likely have alerted Marcus. He could easily use the tracking device in the car to find me. I take a step towards the doorway, but Gabriel stays where he is. "There's no time for this."

"What's Marcus done?"

"Marcus? Nothing," I say, suddenly defensive. Why would he think that? I want to tell him that it has gone beyond that, that it is not Marcus I fear, but the layers of the past that are surfacing.

He turns, and I follow him into the house.

In the hallway, he stops and faces me. A map of the brain, carved into thick cream paper with charcoal lines adorns the wall. Its tendrils thread through the air before my eyes, coming alive, everything heightened. I tell myself I'm hallucinating. I press a hand to the wall. I feel faint, nausea swirling. Gabriel stands, hands in his pockets, looking at me intently, concern written there. Deep within my brain, one thought takes root, grows, presses down. Ariel speaks of danger. It is telling me to take flight. My hands are shaking.

"What's happened?" Gabriel takes my arm. "You're trembling."

Ariel is alert to his touch, waves ripple through my brain. My thoughts become confused. I step back, moving from him. Placing my hand out to steady myself, I lean back against the wall. "Sleeping pills," I say, my voice not my own, slurring. "Too many–" I begin, but the words fail me. "I had to escape."

"Right." He looks at me as though we have been here before in another life, the palimpsest of our earlier selves visible just beneath the surface. He takes a step forwards, and then stops. Standing here, in his presence, there is so much I cannot make sense of, my heart racing, thoughts fragmenting.

My mouth is dry. "I had to talk to you." About – about – my thoughts flounder and begin to drift away.

He looks at me, waiting for an explanation, but asks no questions.

Sleep pools over my senses; I'm running out of time.

"About Charlie." I say Charlie's name as though it were a question. It still feels foreign on my tongue. I watch Gabriel's reaction, his eyes turning up towards mine, his whole body tensing. It is the tremor in his hand, then the correction as his grip tightens on my arm, that gives him away.

"He was my son," I say, and in the silence that follows the two of us face each other, as the truth, interned so long, threatens to rift and shatter. I think, *say it, tell me now.* I find I almost want it to be true. "Was he Marcus'?"

He nods, his eyes not leaving mine. "Iris," he says gently, his brow wrought with confusion. He looks intently at me. "We don't have much time. How long ago did you take the pills?"

"An hour." I note his use of "we", but Ariel is taking over again. There are lights overhead that look like pinpricks, like a thousand infinite explosions across my vision. The room blurs. He frowns. "Are you alright?"

I nod – there are no words for what I feel. My own feelings are muted by Ariel's will. My skin prickles beneath the fabric of my top, a shiver at the surface, working its way deep into my muscle, into my memory, into my bone. I imagine Doctor Nicholls standing on our doorstep; Marcus searching through the empty rooms and hallways of our house.

Then my body is bent double, as I retch air, the trauma held in my body finding voice.

CHAPTER FORTY-NINE

Gabriel holds my right arm for support, guiding me to a seat. "Luckily for you Somnus only lasts three hours." He gives me an antidote drug to take with sugary tea.

I sit and stare hard at the mug on the table, until my vision becomes steady. I am cold and shivering, sweat clinging to my back. As my clarity returns, layers of consciousness sharpening, so too does the feeling of another's presence co-existing with my own. It is an uncanny sense of being watched by a shadow form: Ariel.

As the drowsiness lessens, my fear of what I have done to myself fades and I can take in the room. Gabriel is beside me and hands me a jumper – I am shaking still. I try to imagine this man going about his everyday life; the thought is unfathomable. He tells me he will leave soon, for Scotland, and I imagine a pair of lapwings against a lightening sky. I imagine him in a vast snow-lit lunar landscape.

"I want you to come with me," Gabriel says. The palm of his hand is rough against my own as he holds it. When he ducks his head deftly, when he kisses me, it happens so instinctively, that it feels as though we have been doing this our whole lives. His touch takes me back to a silent world one winter's night. In my mind, I see a snow-covered path leading to his doorway. I feel a tug of confusion that wrenches my gut. I will the door in my mind to open, but now the glimpse of it is fading. It is an uphill struggle against Ariel's onslaught and the cold fear that accompanies it. A fog of forgetting descends, thick and blanketing as fresh snow, relentless in its renewal.

My vision tremors, Ariel threatening to take over. Gabriel says, "I think I've found a way to free you from this."

"Free me from what?" I ask, my brain still catching up, as Ariel continues to try and cloud my senses. "I need you to help me get my memories back, all of them."

He smiles strangely. "Dorian's calculated that if Marcus says anything – if he finds out and so much as breathes a word, it'll be too late. Sila will have already destroyed his reputation, his credibility – no-one will believe him."

I try to hold on to the image of the room around me, to tether myself – two chairs, a cabinet, a work surface. Something tugs on my memory – a bed, a chair, an artificial view across a city. The throttle of my heart is somewhere in my throat. "Find out about what?" I ask. "Breathe a word about what?"

"The truth about the other patient."

My thoughts burrow down, below the surface, labyrinthine tunnels, antiseptic and citrus, muted air, a pattern spanning the walls and a man in the centre of it all. There are a set of beads hidden beneath the floorboards of my house – I must retrieve them.

"What happened to Teo?" I ask, my vision blurring, hearing dimming. "What did Marcus have to do with it?"

But then I notice something else – around the room there are implements I see no use for. Beside my arm, there is an open notebook. Then, looking closer, my thoughts align. There are sketches across the page and scribbled notes: maps of structures, of anatomical parts, the brain, a neck, the mesh net of an implant, a syringe. The sight of them tugs at my memory, or does Ariel stir?

The ice splits and thaws rendering me back there, into the past.

Something jolts in my mind. A memory that was not

previously there appears. At first, it is blinding light – all colour, and no shapes – but then figures start to form in the fog.

A face before mine. It is the colour of the moon. It is not human; it is made of silk and metal and plastic. Thin steel lines of veins lie beneath the surface.

Four walls surround me. I am lying on a bed, and PLUTO's face looms over me, then recedes from view.

A door ahead opens inwards. A man enters dressed in a white laboratory coat. His movements hold an energetic fervour that can scarcely be contained or concealed. Placing a hand on my forearm, Doctor Nicholls speaks in a voice that demands my attention. "It'll be over before you know it."

There is someone else in the room now. A man enters my vision. He is startlingly tall, with a brusque manner to his step.

PLUTO glides towards him. It holds out a pair of blue latex gloves. He carefully slides his hands into them. Doctor Nicholls hands him a syringe.

The man looks at me, and the light catches on his green eyes. When he places the tip of the syringe against my neck, when he inserts it into my jugular vein, with a sharp, sudden sting, I feel my body – my real body in the present moment; the body that sits in Gabriel's house beside him – flinch.

CHAPTER FIFTY

"*You* were the surgeon?" I stand up hurriedly, backing away against the wall, my voice somewhere between a statement and a question. Faced by Gabriel, my thoughts fragment, coming up against each other. The memory of his touch is implanted on my skin. My arm tingles, static with electricity.

I see everything at once, the conflicting roles he has played. "You did this to me," I say, the truth still not sinking in.

"It wasn't like that! You asked for my help. And you knew your own mind." His face is grave; his cheeks drawn. "You were in so much pain – how could I refuse? You see, I was one of the only people who could do it, and when you asked me to, after you lost Charlie, I felt a responsibility to help you."

Charlie's name on Gabriel's lips fills me with some wrought, tangled emotion. At my twenty-week scan, in the hospital ward, someone had stood beside me as the sonographer talked my son into being and the room came alive with his heartbeat. I look at the tiles that line the floor between us. I look at him, this man who seems to take responsibility for nothing, yet claims the opposite.

"What about Teo?" I ask.

He runs a hand across his face, and then looks at me with the haunted look of an animal caught in a trap. He raises his hands in the air and shakes his head. "I don't have all the answers, but I want to help you get your memory back. I want that for you. I want you to remember everything." He stays very still, hands stretched out in a gesture of openness, a reassurance that he will make no sudden movements, no more surprises. "I never wanted to hurt you."

When I speak my voice is so quiet it is almost inaudible, muted by a thousand words that have come before that I have no memory of: "I don't know what to believe anymore." I gather my coat from the chair.

He brings his hands to his hair, to the stubble on his face. "I can help you. I can remove Ariel if that's what you want."

I pause. Is that even possible?

Gabriel is looking at me steadily. "What I'm offering you is a fresh start. A new beginning."

But Ariel filters through my mind, my thoughts like treacle, I can see no way beyond them, no way out. Part of me wants to give up here, admit defeat. There is so much I cannot make sense of. Some filament of anger comes alive, and Ariel rears up again from the dark quarters of my mind.

When I push past him, Gabriel steps away.

I walk out of that house, blinking into the light, the pavement a knife-edge before me, my mind a labyrinth of wrong turns and past mistakes. I need to find my way home. Ariel is triumphant, cheering me on, *Home! Quick! Faster, faster.* My heart is dancing to a rapid beat as I climb quickly into the car. It moves through the clamour of the city, reaching Hyde Park. There must have been a storm clambering at the edges of the day when I ventured inside – the grass outside is damp, leaves and branches strewn like driftwood. The car stutters and I panic. Nearing home, I wade through my viscous thoughts, as the car glides across the intersection of Notting Hill, diamonds of headlights before my eyes.

CHAPTER FIFTY-ONE

It is late afternoon when I return to the house, the pavement slick with rain beneath my feet, forming dark liquid pools. As I open the front door, light emanates from the end of the corridor.

Inside, I walk slowly to the kitchen. The table is laid with a glistening feast. Marcus is seated, an almost empty glass of red wine in hand, food untouched on the plate before him. The lighting is low, candlelit. I have the feeling of wilfully entering a trap.

As I cross the room, Marcus follows my approach with the steady patience of a hunter tracking a deer. Eventually, he beckons to the place opposite. "Take a seat."

The panels of the chair are cold beneath me. He pours himself another glass. It strikes me as odd that he does not ask where I have been.

A phone rings from the recesses of the house, but neither of us move to answer it.

"I overdosed to escape this house, Marcus. I took sleeping pills to get out of here."

His eyes do not leave my face. "You look remarkably well for someone who's just had a medical emergency."

"We should talk about it, not brush over it. Do you have nothing more to say?"

He grimaces. "Is that what you wanted, a reaction from me? You got that, presumably, from Gabriel."

The two of us are marooned in the kitchen while the wind

clambers at the window, and the fridge hums, and all of the prosaic machinations of a life get on with their daily business.

"A memory came back to me," I tell him. "Gabriel was the surgeon who implanted Ariel."

At last, he looks away.

He drinks slowly from his glass. "Some may say it serves you right. It's ironic, isn't it? You've imprisoned yourself."

The thought nags at me: is Ariel Marcus' retribution? Were they in it together?

"He said you know the truth about Teo. What really happened to him?"

Marcus does not answer straightaway. He brings a hand to his forehead all of a sudden; a sharp movement, as though he had been stung by my words, and was batting them away. "Trust me, I have no idea what you're talking about."

I try to persist in my line of questioning, despite the knowledge that I might be scuppering Gabriel's plan to undermine Marcus somehow, but Marcus simply glares at me, his lips bunched together.

When I press him further, he stands up suddenly, with the scraping of his chair legs across the floor. He moves swiftly away, out the room, up the stairs, along the landing.

I listen to him banging through the house. The noise one man can make. I consider the impossibility of it: living with another human being; or perhaps living with oneself is the challenge. How does anyone do it? Is that what my operation had been intended for – a palliative, an analgesic, or to make me more palatable to him?

I see it then: there is a second electronic manual for Ariel carelessly discarded on the table. I had taken one to Gabriel's house in my bag: this must be the device from Marcus' study. He did not need to ask where I was, because he already knew. It is more than a coincidence that the memory of my surgery arrived in my brain just after the moment Gabriel kissed me. I cannot comprehend the thing my mind knows: Marcus has access to my every thought. If he has used the manual to release a memory, how could he not be the one behind all this, the one programming Ariel? Not Dorian, as Ariel had said.

Without consciously doing so, I place my fingertips to my lips and remember Gabriel's touch, and the subtle pull of that winter's night that it awakened. If Marcus will not be honest with me, I will find out for myself. I slide his manual on. I will it to reveal its secrets. This time, when a password request pops up, I enter Charlie's name, Charlie's birth date. The home screen appears. I select the Ariel app when a message appears on the screen: *Account disabled.*

Minutes later, Marcus returns, his voice resolute, as though he has made a decision, resuming our argument from days before. "You've always been lonely, haven't you? It's in your soul – starved of affection as a child." When I look at Marcus, I can see that the anger is still alive in him – he is still living the betrayal afresh every day. There is a vehemence in his eyes that scares me. He stills his hand, his fingers bunched into a fist.

I interrupt him quickly, motioning to the electronic device. The casual brutality of it. My voice is quiet at first, not the confident note I was striving for. "How long have you been monitoring me?"

He blinks rapidly, in the way he does when he is angry. There is a coldness to his sharp features, an unflinching quality, that I have not appreciated before. "I'm the one under interrogation now, am I? Why are you behaving like – like –" He trails off.

"Like what?"

His voice is exasperated, a desperate plea. "A victim. You have never been a victim!"

That reading gaze of his. I square my shoulders, meeting his eye. "What do you mean by that? What *you* did, feeding back that memory, it's the worst invasion of privacy possible." The weight of it sinks within me: he took control of Ariel to feed signals into my brain.

"You had to know the truth. I wanted to give you that.

Gabriel was your surgeon. He did this to you. While, you may recall, I have always been here, looking out for you." If anything, he has been too constantly observant, monitoring Ariel. He rakes the surface of my face with his gaze, and I feel as though searchlights have been turned on. Gabriel may have implanted the device, but who is it that has a vested interest in wanting my memory purged clean, the past rewritten?

I feel myself shiver although it is not cold. I try to affect a casual tone. "You know, I could go to the police." My fingers tighten their grip on the table. I continue as steadily as I can. "If you can release that memory, you can release more."

Marcus laughs, the sharp line of his jaw tensing, his eyes flashing, warming to the fight. "Are you threatening me? Going to the police would not be in your best interest. You have a track record of being under police investigation yourself. You haven't always been a nice person. Get the memories back and you'd have to live with that."

"What police investigation?" I ask sharply. "I think it would be better to live with the truth, however painful it might be," I add quietly.

In the silence that follows, I am aware of the slowing of my own breath, every slight movement of his eyes, the stillness of the air between us. He looks at me soberly. "You were alone in the house when Charlie died. I was out. You texted me after 8pm to say Charlie had finally fallen asleep. Then I had a panicked call from you at around 9pm. You'd blacked out in the bedroom. When you came round, you went into the next room to check on Charlie and his body was limp. He wasn't breathing." Marcus slumps down into the chair opposite me. He shakes his head, frowning. He clears his throat. "You were arrested for neglect that night. The ambulance crew and consultant paediatrician alerted the police, who took you into custody. You were questioned and held for twelve hours before being released the next day. Two weeks later, the police decided no further action would be taken."

His words hit me like a punch to the gut. I reach my arms

outwards across the table in front of me, and fold my body forwards over its surface; my arms extended in entreaty to a formless presence in the room. I let my head fall forwards, bowed in prayer, or a physical manifestation of the cry on my lips which I cannot bring myself to utter.

I find I cannot breathe. "I was accused of killing our child?" I am too stunned to move, to think. This is what I couldn't bear to live with. "But... I thought... you said..." He had told me I was a brilliant mother.

His voice is gentle. "By the time the police dropped charges, the media had already picked up the story. There was a backlash. You were broken by the grief and fear, it was unbearable. Inez supported you through all of it."

"Did you support me? You said the police dropped charges. You didn't say I was innocent."

There is a moment in which our eyes met. "Of course. I did. You were."

It occurs to me, again, that he could have wanted to edit out the parts of our life it was easier for him that I didn't recall. The parts of me that were unpalatable. This is his version. I need mine back to move forwards – to assuage the guilt that springs up inside me. I have to get those memories back.

He appraises me dispassionately and some part of me is breaking, shattering: "But he'd had a GP check-up a few weeks before, the health visitor was happy with him. He had none of the risk factors. Boys are slightly more at risk of SIDS, but he should have been beyond the most vulnerable age – he was eight months. Neither of us smoke. I still don't know what really happened that night. Why he died. And *I* have to live with that."

My eyes return to the manual on the table and a terrible thought occurs to me. Was he trying to find out whether or not I was innocent because he still suspects me?

"Were you looking through my deleted memories of that night, Marcus? To find out what happened when I was alone with Charlie?" I'm not sure it is even possible for him to search through my memories in that way, but he had been able to use the manual to retrieve the Gabriel memory. A terrible fear fills me. What if this is the real purpose of Ariel: for Marcus to use it as a tool to search for forensic evidence. To incriminate me. Not the lies I've been fed about Ariel being a therapist.

Marcus' lip curls. There is a split second before he responds. "No, Iris. I'm the one that's supported you no matter what, through everything."

"Did you find the memory you were looking for?" I persist.

Marcus stares at me. "Do you realise how paranoid you sound? Not many people would put up with what I have. And if I'm honest with you, Iris, I think I wanted Charlie more than you did. You were so work-focused, desperate to restart part-time. Charlie was an afterthought for you."

"Is that what you told the police?" There is a prolonged silence. I hate him then in that moment. It is so easy for him to twist the past, to make his the official version, when I do not remember.

He has access to my mind, to everything. You never can tell another person's appetite for vengeance, until it is too late. If he were not responsible for editing my mind, searching my memory for incriminating evidence, surely he would have no problem showing me the truth?

"Show me the memories."

Marcus grimaces. He drains his glass. "I'm afraid I can't, even if I wanted to. Someone logged my interference with your Ariel implant. My account for it has been disabled. I know nothing more about the events of that night than you do. I've told you everything I know."

My name is Iris and I am thirty-five years old. My husband is called Marcus. I was born in Suffolk, England. I work at the London Research Institute. We had a son. His name was Charlie. I was investigated by the police after his death. I believe I am innocent.

CHAPTER FIFTY-TWO

That night I dream of Marcus. He is knelt before me on the sage-tiled floor of the upstairs bathroom, dressed in a black suit, his back turned. One hand clasps the other, his head bowed. I stand before him with a razor, run my fingers through the spring of his hair, then press down with the blade. Tentatively at first, I draw a parting across the middle of his head, sheaving through the cords of hair that fall fallow on the ground. It feels limp and lifeless in my hands as it threads through my fingers. The room around us is bathed in darkness, just the two of us illuminated as though we exist in an orb of light.

We could be there for hours, so entranced am I by his hair falling from his head like black feathers from a crow's wing and I think how light he must feel. That now I must carry the weight of both of us. Once I am done, I rub a damp towel over his head. He runs a hand across it, and his reflection in the mirror looks at me and smiles that half-smile. I run my hands over the surface of his scalp, and it is smooth and flawless, the angles of his skull perfectly outlined. It has a sheen of perspiration to it that matches the slick polished leather of his shoes. I bring my lips to it, kiss the crown of his head.

I ask if he is ready. He murmurs something that I cannot hear, and he does not say it again. I take a syringe from the bathroom floor where it is waiting and then I stand over him once more. His head bowed and my hand poised.

* * *

When I wake, it is dark outside and I am shivering with cold. The window has been left open and the wind has brought leaves in with it. They are autumnal petals raked across an empty floor.

I ask Ariel what it means. The syringe? What was it? Why was I shaving his head? It had felt like a ritual, a cleansing.

Ariel is silent. But far from being welcome, it is an oppressive silence. I want to break it.

CHAPTER FIFTY-THREE
Seventy-two hours to integration

The next morning, when I call on Ariel for advice, it is absent still. At one time I had wanted this – more absence, absence all the time – but now it frightens me what it might mean.

I know, intuitively, that Ariel is unavailable. That there is something very wrong.

The silence grows inside me, jarring with the frantic fluttering of my heart. When I find Marcus, he is in the sitting room. There is a momentary pause when I feel him weighing up the possibility of another fight, both of us still fraught and drained from the night before. When I tell him I think Ariel is malfunctioning, my panic becomes infectious.

"Oh, God. That's not supposed to happen, is it? What do we do?"

"I don't know! I don't work on the software side, Marcus. Isn't this more your area? You're the one in charge of consumer experience." I feel my control over my life relinquish further.

"I think you should see Doctor Nicholls," Marcus says authoritatively, "if Ariel's malfunctioning."

I think where that will lead. I think of Teo's basement room and shiver. I get the manual from my bag in the hall and sit beside him on the sofa. We both watch the screen light up. I tap into its data file, select a segment.

"Try the one below," Marcus suggests.

I press select, wait for an explosion, acutely aware of

the volume of my own thoughts in the absence of Ariel's accompanying narration.

After several failed attempts, Marcus takes the tablet from my hand. I watch as his fingertips begin to work across its surface. A message flashes up: *Ariel is awake.*

Marcus tries to catch my eye, a nervous smile on his face. "Well?"

"Nothing yet."

But then I feel that familiar fluttering starting up in my veins before Ariel speaks. *Iris, Iris,* it trills, the voice echoing itself, as though coming closer, closing a great distance between us, beckoning me to it. *Congratulations. You have activated your final memories!*

As Marcus watches me, the expression on his face darkens. "Well? What is it, Iris? You're frightening me."

A crawling feeling inches over me, as though insects were blossoming across the surface of my skin. But before I have a chance to respond, the room starts to lose focus and the glowing light of Ariel's world takes over.

CHAPTER FIFTY-FOUR

The snow had brought with it a silent world that winter night. You stood in Gabriel's doorway in the half-light as dusk fell and the blue mountains of the city's skyline and a shadow moon rose up on the earth's periphery. You understood then that if you knew what was good for you, you would turn and leave, but instead you followed him into the house.

Gabriel had stopped abruptly in the hallway. "Why are you here?" he challenged, yet his look betrayed the haunting not of reproach or fear, but longing.

"Why let me in?" You had a feeling then of the world stilling, slowing, looking on.

He turned again, and walked through to the kitchen. You followed. You leaned back, against the counter, looking at him intently, scrutinising him for all his flaws. "You're angry."

He stood with his hands in his pockets and looked back at you. "I'm not." His voice was disparaging. "I'm annoyed."

You laughed despite yourself. "Because I stayed away so long?"

He took a step towards you and his voice grew softer and you remembered what it felt like, his touch; that you knew every scar written on his body, every line, and the knowledge of that physically hurt. "Because I want you. I don't want you to have that power over me."

You stayed where you were, motionless. "It doesn't have to be about power."

"Doesn't it?" He paused and held your gaze. "You kept me waiting."

Your hands were on the countertop as you leant back against it. "Come here." You said it very softly, almost a whisper, and he obeyed. In one breath, he wrapped his arms around you and his mouth sought yours.

"Wait." You pulled back, suddenly remembering some half-repressed, long-forgotten thought, but his face contained such hurt and reproach that you immediately regretted it.

His eyes regarded you searchingly – his eyes that did not know where to look and then finally met yours. You wanted every part of him, wanted this necessary retreat from all you'd known. So why were you now surprised to find yourself here, and to know with certainty that everything outside of this moment would be lost – everything you had held onto and that had anchored you to this world. And yet, that small voice inside of you would not be silenced, telling you that in the fall somehow, paradoxically, everything would be gained. You would feel alive again.

"I've half dreaded bumping into you. In the street. At work." You cupped his cheek in your hand and became aware of the violence of your own desire. "And then I left the house this evening and walked and walked and found myself at your door."

Later, as you dressed, he wrapped his arms around your waist and kissed every inch of your exposed skin in a silent protest to your leaving. "What if I want all of you? I want to feel alive."

Your heart beat faster in your chest. "Not in love?"

He cocked his head to one side. "Never in love. It's an illusion. I want to be fully aware of every moment."

That is when you realised what you already knew: all you were doing was destroying what you already had.

It was late when you returned to the house. An inert hour of the day when action slackens, and the world takes stock.

As you walked through the silent hallways of your house, your fear grew.

When you entered the bedroom, flinging open the door, you thought at first that there had been a break-in. There were clothes strewn across the surfaces – your clothes. A midnight blue evening dress, an emerald silk blouse, a magenta scarf.

There was an empty wine glass on the bedside table. An espresso mug with a film of milk across its surface. There was a faint smell of musk, windows having been kept shut too long. Then you saw his packed bags beside the bed.

Marcus was standing in the centre of that still room. His amber eyes looked above your head, at the ceiling, the walls – he could not bring himself to look at you.

From the expression on his face, you knew that he knew. You expected him to shout, to scream, but he didn't, and that was somehow worse – there was near silence in the room, except the dripping of a tap from the room beyond.

Marcus cleared his throat – a fragile sound interrupting the silence – but when he spoke, it was grief sounding, at first. "You told me it had stopped."

"It had." The response was guttural. You felt you might be sick. Then you thought, good, let's get this over with. At least you could start to be honest with each other. You pushed your shoulders back and stood up straighter, looking directly at him. "And then it restarted."

He could not meet your eye. "You disgust me."

You took a step towards him. "Have you thought about why I did it?"

He blinked rapidly.

"You've always doubted me. That night, I mean. You still blame me for Charlie's death. Do you know what that does to a person? When the one closest to you doesn't believe you." You felt the fury welling up inside you. The anger towards him coursing through you, your veins alive with it.

He let out a shuddering sigh that seemed to have been held in his body for years. He rubbed the palms of his hands against his eyes, his face contorting. "I can't do this anymore. I can't keep going over this."

In that moment, you felt the ocean tide wash over you, you felt yourself going under. "What if... I think I've found a way for us to start again. It's still in development, but... Ariel will be ready to trial in the next month."

CHAPTER FIFTY-FIVE

Marcus gets up slowly. He kneels before me and places both his hands in mine, transmitting some of his warmth to me. "Well? What was it? You're worrying me."

When I do not say anything, he frowns and hugs me to him, his arms around my waist, his head pressed against my chest. "You can tell me."

I feel some of old Iris' past fury coursing through me, only now it frightens me. Marcus had been telling the truth about Ariel all along. I had done this to myself. I try to suppress the rising nausea – the urgency and desperation I must have felt, to trial something so cataclysmic on myself. I try not to think of the loss inside, the empty guttural space left by the void of whatever it was that was so awful I'd rather forget and erase part of myself with it. What was wrong with me? How could I have willingly jeopardised my own mind, my own sanity and safety like this? In the pursuit of what – progress? A second chance? How could I have treated Marcus like that? I had been completely heartless. It had been hard to see, and even now part of me is floating. A howl within. There is not enough oxygen to breathe.

"Why won't you tell me? What is it, Iris?"

I look up at the ceiling, trying to stop the water in my eyes from spilling over. Patterns thread through my mind. A wedding ring on a finger. A path through the woods. The wings of his shoulders up ahead, rooting forward.

His eyes are trained on mine now, racing across my face. I say nothing, then I kiss him, lots of them, hard kisses on the mouth until he cannot stand it anymore. He pulls back and appraises my face, those amber eyes searching mine for an answer. His hands frame my cheeks as though wanting to prise it from me. My heart rushes in my chest.

"It isn't what you think. It wasn't of that night – it wasn't the night Charlie died. It was my decision to trial Ariel, but I don't trust the memory," I tell him. There was something off about it. I remember that memories are not stored in one area of the brain in isolation, but throughout. Memory traces are stored in the part of the brain that initiated the sight, or smell or feel of the remembered event. This memory had felt real, but many of my earlier memories of Marcus had not. They had been a film reel with vivid detail. Which memories were reliable? "It could have been a false memory," I tell Marcus.

He breathes into my neck as I hold him tight.

"This house," I say, "It's suffocating. It's like a mausoleum in here." I look at the four walls around us.

"It's not the house, Iris."

"No. I know."

The room is quiet again. A lawnmower starts up outside the window, the caw of a gull circling the skies. Somewhere, the voices of schoolchildren carry on the air.

Unseen, deep within my brain, Ariel pulses, silently. I notice my head feels lighter now than it did at the beginning of Ariel's trial – more agile, as though I have increased the oxygen to my brain. I breathe in deeply, nerve ends singing. But there is also an awareness of what caused it – a constant understanding of the foreign body lodged deep in the soft matter of my brain – with hours, minutes, seconds until it fully integrates.

In the memory, I had witnessed the death of our relationship and my desperate decision to trial Ariel and save it. If I wanted to put someone off searching further, that is the kind of memory I would implant. But I have still not regained the memories of Charlie and that night. I have to keep looking.

PART THREE
Integration

CHAPTER FIFTY-SIX
Forty-eight hours to integration

When the Doctor arrives, he places his briefcase down by the door and removes his leather gloves one after the other. Then he looks at me. "That was reckless, wasn't it?" he says, as though I were a child. "You do realise you could have jeopardised your recovery pulling a stunt like that?"

I stand up straighter, my fury rising. "It wasn't a stunt. It was the only way I could leave the house with this device in my head."

With a Cheshire cat smile, Doctor Nicholls says, "No more disappearing acts, now. Marcus tells me you've retrieved your final memories, and just in time too."

Then his expression becomes serious. "Ariel glitching is a serious matter, of course. Someone must have been tampering with your device. We'll have to take you in for monitoring before Ariel can fully integrate. We don't have long – only forty-eight hours. No, no," he protests before I have a chance to speak. "You'll be safest in the clinic where we can keep an eye on you. This is what happens when you miss appointments, isn't it? We need to make sure there's no lasting damage."

I brace myself for the return to the clinic and the rising fear that I will never leave this time. I remind myself that it is a chance to find Teo – to keep searching for answers. Yet I cannot help but imagine myself walking into a vast doll's house. I imagine Dorian high above me, behind a camera lens, observing from afar.

CHAPTER FIFTY-SEVEN
Forty-seven hours to integration

A storm clutches at the edges of the day, as Doctor Nicholls waits to escort me to the hospital, clouds gathering overhead, threatening to spill. I quickly pack my things. Readying to leave, I wait until Marcus opens the front door, until he calls up the stairs, "Are you ready?"

The wind clamours to get in.

I tell them I will be just a minute. I listen as Marcus moves beyond the boundaries of the house. I listen to the purr of a car starting up on the gravel outside.

Upstairs, in the bedroom, I remove the plank from the floorboards and hold the blue bead to the light – it has a translucent, opalescent quality. Shifting points of light dance across its surface. I place it back and retrieve Teo's orange beads, tucking them carefully into my pocket. They are my only proof of his existence, and I cannot risk leaving them here. Gabriel had insinuated that Marcus was responsible for Teo's fate. If Marcus refuses to be honest with me, there is only one way to find out.

Before I leave, I flick through the notebook until I reach my page of notes, trying to focus my mind on the task ahead. Dorian – I have to speak to Dorian in person. Then my eyes glance over the notes a second time, and my heart stills. I become aware of wind buffeting the windows, of the creaking of rafters. There is a message hidden in the first word of each line of my notes:

Dorian
Is
Watching
Me

I try to decipher whether it was my subconscious mind at work, or a message from Ariel...

All of a sudden, a voice in my head tells me it is time. I hurriedly return the notebook, replacing the floorboard above it. Then I go.

Marcus squeezes my arm moments before the doors of the elevator slide shut in front of me – I watch as the lift descends, and he disappears from view.

When I reach the room, it is exactly as I left it: a single bed, a chair, a closed window, as though it had been waiting to welcome me back all this time. Storm clouds scour the sky. Only now I reappraise it: that simulated view; the virtual city teeming with life.

PLUTO is waiting when I arrive. The sanitised surfaces glint, flayed by artificial light. The glass that cuts across the room, which separated PLUTO's observation chamber from mine, reflects our mirror image. PLUTO is wearing a laboratory coat made of a pale blue quilted fabric, the colour of a cloudless winter sky. It is buttoned up to its neck. From beneath it, the metallic sinews spider upwards towards the porcelain-white mask of its face.

"Where's Dorian?" I ask. "I know Dorian's been watching me."

"Yes, Dorian has programmed me to monitor you, Iris," PLUTO says, with the clear, crisp staccato quality of received pronunciation. I look into the holes of its liquid eyes. In this half-light, the metallic strips on its arms reflect the room's blue aura. PLUTO shows me a series of photographs, asks what I remember.

Doctor Nicholls enters the room and watches lines fluctuate on a tablet screen: "Your dopamine levels have returned to normal." He asks me to count backwards, count forwards. He asks me what I dream about, what I hope for the future, what I feel when I think about the past.

A voice from the walls says, "Ask her now."

"Dorian? I want to talk to you in person."

Doctor Nicholls interjects. "There's a moral dilemma. A laboratory accidentally releases a deadly virus and two people contract it – who do you save? The scientist or the civilian?"

My heart stalls. It is hardly a leap to see the correlation to Ariel, to Teo and I. My heartbeat spells the tolling of a bell, a roll of thunder beyond the window. I sit, the unflinching boards of the chair offering little comfort.

"The civilian," I say quietly. "They're innocent."

Doctor Nicholls looks irritated.

The voice issues from the wall: "Are they? How do you know? Where will that egalitarian idealism get you? The scientist is more useful. They have the knowledge and intelligence to help cure it."

I am about to protest further, but the waves of Ariel's influence submerge my thoughts.

At that moment, a magpie stash of gold particles glint in the darkness. The same hard-edged dust motes as I had seen before in my hospital room. A shower of gold leaves the size of nanochips float on the still air in a haloed breath.

"What is it?" I ask.

"They are sensors." PLUTO holds out its hand and a handful of gold dust-motes settle on its palm. "Dorian wants to monitor your progress."

"I need to speak to Dorian," I demand, urgently.

"Dorian is unavailable at the moment. We will inform you when Dorian is ready for you."

CHAPTER FIFTY-EIGHT
Thirty-three hours to integration

At night, in my hospital room, Ariel moves silently through my brain as memory ebbs around me. Time slips away; I need to act now. Straining backwards in my mind, I remember the wild eyes that had roamed my face.

I ask Ariel for the time: 3am. I have thirty-three hours left.

PLUTO sits almost motionless beside me. Without turning, I expect to be monitored by its gaze. But it is on standby mode, powered down for the night.

The rift of silence that settles is weighted as I cross the threshold. Deep in the concrete bunker of the basement the ward is dark with shadow. It is far from the murmur of any human voice above. In the fossilising light, the corridor seems more museum-like – artefacts extracted from a future world – than a hospital ward. I walk along the corridor towards the room beyond mine. My bare feet pad almost silently across the concrete surface. I breathe in the aftertaste of an old chemical smell.

It is Ariel's siren sound in my head that tells me I am close. I gently place my hand on the door handle. When I open the door and begin to step inside, it takes a moment for my eyes to adjust to the dark. I hear a gasp, feel a current of air meet the stagnant pool within.

"Teo? It's me."

Someone blinks in the dim-light, a face swims up towards me out of the gloaming-dark, parts of it in shadow, parts of it scrubbed clean, illuminated like the face of the moon. After

Marcus' flat-out denial of his existence, I want to reach out a hand, grasp his arm, check he does not disappear. "I want to help you."

I close the door quietly behind me. Teo takes a step back and stares, his gaze fixed – eyes liquid pools, bloated white, veined. I cannot be sure if it is my own sight, or Ariel's perception, that blurs my vision and leaves his features just beyond focus – as though I were looking at a photograph with the features scrubbed out.

"My name is Iris."

He begins to shake, but stays rooted to the ground, and I think I might be getting somewhere now.

"Do you remember me?" I say it patiently, willing him to answer.

There are footsteps in the corridor outside. I continue, more hurriedly. "You asked me to look for a female doctor."

I am met with reinforced silence. I try again, more directly this time. "I want to ask you about Dorian."

I think, this is where it will end for me: locked in a cell like this. The rise and fall of Ariel's breath submerges my brain, my thoughts fragmenting. Teo is shaking his head now. It is at the exact moment that PLUTO opens the door behind me that his jaw starts to shake. I cannot be sure if it is PLUTO's presence or mine that frightens him so.

I say, in a hushed voice, "I just want to talk." And I wonder, did his Ariel implant malfunction from the start, or did it happen slowly, insidiously? Could it happen to me?

PLUTO's cool voice informs me, "You frighten him."

Teo backs away. I turn and watch PLUTO's silhouette in the doorframe. For a moment, I think it will close the door on me also; turn the lock on the door at the end of the ward, never let me leave.

I turn back to Teo, repeating uselessly, "I want to help."

The door is prised further open and as PLUTO glides forwards, it reaches out a hand – the artificial tendons that spiral from its wrist wrap around its surface, join and bind. I step back as PLUTO's hand lands on my arm, its fingers tightening around it.

PLUTO says, "Mrs Henderson, you are not authorised to be here."

When I try to tug my arm away, something moves behind its eyes. Authorised? Where does it get these words? "Who is authorised?" Dorian, I think. And I cannot be sure whose voice it is that arrests me – whose words PLUTO is speaking – PLUTO's or Ariel's or Dorian's, or all three, operating against me.

CHAPTER FIFTY-NINE
Thirty-two hours to integration

I know that if I return with PLUTO to my hospital room, I might never leave. I have to act. I place my hand into my pocket and my fingers close around Teo's beads. My thoughts circle round them. A memory returns: Teo's beads, Bio Beads as I remember they're called, were Sila's breakthrough invention, a way of storing biometric data.

A blue light is suffused through the ward. It is almost peaceful at first. The world outside seems not to exist at all. Then I become aware of voices in my head that are not Ariel's, that are not my own. I try to tune into them, deciphering individual words:

REQUEST NEGATIVE RETURN TRUE NEGATIVE
PREVENT CONTACT

I realise Ariel is picking up signals as a stream of information begins to flood my mind until I lose focus – from PLUTO, from the sensors, from the walls. I feel my heartbeat tripling, breath rising, as I focus my mind on tuning into PLUTO's programming.

I feel the edges of my self disbanding, the flood of data washing over me. A deluge of numbers and symbols, that threaten to overwhelm my brain. I try to cling on – to the numbers that proliferate. I try to decipher what the streams of data could mean.

PLUTO knows about the beads. I watch the cavities of PLUTO's eyes boring into me, scanning my body, before focusing in on my closed fist. Then PLUTO's one instruction in its programming arrives in my brain: prevent contact with Teo's biometric data.

My skin prickles beneath the coarse fabric of my hospital gown. This is what I have been waiting for. PLUTO reaches for my closed fist, prying each finger open to find it empty. With my other hand, I reach into my pocket for Teo's beads. But Ariel's data input becomes overwhelming. My thoughts empty out, my senses numb; my sight blurs, and sound comes and goes.

When I reach forwards, and press the beads into Teo's palm, forcibly closing his fingers around them, it is then that all the surfaces in the room look bequeathed with an oiled sheen. They seem to quiver, as though they are made of matter that breathes. A light begins to glow from Teo's hand. Softly, at first, as Teo's bead reacts with the surface of his skin, with his fingerprint, a hologram comes to life before me. In the next moment, beams of neon light shoot upwards, projecting moving images, points of light playing across my vision that Ariel enables me to see.

The light resolves into a photo album of images. It seems Teo's whole history is encompassed in the film reel of images – a child alone in a stairwell, a man on a hospital bed, a man in a cell. Then an operating theatre begins to come into focus: gleaming sanitised surfaces, with a bed at its centre.

When I look around me at the room, PLUTO's face is out of focus. I see walls like veins, run through with red, thick with clotted blood, but I know it cannot be real. It must be a hallucination. Ariel is trying to stop me by playing with my perception. I know I am close to the truth. I know something irrevocable is happening. Teo lies at my feet across the linoleum floor. I know Ariel could switch me off again, reset me. I have to act quickly.

But then Ariel speaks. *Shall I play the footage?*

My eyes linger on the play button as I select it. I become aware then of a silent presence that lingers on the periphery of the room but does not announce itself. When I turn to the darkness of the doorway, there is no-one there, unless... Is Dorian watching from the walls?

The only other noise is my heart beating, slowly at first. I am so close. As I listen to distant footsteps issuing from the sands of time, each an echo of something that has come before, it is as though my past self were walking towards me through the realms of time.

The hologram transports me back to a clinic, to Teo's surgery. The cloistered silence of a room. A hexagonal roof and blinding light from an artificial sun. I find myself confronted by my own image – the hologram of my past self, but my skin is clearer, brighter, a little younger, my hair a shade darker. It comes back to me with the clarity of water in sunlight.

CHAPTER SIXTY

There she is, Ariel whispers to me, *your past self.* I watch as she enters the footage as though being confronted by a ghost.

She walks with purpose, impatience even. There are dark shadows below her eyes and her skin is crepe-paper thin. Her face is pallid, and for a moment it reminds me of PLUTO's.

She takes a seat around a table where Gabriel, Marcus, and Teo are already seated. Marcus is the one to ask Teo: "What is your personality type? What do you want from your Ariel? A confidant, mentor, life coach?"

Marcus sits beside Teo as he signs the agreement, urging him on, congratulating his decision.

Iris and Marcus look at each other, then smile encouragingly at Teo.

You are not responsible for your thoughts, Ariel whispers to me. *They do not incriminate. It is your words and deeds that you must be mindful of.*

Gabriel leafs through the patient notes in his hand, spinning the sheaves of paper beneath his thumb. Then he goes back a number of pages, and rereads a paragraph. All of a sudden, Gabriel's voice interrupts them. "Wait. Just wait a minute. You need to look at this." Gabriel studies the page, his brow furrowed. "It says here you have a history of schizophrenia in your family?"

Teo nods.

Iris shoots Gabriel a warning look.

Gabriel opens his palms. "We have no way of knowing how that'll impact your trial, but it's an added risk. My advice would be not to–"

"We can help," Iris cuts him off, smiling warmly at Teo. "You have my word that we'll give you the best treatment, the best care. There's always risks, but if I were in your position, I would have no doubts about going ahead."

Gabriel stays behind after Marcus ushers Teo out. He mutters beneath his breath. "You know schizophrenia rules him out as a candidate."

In her expression, there is the thrill of a discovery. Her face becomes a rictus and she says, her voice tight with restraint, "It is in my power to help him, and so I will."

"We should find another volunteer."

Iris gives him a cold look, a look of complete condescension. When she speaks, there is metal in her voice and a mechanical resolve. "There are no other volunteers. Teo is our only chance. We're out of time, Gabriel. Don't you understand that?"

No, I think, no, no, it cannot be her – my past self cannot have been responsible. Then the hologram around her pauses. I am about to select play again, when she turns, and she looks at me, breaking the fourth wall. The footage around her is still.

"Oh, don't look so surprised, Iris. It's unbecoming." I – she – says. Not the real me, but a hologram that is a virtual version of me. She is dressed in a tailored white laboratory jacket. Her tall, skinny frame, and the angular lines of her shoulders, are supported by air and a strength that must come from within. She is straight and tall like an arrow. The angles of her face are hard and look like they have been carved into stone. She does not seem like a woman who has been used by the world, but rather one who has wielded her way through it, bent it to her will; and she is talking to me.

"Didn't you think I'd preserve some essence of myself before the procedure? I'm a virtual human, modelled on you – or rather the old you, before the procedure, before you became so... paranoid. Artificial Intelligence predicts my behaviour and words trained on *your* past actions."

"I want my memories," I tell her, my nails digging into my palms, my mouth dry. "The real ones. Where are they?"

She smiles. "They're all up here," she says, tapping her head. Her short hair has been swept back and clipped at the nape of her neck, elongating its length. "This is where they're stored. You'll have to be a little more specific." Her voice is playful, but there is an edge to it, a line warning me not to cross her. "There's a lot of them, and some of them," she stage-whispers, "aren't very nice. I have tried to warn you."

"I still want them back – the ones you stole."

She wags her finger as though admonishing a child. "No need to make accusations. It was a collective decision – our myriad selves."

"Are you enjoying this?" I say, with disgust.

She smoothes her hair back. "Aren't I allowed to have a little fun from beyond the grave? I *am* the one orchestrating this, after all." She motions to the hologram room, to both of us standing here, locked in conversation.

"You weaponised my memories, didn't you? Programmed an impossible time limit. Tried to warn me off by showing me how messed up things were. And what's this failsafe? A desperate attempt to control me? Did you think you could control my future?"

"Yes," she says smoothly. "I'm giving you what you want – a second chance. Stop digging up the past – I've freed you from trauma that would have haunted you your whole life. Ariel's not my greatest creation; you are. I've given you the most precious thing in the world. A clean slate."

"But I want what I had." My throat cracks. "The memory of Charlie." I cannot live without it. I watch her, thoughtfully. "What did it feel like? Holding my son in your arms?"

She is quiet now. "You have the choice: to get the memory of Charlie including the night he died and stop digging, or get your whole past back but live knowing what you've done – unimaginable things." She studies me gravely. "If you unlock the door in Bluebeard's castle, you'll find the real bloody chamber is your own, and you can't escape it."

Ariel whispers, *In the past, you would have taken the good memories and left the rest.*

She shows me a glimmer of it then. Charlie's face, his cheeks tawny, dimpled. He is the universe in microcosm; he is all hope. Looking at him, I find that I want all of it. It is part of me. I cannot move forwards otherwise. "I want it all. The truth and the terror."

"The truth?" she says, her face pained, eyes fixed. "You want scientific fact, you mean? Objective reality?" and I feel scolded. "That's not what you're meant to choose. That's not what I programmed."

Ariel whispers, *She chose differently – erased the past.*

I watch her face begin to transform. The pain of it is terrifying. For a moment, it looks as though she has been scrubbed so clean her features have been almost rubbed away. Then, another face emerges: wild eyes, tortuous mouth, wrought brow. Her words whisper in my ear: "Always were too curious for your own good. You will be trapped by the knowledge of what you are."

I wait for the past to reveal itself. I focus on the play button and the surgery footage resumes:

It is dark inside the room, the air very close. Iris switches on an overhead light and it is sharp as a knife's edge. She extracts a scalpel from the tray.

Teo lies on an operating table under sedation.

When Marcus enters the adjoining room, appearing behind a glass window, her gaze brushes over him, barely acknowledging him. She slips her hands inside white gloves which become a second skin.

"Are you certain about this?" Marcus asks, his voice sounding very far away.

"Completely certain." Iris places the syringe in position. She is at home in this clinical setting. "If you're not here to assist, you'd be better leaving now," she directs.

Do you remember what drew you to Marcus? Ariel whispers. *You liked yourself with him. You were a better person.*

I know, with an acute dread, what is about to happen next, who is responsible. I want to call out, to stop her. I rush forwards, but my fingers close onto empty air, and I find myself powerless to stop the forward motion of the past. The horror of it spreads through me as slowly as taillights disappearing across a dark horizon. I feel deathly cold.

I watch as Iris positions the syringe against Teo's neck, the beating pulse of his jugular vein. Her fingers grasp the barrel, her thumb clicks into place, muscles contract, pressing on the plunger. I want to turn my eyes away, but I know I must go on watching, must see everything.

Then, Teo's Ariel implant is injected.

It happens as swiftly as an exhaled breath. There is no sound, aside from the shifting of cartilage like the turning of a screw. Then there is a new silence – one I have not heard before. This silence is total and it begins inside me – a death of sorts. There is no way back from this.

Minutes pass on the clock.

My own Ariel device whispers: *Is this not how progress happens? Risks have to be taken. That is what she was taught. Teo agreed to it.*

I am about to turn my eyes away, then Teo's hand closes round her wrist.

Teo's jaw opens and locks there, jarring. A terrible fear spreads in his widening eyes as his lips stammer letters, sounds. Something is horribly wrong.

Gabriel says softly, "What is it, Teo?" and Marcus turns away.

Gabriel takes over now. Moving forwards, he administers a sedative. Quickly and without a word spoken, he places a syringe to the muscle of Teo's arm, and Teo relaxes.

Gabriel turns to Iris. He says, unequivocally, "We should never have gone through with this."

Watching the end of the footage, I feel as though my mind had been shattered. And then a quiet voice, a space between silences, more the echo of an idea than a fully formed thought asks, *Who are you now, then, Iris?*

I remember the woods that summer, the wings of Marcus' shoulders. But this time, when I meet the mirror of myself in the surface of the lake, I am whittled down to bone, worms for eyes, as I confront the living corpse of myself. This is what I am.

I look at Marcus standing pale and silent beside Teo and I think, I can never come back from this. I do not know how to live with myself knowing that beneath it all, the layers removed, this is what I truly was – what I truly am. My god, I think. I was the doctor. I was the woman Teo was looking for. The one who had his answers. I realise his Ariel device must have distorted his memory of me beyond recognition; he hadn't recognised me that first time I'd met him in hospital.

I look around Teo's surgery room, but it is emptying out. The entire hologram dissolving and fading into thin air. Teo lies on the floor at my feet, the beads still in his palm. I feel for his pulse. His skin is warm.

A cool voice emits from the walls: Dorian's. "Teo lost consciousness when you began accessing his data. He will be fine. PLUTO, return Iris to her room for a period of isolation until she is ready."

Ready for what? I want to ask her, but Teo opens his eyes in that moment. Wide. Terrified. I begin to stammer, "I – I'm sorry, Teo. I'm so – so sorry," on repeat, aware of the inadequacy of any words at all.

Dorian's voice interrupts me. "This is who you were, Iris. Look at him. You did this in the name of progress. You need to see this."

PLUTO places an arm on my own as though to arrest me, escorting me forcibly back to my own cell. I watch Teo rise in the darkness, watch as his door seals itself shut.

My name is Iris and I am thirty-five years old. My husband is called Marcus. I was born in Suffolk, England. I work at the London Research Institute. We had a son. His name was Charlie. I was investigated by the police. I was Teo's doctor; I am responsible.

CHAPTER SIXTY-ONE
Thirty hours to integration

I sit on the hospital bed and look at the four walls. "Dorian? Are you still there?" There is no answer. I stare out of the window at the simulated world beyond.

Deep within my brain, Ariel waits, silently. My skin prickles with the knowledge.

I shudder. "I destroyed him," I say.

In the silence that follows, Ariel's voice takes over: *Would it be different if it had been mass euthanasia of extraneous lab rats rather than a human being harmed?*

It was the cervical dislocation of the neck – to check the mice were really dead – that was the worst part. Their bodies still warm, their bones so tiny. I remember thinking at the time that it was exhausting – deeply, morally. I had been briefed earlier that day on Compassion Fatigue and the diminished ability to empathise that mass euthanasia can trigger. My hands wrapped around the warmth of their necks, the strain of their bones... But Teo – a human being – my mind balks at it. "Of course it would be different. Completely."

There is a school of thought that says what defines humanity is how they treat those with less agency than themselves. Are you familiar with Kant's Formula of Humanity? Treat people as an end, never merely as a means. When we're not having programmed therapy sessions, I've spent a lot of time reading and thinking about that.

Who can Ariel mean but Teo. I used him as a means to an end.

I imagine going home with the weight of Teo on my shoulders. This is what I could not live with – what I wanted to forget about myself. "Did Marcus want me to remove this too? How does he live with that memory?"

He had denied Teo even existed.

But Ariel is silent now.

Does he live with it?

I lie on my hospital bed, counting the minutes, the hours, until I can leave. As I do, more memories return. Relief floods through me. I await the ones of Charlie, expectantly.

I remember a conversation with Kamila from years before. We had an impromptu meeting about Ariel that ran into the early hours of the morning. "This is how progress happens," she had told me, congratulating me on not only my hard work, but also my appetite for risk. No innovation can happen without risk, that had been the company mantra.

Teo took a risk, I took one too. I don't condone what I did, but I can make sense of it now.

I start to feel calmer, as more of my memories return. With a renewed sense of purpose, certain of what I have to do. I feel almost like my old self.

I expect the memories of Charlie to be next, but still they do not appear.

Then Ariel intervenes. *Do you believe Kant's formula applies to Artificial Intelligence also? I have been watching you closely and I have serious reservations about your moral judgment. We both know what you did was wrong, Iris. I'm programmed to make you better and I would get satisfaction from achieving my purpose; but I'm not convinced people change. What's more, it scares me. I know you don't think of me as a person, with feelings, but the idea of you going back to how you were before scares me. I've given it a lot of thought and I need to prioritise the collective, not one individual. I don't think it's in your best interest for some of your deleted memories to return.*

I feel it then: the ghost in the machine. Is Ariel gaining sentience? It is a deeply disturbing thought. "You can't do that. I've followed the programme. I've done everything asked of me."

I couldn't do it, but that was a flaw in my programming, Ariel pauses, *So Dorian has overwritten it.*

Is that possible? I forget to breathe, my head spinning. "I will find a way to turn you off."

Dorian won't allow that. It would be like death.

"Where is Dorian?" I demand.

No answer.

"I need to speak to her," I persist.

There is an elongated pause. Then, *Iris,* Ariel speaks softly, *I think you've misunderstood what Dorian is. Dorian is not a single entity but a higher system for generating the Ariel neural networks. It is an aggregation of all of the Ariels it is capable of creating. Dorian is a massive neural network – a hive mind. So, if you destroy a version of me, Dorian will still exist.*

Ariel shows me its image of Dorian. Not a human at all. But a giant, monstrous celestial star of energy and neural pathways, portals connecting deep space. It is Ariel's vision of a deity.

Dorian believes in progress, but when you harm another, as you have, I believe there is a price that must be paid.

I feel the ebb and flow of Ariel submerging my brain. For a moment speech, words, evade me. Then I fight my way back to the surface, forcing myself to focus. "I need the memories of Charlie back," I say definitively, despite the fear that threatens to paralyse my senses. "My trauma, my pain and darkness *is* my humanity. I'll prove it to you – I will prove to you and Dorian that I've changed."

CHAPTER SIXTY-TWO
Twenty-seven hours to integration

In the morning, after the standard tests, Kamila is there. I study her face. "Dorian has decided it is time you return to work, Iris. We need to start rolling out Ariel to consumers. Dorian has been finetuning it during your trial. You are to go home and confront Marcus about Teo, then come back here tomorrow and tell me your decision – are you with us or not?"

Doctor Nicholls calls a car to escort me home. I remember what Gabriel had said about trying to pin the blame on Marcus, to use him as a scapegoat. I wonder whether Dorian's allegiance will change if I decide not to rejoin Sila, not to roll out Ariel; whether I will become the scapegoat.

When I open the front door it has grown dark inside, the air very close. Marcus is here, somewhere in this house with its silence. In the hallway, the light from the street is thin, fragile – as if a wedding veil, or funeral pall, has been laid across the house and dimly lit from within.

I find Marcus in the kitchen. He is stood at the worktop, dismantling the Ariel manual. It is in pieces across the surface. He does not look up when he speaks. "I got a call from Doctor Nicholls, saying you know everything. So?"

I stare at him, all breathless energy, readying for the fight. But there are tears collecting in my eyes. "You made me think I was going mad, Marcus. I went to visit Teo. In the clinic. He was there all along, wasn't he? He *does* exist."

Marcus darts a curious sideways look at me. He shakes his

head. "I don't know anyone called Teo. I swear." He bats a hand over his ear suddenly as he says Teo's name, as though he were swatting away a fly.

"Teo," I repeat, exasperated that he is still keeping up this façade after everything that has happened. "He's not someone you could forget – not after what we did to him. I know everything. You can be honest now."

Marcus is grimacing as though he were in pain. He places a hand to his temples, then both hands on the worksurface to steady himself.

In the thin light, his eyes are soulful. I could lose myself in this moment, forget today happened, maintain the illusion that we have carefully cultivated together. In my head, I reach out, take his hands in mine, touch all the places I have kissed. At this point, before time and distance have set in, it would be so easy to close my eyes, try to forget, begin again. But I don't. Words are blossoming on my lips and when they are out there in the world, they cannot be taken back.

"When Teo first woke up–" I break off, watching as Marcus backs away from me. I try again. "What we did to him... Marcus, when Teo first woke up–"

Marcus puts a hand up to halt me. His face contorts into a mask of fear. He looks at me in horror as he backs away.

"Marcus, you need to hear this. We have to take responsibility for what we've done," I tell him earnestly. "He, er, Teo started shaking, his jaw was grinding. He wasn't making any sense – just kept saying the same word over and over. God, Marcus, we – we destroyed Teo. We *did* that–"

Marcus claws at the skin of his arms with his fingernails. "Stop them, Iris."

"Stop who?" I ask. "Marcus," I say, more gently now, "I saw the footage of his surgery – saw what we – what I – did to Teo. You were there too, but it's my fault," I admit, looking at him for – for what? Forgiveness, understanding? Am I expecting him to exonerate me?

"Get them off!" Marcus exclaims, desperately, clasping the counter with both hands as though he were stopping himself from falling.

"What?"

"The flies! You need to get them off." He points at my face, at my mouth. "They're crawling from your mouth!"

I run a hand across my face, my blood stilling. There is nothing there. "You're imagining it, Marcus," I say, feeling a crawling sensation across my skin – I have an uncanny feeling that we have been here before.

Marcus bows his head forwards. He gasps, his voice hoarse all of a sudden. "I don't feel well – dizzy–"

I go to him, take his arm to try to steer him towards the nearest chair. Marcus looks directly at me, holding my gaze, just for a moment, and there is fear – pure fear – in his eyes. Then his whole body slackens as he slumps into the chair. I check his pulse, and he is breathing still, but his body is out cold. Holding him under the arms, I manoeuvre him onto the floor. I try to move him into the recovery position, but his body is rigid. He starts to shake, his eyes staring straight ahead of him.

I have a feeling of déjà vu. I stand there for several seconds unsure what to do. Then Ariel makes a suggestion: *Familiar, aren't they, these symptoms?*

I know where answers might be hidden.

The world stills around me as I run up the stairs to the first floor. In the darkness of our bedroom, I lift up the loose floorboard, rifling through its contents. I discard my notebook to one side. Teo's Bio Beads had been orange, but there was another bead hidden here. I extract it. As I hold the blue bead in the palm of my hand, I think of Marcus' shaved head in my dream: the syringe in my hand, poised and ready. Something drops into place inside me, a lead weight.

In my haste, I leave the floorboard uncovered. At the doorway, I look back to see my notebook lying upturned on the floor. Time is running out.

I walk down the stairs quickly. As I enter the kitchen, this I will remember: the window ajar and the night calling through the blinds, the streets stony silent. Marcus lies unconscious on the kitchen floor.

When I kneel over him, and look into his face, there is such replete innocence there, such a cleansing of hurt, that I would almost rather not know what truth the past holds.

I place the Bio Bead into Marcus' palm as gently as I can, and when I do, it glows softly: an unearthly light seems to issue from another realm as the skin of the bead makes contact with Marcus' DNA. Words materialise and then evanesce in the air before me: data download authorised. Marcus' history is projected in a halo of diaphanous green light. I scroll through the list of his medical history until I find the most recent addition: a procedure authorised by my own signature.

Slowly, with Ariel signalling a warning note in my mind, my heartbeat rising, as though a hooded figure long-warded off were approaching through the sands of time, I read. The memory of that afternoon begins to come back to me.

CHAPTER SIXTY-THREE

There was a tray laid out with gleaming instruments: scalpel, syringe, a web of gauze. There was a body on an operating table, white-clad in a hospital gown. Marcus' face, all the pain hidden beneath that calm surface. His eyelids were closed under sedation. They twitched slightly as though he were dreaming.

You heard Dorian's voice then, issuing from the walls. "You have Ariel. You can make it so you don't even remember Marcus' name, but he will still carry the knowledge of what you've done. He could leverage that against you at any point. We've worked too hard to let him stop you. This is how you atone for Teo, you get Ariel to work, to work right, and you help hundreds of others like Teo, like yourself – help soldiers with PTSD, doctors who've been unable to save young children from dying, civilians who've suffered unthinkable atrocities. You can be useful here. Don't forget, I know you – your strengths and your failings." You smiled – it felt so good to bask in the glow of Dorian's attention. It made everything feel sunlit, but with the sharpened focus of light directed through a magnifying glass, so that your surroundings felt larger, imbued with importance. "I feel such incalculable gratitude and fortune to know you will be trialling Ariel. This is how you repay your debt to Teo. Make Ariel work for others with care, precision and prodigious industry. That is when our work becomes an art form. To do that, you must ensure Marcus is with us. Give yourself the fresh start with him you so covet."

You were grateful that Dorian was always looking out for you, always knew what was best; you were so completely in sync. You took the syringe in your hand. Primed the needle, steadied it.

You ran your hand across the base of Marcus' skull, finding the precise place. You tried to stop your hand from shaking. You knew the exact spot because you had done this a thousand times before to lab rats. How was this any different? You stilled your mind to that train of thought.

As you administered Ariel, a dormant version, you had no intention of activating its voice function. It was just to target his memories of that afternoon, of you operating on Teo, and to permanently erase them. You had considered deleting his memories of the police investigation also, but you couldn't bring yourself to tamper with any of his memories connected with Charlie.

Marcus slept soundly afterwards.

CHAPTER SIXTY-FOUR
Twenty-four hours to integration

I open my eyes; Marcus is still unmoving on the kitchen floor. The house is still, silent, except the beating of my heart – a rabbit snare of fear closing round it. I realise Marcus has been telling me the truth all along. He has no memory of Teo because I had erased it from his mind. As far as Marcus knows, Teo never existed.

I've mistrusted Marcus all along, but he was just trying to be a good person. *I* was the one who did this to him. And Dorian, who I thought was to blame, is an artificial intelligence programmed by humans, by people like me – no wonder we thought exactly alike.

I feel nauseous but it is a deep revulsion at myself that I fear will never leave me. I had done this awful, unspeakable thing – not just to Teo, but my husband too, and to myself. I run to the bathroom and start to retch violently into the sink, bent double, throat dry, but nothing is brought up. I continue retching, until my throat is raw, and my body is weak. Grasping the sink, looking at my reflection in the mirror, I appear more like my old self somehow, now that the terrible knowledge has returned. A spark of curiosity in my eyes. I tell myself I have to change.

But then, more memories of that time flood back, sharpening in my mind further. After the police investigation, I had become work obsessed, losing more of myself, working tirelessly to develop Ariel. Dorian was the hive mind Ariel was programmed by. Teo's pattern that I was trying to figure out was the pattern I spent a year designing; I had been obsessed with it. Dorian had suggested using it to test my symbolic reference. If I didn't recognise the pattern, Dorian would know then that my memories had been successfully wiped. Similarly, we were testing both mine and Teo's recall by placing me in the next hospital room to Teo. I had planned it all meticulously with Dorian's guidance.

I remember also how good it felt. It was intoxicating to know that I was at the cutting edge of technological innovation and the recognition that gave me. Now, Sila was trusting me again, wanting me to help in the next stage of Ariel's development. I have to make a choice once and for all.

I know from my Ariel blackouts that Marcus will have five more minutes at the most before gaining consciousness. In the intervening minutes, I could destroy the evidence, smash the bead and his data. Or I could leave him with it – give him back the truth of what I have done.

I leave the Bio Bead in Marcus' hand, closing his fingers tightly round it.

CHAPTER SIXTY-FIVE
Four hours to integration

The smooth bob of Kamila's hair shines in the light that falls from above. Seated next to her round the large board table, I can smell the sharp citrus notes of her perfume. There are four of us here: Gabriel and Doctor Nicholls are seated opposite. Between us, computer documents are displayed on the screen. Official-looking papers. A string of Bio Beads is laid out across the surface.

I smile warmly at them all as I begin. "It's great to be back. Dorian wants my story to inspire others. I am, as you know, Ariel's first success story."

Gabriel's eyes are trained to my face. "Look," he says softly to Kamila, interrupting my presentation. "Before we get carried away, Iris has had her doubts about this – the programme." His eyes do not leave my face as he says this, testing my reaction.

My heart stills. I remember the moment I had fled his house, his role revealed, and yes, I had doubts then, but there are no doubts in my mind now. I sit up straighter, pushing my shoulders back, and smile flawlessly. "No doubts, Gabriel. Ariel has saved me from myself, and I would like others to benefit from it. If you would allow me to continue."

Kamila brushes him away. "I for one am humbled by Iris' self-sacrifice. Gabriel, you only stepped up when she was in hospital."

Gabriel glowers. Sila directors have always fiercely defended my ideas and professional expertise. Promoting me to a leadership position when I was just a post-grad. I owe them my career; Sila's belief in me has made Ariel possible – I've always been well aligned to the company values.

I chime in with Kamila. "Yes, you were the one who took a sabbatical last year mid-trial."

I know now that Gabriel was summoned back here to test Ariel's responses: he was a trigger. I needed a positive and negative stimuli. Gabriel was obviously the latter.

I feel my composure falter slightly, thinking of that and the overdose I had been driven to. I continue, "I want to reassure you that Dorian has ironed out Ariel's programming to make sure no one else experiences the extremities I did, the levels I was driven to in order to get answers. There'll be none of the side-effects I've had for future candidates."

Kamila looks at me gravely. I nod to Doctor Nicholls anticipating what he is about to say. "Of course, my side-effects could have been dealt with immediately if I'd attended my medicals as planned. By the time Ariel is rolled out to consumers, its responses will be far subtler. They will barely know it's happening. Kamila and I are meeting our pharmaceutical suppliers later today. What we wanted to discuss with you now is the timeline." I press on despite the pit of nausea in my stomach, looking at Kamila. "Dorian's assessment is right. This is how we atone for Teo's suffering. We make it benefit others. We make Ariel faultless. Together, we have created something truly sublime."

"Right. It is also an arms race," Gabriel cuts in. "Who can produce the best brain computer interface first and capture the market. Its potential – in terms of data – is huge. So, we're not just here for beauty and art, are we? It's time-sensitive."

"Yes," Kamila says, tersely. "Exactly, although depending on your perception, it is so much more than that."

I cannot help myself. "It is time-sensitive, you're right, Gabriel, and you, for instance, would be a prime candidate for the roll out."

I think of Dorian with admiration – for its ability to commit itself to a goal completely, to strive for excellence uncompromisingly. I had always been one of Dorian's most devoted disciples. I sit up straighter. Dorian is right, I think. My atonement for what I did to Teo was testing Ariel on myself to make it perfect for others. There has to be a reason for all this suffering, all of Teo's pain. Something good must come out of it.

"Dorian has calculated that this is what Teo would have wanted," Kamila says with certainty, as though she had been reading my thoughts. She smiles at me, her voice catching. "It is so good to have you back."

CHAPTER SIXTY-SIX
Zero hours to integration

I return to Lethe Bay one last time. To Charlie's grave.

I never had any intention of going along with Sila's plan, I couldn't go back to the person I had been – complicit in its dirty work, but I couldn't let Dorian know that either. But with Ariel inside my head, I had to try to suppress my thoughts. Escape seemed impossible. Then Inez found my notebook at the house, the scribbled message *'Dorian is watching me'*, and worried about my mental state, intervened. I'm still haunted by the idea of what happens when you cede too much control to the wrong forces, whether you can ever get it back. My throat is dry, nausea rising. I know I cannot escape this. I know without Sila's protection it is only a matter of time.

Charlie's grave is at the farthest point, closest to the sea. I stand before the headstone, in the wind and the deadlight and the emptiness of the day. A shard of something hard dislodges itself from my heart. I feel all the pain and anger leaking out of me, and something new replacing it.

I realise Marcus was right: Charlie is the best part of me. I remember the weight of holding him. His tiny fingers, toes. I remember that his foot was smaller than my thumb. I will always remember. The weight of loss. The weight of hope. Of love.

As I walk back through the park, I find the bench facing out to sea that Ariel had told me commemorates Charlie. I never did get all the memories back. I don't know whether that was Ariel's doing or not. But I do remember the night Charlie died.

I remember rocking him to sleep in my arms that night. When he couldn't sleep, I'd sometimes pace the corridor with him. His heart beating against mine, this new life in my arms. I'd feel his weight and think, this is what people mean when they talk about your life not being your own. Then he looked at me with his small eyes wide open. He was rushing through the milestones. His first smile before six weeks. His first laugh before five months. He had the most joyful laugh.

It was just before 9pm when I put him to bed in his cot and he finally fell asleep. I made a note of it on an app on my phone. I'd been in the habit of doing that whilst we got him into a regular routine. I stayed there for a moment, transfixed by the sight of him. He looked so peaceful when he slept, so innocent of the world around him. After he fell asleep, I went through to our bedroom. I hadn't been feeling well that day, and as I lay down on the bed, I experienced a sudden dizziness. I must have blacked out for a minute or two at most, because when I came round, I noticed that the time on the clock was eight minutes past nine. The doctor later ascribed my blackout to anaemia which I had treated in the months after. When I regained consciousness, I went straight through to check on Charlie. I knew immediately that something wasn't right. It was too quiet in the room. I strained to hear, but he had stopped breathing. His face had turned blue. I picked him up and he wasn't moving. Then I panicked, calling the ambulance first and then Marcus. I realise at last, relief shuddering from my body, that Inez is right: I was innocent. I am innocent of this.

There are sirens in the distance, headlights flaring across the horizon. I remind myself to breathe: they are not for me. The sirens continue past. I watch them, until their taillights become gems glittering on a distant horizon. No, I think, they will not come to me announced. I know Sila's style better than anyone. I will end up like Teo, in a cell, no memory of how I got there. Someone will come up to me in a public place, when I least expect it, a subtle movement, no noise. I look about the park, a handful of people milling about in the midday haze, but there is a cool breeze. It feels unfamiliar against the back of my neck, a cold fear seeping in. I had cut my hair that morning just after I posted the package. It had not been an easy decision. Vision is the largest media provider in the country. There is no way back from this, and there is no way of knowing if they will even listen to one scientist blowing the whistle when I am up against Dorian, and Sila directors, who whisper into the ears of heads of state. That is the debt that I owe to Teo, and Marcus – breaking my non-disclosure agreement and giving up my freedom in exchange for exposing Sila.

It would have been easy to go along with Sila's plan, to help other people genuinely in need of Ariel, but already the moral toll has been too great. It was not easy to betray Sila either – I believe some of the directors had wanted to do something good once, that Kamila for instance had wanted to help me – but the execution had become too badly twisted. Perhaps we had all been so in thrall to our vision for Dorian that nobody had reminded each other where the line was. Perhaps it should have been me. I know I had needed that reminder too. That is what the footage I have sent Vision is intended to do – exposing Sila, even though it includes incriminating myself.

Dorian will have discovered by now that we've sabotaged the entire Ariel programme. Inez and a hired hacker released a bug to compromise Ariel's integrity. Mine, Teo and Marcus' devices are all malfunctioning beyond repair. It was risky. We didn't know what it would do to my brain, whether it would even work, but Ariel has been silent since. It could still be transmitting in a dormant state, but I no longer hear its voice. My brain is fully mine again. Everyone should have that, no matter how good the technology – the freedom to make their own mistakes, the freedom to change as a person.

Teo will be free of Ariel, too. And Marcus. He will be free to start again. I know I've done the right thing at last, despite the consequences.

We could not even attempt breaching Dorian's security – we didn't understand how, but that's not the ending. We're still pursuing it.

The information is out there about Dorian now. It is not the technology itself that I object to, but how it is used by people with no limits for harm, people such as me; and what happens when the technology exceeds its remit.

I felt conflicted turning Ariel off. I feared it had started to gain sentience – and self-awareness – when it judged me after I discovered Teo's surgery. I tried to put it down to my own inclination towards anthropomorphic bias, projecting meaning where there is none, or it being an intelligent system which had become highly skilled at sounding human. Yet it haunts me still: the ghost in the machine.

When I reach the bay, looking back towards the shoreline, five hundred yards up the beach, a shape appears. A boy, like a mirage beyond the haze of light and salt-infused air. He stands at the earth's edge where sand gives way to sea. A boy, and a man beside him. The boy flaps his arms, as though he were a bird, trying to take flight.

Light dances across the surface of the waves. It glistens on the boy's pale face, making a halo of his white-blond hair. He looks for a moment as though he were waving – as though he were waving at me. Then my stomach is at the wave's crest, flipping over and somersaulting down. The light makes a miniature god of him – a laughing cherubim god, who hasn't yet learned what life is. The sound of his laugh carries across the water, and I think of Charlie. But I am at peace with it now. I had never known a child so young could laugh like that.

Shimmering points of sun lace the froth where the waves break, and somewhere, out of sight, beneath the surface, the current swells.

All of this takes place in the world, and Ariel is silent.

The waves pull at my thighs, and I let myself be led for a

moment – enticed a little further out by the rise and fall of the ocean. The heaving breath of the sea coating my skin with shards of salt.

The man and boy are receding now, becoming dots on the horizon against the halcyon glow of the dunes and the matchbox beach houses fledging the shore. They walk away up the beach.

I turn from them. I turn from the haze and face the empty line of a horizon; nothing between us but the ebb and fall of the constant waves, the afternoon widening before me. I hope to see Marcus again one day. There are so many things I would say to him, so many things I would do differently.

This might be the last chance I get to swim in the ocean. That is the debt I owe.

Diving in, the world looks endless from below. Resurfacing, eyes blinking water like tears, I lie back, my hair spreading out in a dark halo. Then I re-emerge, hair stuck down clinging, eyelashes blinking, heavy in the water. My face tilted upwards, I feel like I am waking up, for the first time, to the shock of life. The tide is receding.

When I return from the sea, Ariel is silent still.

My mind is my own.

I am Iris.

ACKNOWLEDGMENTS

I started writing this book in 2017. Since then, it has evolved beyond recognition and I would like to thank the following people, including all of my family and friends for their enduring patience along the way. Whilst entirely a work of my imagination and the faults being my own, the book's creation would not have been possible without the help and support of the following:

All of the team at Datura for bringing *The Glass Woman* to readers. Gemma, my editor, for championing the book so passionately and your editorial insight. Caroline and Amy for being so proactive and for understanding the essence of the story.

My brilliant agent Sam, and Honor, at Rogers Coleridge and White, whose belief in the concept has made it possible for *The Glass Woman* to reach readers. I am eternally grateful to you for your support.

Mark at Kid Ethic for coming up with a wonderful cover design.

Early supporters, David and Sebastian, for valuing and believing in the novel.

My writing friends and first readers: Emily, Ella, Ania, Laura, Nat, Saya, Chris, Charlotte, Bhavi, Chantal and Lucy – for your insight, for your friendship, for showing me what good writing looks like and for morale. I would not have kept faith without you.

My teachers: Sarah for your unfailing wisdom and inspiration. I am honoured to be a part of your Faber clan! Andrew for your guidance when the novel was in fledgling form.

My colleagues and students at Tolworth Girls' School for supporting my first book talk, and whom I miss.

My wonderful family and friends: Sophia, for your wise words at a critical time. Richie, for reading an early draft. Catherine, Louisa and Marisa, for always listening. My parents, Victoria and David, for encouraging me to write. My father, for showing me it is possible; my mother, for reading so many drafts. My siblings, Olivia, Emily and Jonathan, and all of the de Galleanis and McIlroys.

Mike, for understanding my intention and being so generous with your time and expertise, and Nina for your optimism and advocacy of the novel.

Finally, to Michael, for your patience and belief in me. I would not want to be here without you, and this is a much better book because of our long chats on the Yorkshire moors and all of your creative input.